T0171289

Becoming a Man in Thailand

A Young Man's Journey of Self-Discovery

C. J. Fawcett

Edited by the Russian Mig

iUniverse, Inc.
Bloomington

Becoming a Man in Thailand
A Young Man's Journey of Self-Discovery

Copyright © 2011 by C. J. Fawcett

All rights reserved. No part of this book may be used or reproduced by any means, graphic, electronic, or mechanical, including photocopying, recording, taping or by any information storage retrieval system without the written permission of the publisher except in the case of brief quotations embodied in critical articles and reviews.

This is a work of fiction. All of the characters, names, incidents, organizations, and dialogue in this novel are either the products of the author's imagination or are used fictitiously.

iUniverse books may be ordered through booksellers or by contacting:

iUniverse
1663 Liberty Drive
Bloomington, IN 47403
www.iuniverse.com
1-800-Authors (1-800-288-4677)

Because of the dynamic nature of the Internet, any web addresses or links contained in this book may have changed since publication and may no longer be valid. The views expressed in this work are solely those of the author and do not necessarily reflect the views of the publisher, and the publisher hereby disclaims any responsibility for them.

Any people depicted in stock imagery provided by Thinkstock are models, and such images are being used for illustrative purposes only.

Certain stock imagery © Thinkstock.

ISBN: 978-1-4620-0452-2 (sc)
ISBN: 978-1-4620-0453-9 (ebook)

Printed in the United States of America

iUniverse rev. date: 03/04/2011

Chapter 1

Recruit Nathan Foster took a faltering step forward into the flattened, sandy ring. His breath started coming in short gasps, and his vision began to constrict. Feeling faint, he was covered in a cold, clammy sweat. Nausea warred to empty his stomach.

"Recruit Foster! You can't hide here. It's just you and him. Now get out there and kick some Platoon 1601 ass!" Drill Instructor Garcia's gravelly voice sounded distant and tinny. Normally blessed with the kind of voice which penetrated a recruit to his very soul, the power of that voice somehow dissipated, unable to pierce the rising panic in Nathan's brain.

He had been dreading this since arriving at the Marine Recruit Depot, San Diego. Training Week Five: pugil stick training. All this morning, after chow, while the martial arts DI had given them their fighting techniques and safety training, Nathan could feel his anxiety level rising. Merely putting on his red Riddle football helmet, his groin protection, his flak jacket and his neck roll sent his heart hammering. Trying to practice his first strike, he dropped his pugil stick, something not too smart for someone trying to escape the notice of his DI's.

When the two platoons gathered around their respective ends of the fighting pit, he tried to drift back, out of sight. The roars of approval from his fellow recruits as their platoon mates delivered blows made him cringe. When Drill Instructor Garcia called out his name, he literally froze, a deer in the headlights. Garcia, a swarthy, barrel-chested staff sergeant, physically grabbed Nathan by his flak jacket and jerked him to the edge of the fighting pit.

Already halfway into the fighting area, his opponent eagerly waited. Recruit Andersn was in Platoon 1601, and Nathan did not know him well. A somewhat slight young man, he nevertheless shook with eager anticipation, his platoon mates egging him on.

The stale smell of old combats lingered inside his helmet. The clammy sweat pouring from his brow ran down his forehead, making the helmet slide down. He pulled his right hand out of the padded handhold on the stick to push his helmet back up, and his nerveless left hand released its grip on the stick, causing it to fall and bounce on the sand. He bent over to pick it up amidst the hoots of the other recruits and fell to his knees as his tunnel vision and nausea threatened to overcome him. He tried to stand up when Drill Instructors Garcia and Williams rushed into his face, rage making their veins literally pulse with anger.

"What the God-damned hell is that, Foster? You just going to lose your weapon like that? You going to give up and die like that? I've never in all my Marine Corps days seen anything like that, recruit, never!" Drill Instructor Williams was in a rage, spittle flying from his mouth as he yelled. One string of spit hit one of the facebars on Nathan's helmet, where it slowly started to drip down.

"Foster, you are one sorry excuse for a recruit." Garcia was yelling, but did not seem about to go into cardiac arrest as Sergeant Williams had done. "What the hell are you thinking?"

Not knowing if the question was rhetorical or not, Nathan tried to respond. "The recruit's helmet does not fit, Senior Drill Instructor. The recruit feels that he needs to get the proper fitting equipment!"

There was stunned silence for a second from the two DI's. Williams spun around as if in mortal pain. Garcia grabbed Nathan and thrust him into the fighting area.

"Do you think the friggin' Taliban cares if your helmet fits or not? Do you think the Taliban will give you a time out? They'll take every opportunity to kill you, Recruit Foster, if my Marine Corps doesn't put you out of your misery first." He gave Nathan a push forward, towards Recruit Anderson, who was now standing slightly perplexed, not sure what to do at this turn of events.

"Recruit Foster, that is not Recruit Anderson there from Platoon 1601. That is a Taliban insurgent. He wants to kill your family. He wants to rape your mother and sister. He wants to kill you and piss in your skull." He turned to include Recruit Anderson. "You hear that Recruit Taliban? You are a Taliban now, and you want to kill this sorry son-of-a-bitch."

Anderson belted out a happy "Ooh-rah!" followed by some sort of yodel-like trill, which he obviously thought of as something coming out of Afghanistan.

Garcia pulled the taller Nathan down so he could whisper, as much as a

DI could whisper, that is, into Nathan's ear. "You better get out there and kick some ass Foster. Show something here of your father, at least." He released his hold on Nathan and stepped back out of the ring.

Nathan looked up at the excited Anderson. All he could see was a pair of malevolent eyes, eyes intent on killing him. His entire world narrowed down until all he could see were those eyes, eyes piercing into him.

"Attack Anderson! Go get that limp dick!" one of First Platoon's DI's shouted out. Anderson started to bolt forward, pugil stick raised for a blow.

Nathan froze again, watching his opponent's eyes get bigger and bigger in his tunnel vision. His nausea finally won through, and he forcefully vomited out that good Marine Corps chow he had had for breakfast. Eggs and bits of bacon splashed on the onrushing Recruit Anderson.

Anderson skidded to a halt, pugil stick still upraised. He stared in horror at the vomit on his legs. He looked up, and if Nathan thought he looked malevolent before, then this was something from the very depths of hell.

Anderson's pugil stick came back for a roundhouse swing, a technique not taught in class. That seemed to release Nathan's locked nervous system. Dropping his pugil stick, Nathan turned and flat out ran. Drill Instructor Williams reached out to grab him, but Nathan never saw the sergeant and ran right over him. He ran out of the ring and out of the Marines.

Three days later, he waited outside the Separations Platoon squadbay in the same civilian clothes in which he had reported to commence recruit training five long weeks before. He felt deflated, but not really too upset. Becoming a Marine had been something he was expected to do, not something he really wanted to do. Truth be told, he was somewhat relieved. He could hear the chants of a recruit platoon marching somewhere off in the distance, and he was not really upset that he was no longer part of the program.

The last few days had been somewhat hectic. After running from the pugil stick ring, he somehow ended up in officer's housing, sliding his back down against the wall of a home to sit there, head down between his knees. He sat there until the MP's showed up and escorted him back to his squadbay. He was told to wait there by the platoon's 4th hat, Drill Instructor Lin, and wait he did. He sat on the edge of his rack and stared out the squadbay window. When the rest of the platoon burst in to get ready for chow, they studiously ignored him, perhaps afraid that his cowardice was infectious.

While he waited, the company staff was determining his fate. He sat there, seemingly forgotten, until later that afternoon when he was finally ordered to report to the company commander's office. He straightened out his uniform the best he could, then marched over to report. His senior drill instructor was there waiting to enter Captain Broadnax's office, his eyes roaming everywhere except for catching Nathan's eyes. The hatch opened and First Sergeant Henry ordered him to report. He marched in, followed by Staff Sergeant Garcia, positioned himself in front of the captain's desk, and reported.

The captain asked Captain Kunckle, Nathan's series commander, the Series Chief Drill Instructor, Gunnery Sergeant Mendez, and Senior Drill Instructor Garcia their opinions of the future potential for Nathan in becoming a Marine. All three succinctly opined that perhaps Recruit Foster was not cut out for the Corps. His previous refusal to climb the Stairway to Heaven on the obstacle course back on Day 12 had resulted in his first WNOD, or Written Notice of Deficiency. Now, his recent actions with the pugil stick cemented in their minds that Nathan Foster was a coward, something incompatible with being a Marine.

Captain Broadnax thanked each Marine and looked down at the papers in front of him, seemingly composing his thoughts. He folded his hands and finally looked up. He sounded almost apologetic as he addressed Nathan. "Recruit Foster, it is our combined opinion that you are not capable of becoming a Marine. Consequently, we are giving you your INC separation, your Incapability sep." He paused for a second. "Foster, I served with your father. A better Marine, well I don't think they make them any better. With respect to him, I would love to give you another chance because this is going to flat out kill him. I even brought your case up with the battalion commander. But we've decided that it will be best for everyone, for the Corps, for you, and even for your father, that you be separated. I do respect your father enough that I will personally do the Next of Kin notification." He looked back down at his papers again before looking up. "Do you have anything you would like to say?"

Nathan felt numb. Not horrible, not devastated, just numb, as if he had been drugged. "No sir," he managed to get out.

"Very well, you are dismissed."

Nathan did a credible about face and marched out of the office. The next two days were spent at the Seps Platoon, turning in his gear, getting a final physical. Now, he was sitting on the bench in front of the platoon headquarters, discharge papers in hand, waiting for his ride home. Lost in his thoughts, he felt a presence and looked up to see First Sergeant Henry standing there looking at him. Five weeks of boot camp had their effect, and Nathan jumped up to attention.

"Take it easy, Foster. You aren't a recruit any more." The tall, broad-shouldered Marine placed his hand on Nathan's shoulder. "Have a seat."

Nathan quickly sat down, acutely aware of the First Sergeant still standing there.

"Mind if I sit down?" he asked congenially.

"No sir!" Nathan scooted over a bit to make more room on the bench. The big first sergeant sat down and stretched out his legs in front of them both. He sat there for a few moments, quietly staring off into space.

"You know, I served with your father twice, once in Kuwait, and once at Pendleton. I served with your uncle, too. Both are fine, fine men. Sergeant Major Foster, well either Sergeant Major Foster for that matter, but your father most of all, you know, people think he can become Sergeant Major of the Marine Corps."

Nathan shifted a little uncomfortably as he sat at attention, back straight, hands on his knees. He had spent his lifetime hearing about how great his father was, how great his uncle was.

"And now your cousin, your uncle's boy, he's a corporal now. I heard he got a Bronze Star in Afghanistan." Nathan merely nodded.

"Your other cousin, your uncle's girl, she's getting ready to leave for Afghanistan, too. You see, people follow the Foster clan. It's not too often that twin brothers join the Corps, even less often that they succeed as your dad and uncle have. We know about them, we know about your cousins. So pretty much everyone is going to know about you, too."

Nathan felt a deep gnawing in his gut. He really didn't mind not becoming a Marine. But he did mind letting his dad down. He wasn't sure how he was going to face him. Ever since his mother died some six years ago in that car accident, hit by a drunk driver on the 78 going through Vista, well, his father's life centered on the Marines and on Nathan. Nothing else mattered. And now Nathan had let him down.

"I want to tell you, that you can weather this. Your dad, too. Captain Broadnax got a hold of him yesterday. He's at Quantico for a general officer/ sergeant major symposium. I guess he took it pretty hard, but the captain told me that the sergeant major was more concerned about you, how you were taking it."

Nathan looked up to the broad, ebony face of the first sergeant, trying to read the degree of sincerity that might be there.

"Anyway, your dad will be flying back Friday evening. He asked that you go to your uncle's house until he gets back. Or if you want, I called my wife, and you could stay with us until Friday. It wouldn't be an imposition."

Nathan considered it. He didn't want to go to Uncle Bedford's home, that was for sure. But he really didn't know First Sergeant Henry, and he knew he would feel uncomfortable there, not just because he would feel that he was imposing despite the first sergeant's assurance, but also because he would be constantly reminded of his failure to complete his training.

"Thank you First Sergeant, but no, I think I will just go home and wait for him there. He and I have lived there since before my mom died, and that is where I'm going to feel the most comfortable.

"I kinda figured you would say that. Well, the duty driver will be here soon, and he's going to take you right to your doorstep. At least you don't need to be going to the airport to catch a flight. That's one advantage of living in Oceanside." He cleared his throat. "I know the docs asked you this, but you aren't going to do anything stupid now, are you? You know, hurt yourself?"

Nathan finally cracked a smile, something he hadn't done for the last several days. "No First Sergeant, you know I can't do that. Haven't you heard? I'm a certified coward, and I'm too scared to kill myself!"

The first sergeant spun to look at Nathan for a moment in shock before he burst out into a loud, raucous guffaw. He slapped Nathan on the shoulder, a huge blow which almost pushed Nathan off the bench. "You're going to be OK, Foster, you're going to be OK!"

The first sergeant got up and walked off, still chuckling and leaving Nathan on the bench, waiting for his ride home.

Chapter 2

Nathan got out of the duty vehicle without a word. The driver had been quiet on the 45-minute drive, only asking for directions after they left I-5. Nathan opened the door to the back seat to get his small bag, then shut it, not even looking as the car backed up and took off down the street, seemingly taking Nathan's short Marine Corps experience with it.

He stood still for a moment in front of the small ranch house which had been his home for most of his life. The yard had been changed over to a xeriscape a few years back as his father had neither the time nor inclination to take care of a lawn, and he had given up trying to get Nathan to take care of it. The senior Foster, then a sergeant, had bought the house using a VA loan, and with Nathan's mother working at a Denny's in Carlsbad, they had managed the payments. His mom had been so proud of the run-down home, and weekends had been spent painting and fixing it up. The family had been fixtures at the Vista Home Depot.

Emily Foster had loved roses, and she planted a profusion of them. She even won a Best in Class award one year at the Del Mar County Fair for a Dawn Chorus. But after she was killed, the roses withered despite Nathan's constant watering. When they finally gave up the ghost, he pulled each one out and left them in four large black plastic bags for the trash collectors to pick up, never to lift a finger in yardwork again. With neither of them willing to work on the yard, and the yard looking pretty ratty, Nathan's father called a landscaper to xeriscape it.

Now Nathan looked past the stones, the cacti, and the yucca at the non-descript house. It almost seemed like he hadn't left it, like he was back in high school. He reached under a potted ocotillo beside the front door and picked up the key. Opening the door, he stepped into the quiet, dark house.

The shades were drawn, and Nathan didn't bother to open them or turn on the lights. He walked down the hallway to his bedroom.

It was exactly how he left it. He put his bag and his discharge papers on his small desk and flopped down on the bed. He realized that he had absolutely no idea on what he was supposed to do next. Being a Marine had been an accepted fact, something as sure as the sun rising in the morning, something taken entirely for granted. Now, he had to face a future that he had never considered. His grades had never been too high, so college was probably a non-starter. His only work experience had been at McDonald's, and he shuddered as he considered going back to that. Well, he had until Friday before his father came home, and as much as he was dreading that meeting, he knew he should have some sort of plan, some sort of idea of what he was going to do to present to his dad.

With a sigh, he sat up. He wasn't hungry yet, but he felt he had to do something. He walked out of the room and down the hall, pausing outside the third bedroom which had been converted into his father's office. He stepped into this inner sanctum. The light coming through the blinds was enough to see his father's I Love Me Wall. Nathan knew all of the plaques, photos, and certificates there. But still, he moved over to look at them once more. Each promotion and re-enlistment certificate was framed and hung along the very top of the wall in chronological order. His latest promotion, to Sergeant Major, would be his last as there was no rank higher that an enlisted Marine could achieve. Prominently displayed in the center of the wall was his citation for his Silver Star, earned in Kuwait when then Corporal Nathan Foster drove his LAV into the attack against an Iraqi T72 tank, destroying the much larger and better armored vehicle. Under the citation was an article from *The News Herald,* Morganton, North Carolina's newspaper, telling the story on how a local boy made good. There were photos of First Sergeant Foster with Lieutenant General John Sattler in Fallujah, the general's huge smile beaming with his arm draped around him, and a photo of Sergeant Major Foster with General Conway during one of the Commandant's visit to Camp Pendleton. The center-most photo, though, was of Sergeant Major Nathan Foster shaking the hand of newly promoted Sergeant Major Bedford Foster, his twin brother. Perhaps no twins in the history of the Corps had succeeded so well. Nathan stared at the photo for some time, his thoughts drifting.

To the right of the photo of the twins were some family photos. There was a photo of a young Grandpa Will when he was a sergeant, shirt off, sitting on a 155 howitzer in Khe San. Though the photo was a little faded, the green of the surrounding vegetation was in sharp contrast to the almost orange dirt all around the big gun. Then there was Corporal Bedford Foster, Nathan's cousin, in an AP photo taken in Afghanistan. Above that was a photo of a smiling Private Jennifer Foster at her boot camp graduation at Parris Island, with both sergeants major flanking her, pride threatening to burst open her father's face. Nathan morosely wondered if his father would ever feel the same pride for him.

Although not family, above the rest was an old print of General Nathan Bedford Forrest, CSA. Nathan's grandfather was such an admirer of the man known as the finest cavalry officer ever produced in the US that he named his twin boys after him. Although the Fosters were Tarheels tried and true, the Tennessee–born Forrest was elevated, both by his actions and his myth, to an almost god-like status. Although also named for the general, Nathan had never felt a kinship with the man. He couldn't quite understand the hero-worship for a man who, after all, fought for the losing side.

Nathan started to turn away when his eyes caught one more photo. He reached up and took it off the nail holding it on the wall and brought it down in front of him. It was of the twins as Staff Sergeants, sitting at a bar in Phuket, Thailand, with Nathan's mother and Aunt Sandy. The two brothers were in the middle of the photo, the two wives flanking their husbands. Each had a stein of beer raised in a toast; each had broad smiles as they posed for the camera. Nathan remembered when the photo had been taken. He and his cousins had been bundled off to stay with Grammy and Gramps back in North Carolina while the two wives flew out to Thailand to meet their husbands when their Marine Expeditionary Unit pulled into Phuket for a 5-day liberty port after a long Indian Ocean deployment. The men hadn't known the wives were coming; everyone had kept it as a surprise.

Nathan looked at the image of his mother. *God, she had been so young and pretty!* He felt a lump form in his throat. He didn't know if he was ever going to get over missing her. He put the photo back and walked over to his father's desk. Pulling out the bottom drawer, he reached in and found the album he knew was there. It was a scrapbook his mom had made of that trip. There were his mom and Aunt Sandy's boarding stubs for their plane, a photo of the two women at the hotel pool while waiting for the ships to pull in. There were photos of the ships moored way out to sea, then photos of the two men getting off the liberty launch. His mom had told him later that his dad's company and his uncle's squadron had been in on it and had sent them ashore at the same time, ostensibly to check out a site for a staff non-commissioned officer's dinner.

The rest of the photos were of various touristy things. Getting a massage on the beach. The two of them beside a lighthouse while the sun set in the background. Holding a huge live lobster, then a photo of them eating said lobster. Dancing at a disco. Riding jetskis. Out drinking at a bar. That particular photo had always caught his attention. In the photos, the four of them had been surrounded by a bevy of pretty Thai girls smiling for the camera. All dressed in short skirts and tank tops, all with long dark hair. Of course, as with any military brat, he had heard stories about how a wonderland Thailand could be for a guy, and with teenage hormones raging, the images of those petite bodies had raised more than a few daydreams over the years. He had vowed to go to Thailand to see how much of the hype was true as soon as he could, maybe as soon as his first leave. Well, he wasn't going to get that leave now.

Holding the scrapbook, he looked at one of the girls in the photo, a small girl with a huge smile. Nathan had always fixated on her since he had first seen the photo. Neither his mother nor father had remembered her name, but Nathan thought he could read into this young woman's eyes. He wondered where she was now, what she was doing.

He closed the book with a sigh. Well, fantasizing about Thailand was not going to get him anywhere. He was no longer in the Corps, and he was not going to get leave so he could get there. Then it hit him. He wasn't ever going to have military leave, but why should that stop him? He had absolutely nothing on his plate now. What was stopping him from taking off for Thailand right then and there?

A sudden sense of excitement washed over him. Could he really do this? He was dreading Friday when his father would come home, and taking off at the spur of the moment for Thailand sounded like a much, much better alternative.

He bolted back to his room and opened his desk drawer, pulling out his last statement from the Navy Federal Credit Union. $1,243.65. Wages earned from making untold numbers of fries and Big Macs. He reached up under the drawer and felt for the envelope taped there. Pulling it down, he opened it up, pulled out the bills inside, and counted out seven crisp $100 bills. This was a covert graduation present from Gramps. Nathan kissed the bills and slid them back into the envelope. Could he manage to get to Thailand with a little less than $2,000?

Rushing back to his dad's office, he turned on the computer, waiting impatiently for it to boot up and come online. Excitement rising, he pulled up Travelociti and Orbitz. Neither one was a help as he wanted to leave before Friday, and neither site had flights available. Undaunted, he pulled up United, the airline his mother had taken to meet his dad. Going through the online reservation system, he entered his departure airport, SAN for San Diego, and his arrival airport, BKK for Bangkok, leaving tomorrow. And now his excitement faded. $2,454.95. He didn't have that much to his name. He closed the site and opened up Delta's website, which he had seen from Travelociti also flew to Thailand. The results were basically the same.

Nathan leaned back deflated. Well, it had been a good idea while it lasted. He just didn't have the money to pull it off. There was his father's emergency credit card, of course, but that might be just too brazen a move. Knowing he couldn't use that, he nonetheless opened the right-hand drawer on his dad's desk and went to the Navy Federal Credit Union credit card file. His father kept things remarkably organized, and the file had sub-dividers for the VISA and MasterCard his father used, and then a slot for the extra, emergency MasterCard, the one that wasn't normally used. Nathan reached in and pulled out the card, looking at it. It looked brand new, never used. Tempted, he decided to put it back before he gave in and used it. Almost $2,500! That was too much to put on the card.

As he closed the file, his eyes caught on the United Airlines file. Something made him pick it up and open it. Inside, in neat chronological order, were his father's Mileage Plus account statements. The last statement labeled Nathan Foster as a Premier Executive, with 352,615 miles in his account. That seemed to Nathan Junior as a lot of miles, surely enough for a ticket to Thailand. He hesitated for only a second. It wouldn't hurt to find out. Calling the number at the top of the statement, he moved through the phone tree to international reservations, award travel, entering his dad's account number when prompted.

Finally, a live voice came on the phone. "Hi, this is Becky with United Awards Travel. Am I speaking with Nathan Foster?"

He hesitated for only a second. That was his name, after all. "Uh, yes, this is he." He winced. That sounded awkward.

"Good afternoon Mr. Foster. I want to thank you for being a Premier Executive with United. We appreciate your loyalty. How can I help you today?" Becky's cheerful voice helped calm Nathan's rising apprehension.

"Well, Becky, thanks. Um, I was wondering how many miles it would take to fly from San Diego to Bangkok, Thailand."

"Certainly I can help you with that. When would you like to travel?"

"Tomorrow?" Nathan sounded hopeful.

"I'm afraid that won't be possible, Mr. Foster. Award tickets must be at least two days in advance, and that is only with a $150 expedition fee. And flying over the Pacific is pretty hard right now, but let me check for you. I'll check United and our Star Alliance partners for the first available date. Is that OK?"

"Yes, that's OK. Any way to get there is fine with me."

"Well, there are no seats from LAX for the next week at least. No business class, no economy. That's as far as I have checked. Let me check SFO, but it will probably be the same. I checked the same routing this morning for another customer, but you never know."

Nathan could hear the faint clack of computer keys over the phone. "Well, Mr. Foster, you aren't going to believe this, but I do have one seat which has opened up for the 18th, which is Friday. The seat is in economy, and that would be our standard award of 65,000 miles. You are really quite lucky, because there were no award seats available this morning. You would be leaving from San Diego on flight UA 853 at 9:25 AM to SFO for a plane change, then a continuation on 853 to Narita, arriving there at 3:45 on the 19th, on Saturday. Then, you would take flight 891 from Narita to Bangkok, departing at 6:45 and arriving in Bangkok at 11:30 on the 19th. When would you like to return?"

Friday morning at 9:25? That would get him out well before his father got back. "My return isn't so important. How long can I stay?"

"Let me look at the terms of this ticket. OK, I see this now, the terms of this ticket stipulate no longer than 30 days."

"OK, then 30 days would be great."

There was another pause. "There are lots of award seats available for the 19th of next month. I can book you through LAX, leaving at 6:55 in the morning on UA 891 to Narita, then UA 861 to LAX, then United Express flight 6523 to San Diego, arriving back in San Diego at 2:35 PM, still on the 19th. Do you want me to grab that ticket for you?"

Now Nathan got a little nervous. Using his father's miles to get his ticket seemed wrong. But the idea of actually getting to Thailand was almost overpowering. "Can I just hold the ticket for awhile, so I can make up my mind?

"I am sorry, Mr. Foster, we can't hold it. And someone might grab this ticket at any time." She sounded apologetic. "If you want it, I would take it now. I didn't see any other flights on my computer anytime in the near future."

Nathan took a deep breath. This might be his only chance. Who knew what job he would have to take, and when he might get the opportunity to take the time for a trip? He made up his mind. "Yes, let's do it!"

"That's great, Mr. Foster. Glad I can be of some assistance today. OK, we have $98.12 in airport taxes and the $150 expedition fee, so that comes to a total of $249.12. What credit card would you like to put that on?"

Nathan didn't have his own card, and not giving a card would mean no ticket, no trip. $250 was better than $2500, at least. He reached back in the drawer and pulled out the MasterCard, giving Becky the card information.

Becky thanked him and ran the information, telling him that an itinerary would be e-mailed to him. He thanked her and hung up. He had done it: he was going to Thailand. He had been to Mexico before, of course, and he and his dad had gone on a fishing trip to Canada, but this would be his first real foreign trip in his life,

And he was going to be gone before his dad got back. That put off, at least for now, that upcoming confrontation. He put back the United file, then went back online. He needed to get a hotel, arrange for a ride to the airport, and go online to get whatever information he could about Thailand. He was actually doing it! Thailand!

Chapter 3

Nathan gave the flight attendant his dinner tray and pushed up the folding contraption which served as a table, locking it onto the seat back in front of him. It hadn't been a great meal, but food was food. He wondered if there was such a thing as seconds on a flight. He glanced at his watch. An hour-and-a-half down, four-and-a-half to go to Bangkok.

It had been a long 20 hours or so. He had gotten up at 4:30 in Oceanside after a fitful few hours of sleep, then showered, dressed and waited for the Cloud 9 shuttle to take him to the airport. While waiting for the shuttle, he wrote his father out a message saying he needed some time to think things out and not to worry about him.

At the airport, he nervously waited in line. He was sure there would be a strong hand placed on his shoulder, nabbing him for impersonating his father. But the woman greeted him with a smile, and after checking his passport, checked in his bag and gave him his boarding passes. As "Nathan Foster" was a Premier Executive, he was able to wait in the small lounge in the front of the circular terminal. He sat there, drinking hot chocolate and watching CNN. He boarded the flight for the one hour trip to San Francisco, then went to the Red Carpet lounge there to wait for his flight to Narita.

The Narita flight was almost 10 hours long. After eating and watching a couple of forgettable movies and two episodes of *The Office*, Nathan had finally fallen asleep, waking up as the flight descended into Japan. Going through another security check, Nathan went to the United's Star Alliance lounge, but he was getting too excited to just sit. He got up and wandered the terminal. The terminal duty free stores were full of booze, electronics, and perfumes. One pretty young woman offered him a small paper cup with some sort of alcohol in it. More mesmerized by her cute face, Nathan took it. At nineteen, Nathan was not old enough to legally drink, but he'd had his fair share of beers. This, though, was rather stronger, and he unsuccessfully tried not to choke on it. His face reddened, and he hurried away in embarrassment. Walking further along, he was surprised to see a McDonald's in the terminal, and hungry as usual, he stopped and bought a filet of fish value meal. He paid in dollars and got a few yen back in change.

The time moved glacially, but just as glaciers eventually do flow into the ocean, the Bangkok flight was finally ready to board. He found his seat, 32K, up against the window. Two middle-aged men sat down in the adjoining seats.

Now, with the dinner service over, he really didn't want to jump midstream into the movie which had already started. He had already read the in-flight magazine, even trying the sudoku puzzle in the back before giving that up after fifteen minutes of futility. His attention drifted to his seatmates. With a start, he realized that they were talking about some sort of experience with a dancer in a bar. Totally focused on what the first man was saying, he shifted a bit, something which didn't escape the notice of the man in the middle seat.

He stopped, lowered his drink, and turned towards Nathan. "Can I help you, son?"

Mortified, Nathan managed to stammer out, "I'm sorry sir, it's just that, I mean, I haven't, I've never been to Thailand, and I heard what you were saying, accidentally overheard it, I mean, and I don't know how to meet someone there or do anything there!"

Both men stared at Nathan for a moment before bursting out into laughter. "First time, huh, son?" asked the nearest man, a slightly-built 50-something guy with blondish, thinning hair.

"Yes sir," Nathan admitted.

"Well, I guess there is always gotta be a first time. And what are you? 20? 21?"

"I'm 19, sir."

The man on the outside seat whistled. "19? Man, I would love to be in your shoes. The bargirls are going to love you."

Nathan could feel his face flush. He was glad that the lights on the plane were turned down low. "I hope so," was all he could think of to say.

Both men laughed. "Oh, they will," said middle-seat man. In the close confines of the seats, he shifted his drink to his left hand and awkwardly stuck out his right hand. "I'm Chuck Wright, and my partner in crime here is Jan Levin."

Jan reached across to shake Nathan's hand. "The 'crime' part of that is right, at least!"

Nathan took the offered hand. He hesitated. He started to say his name, but something in him wanted to make a break from his past. Nathan Foster was supposed to be a Marine. That person was no longer around. He started to say "Nathan," but he suddenly changed it to "Nate." The shift made it come out as a two syllable word. Na-ate."

"Well, Na-ate," Chuck mimicked, "let us be the first to welcome you to the Land of Smiles. So what're you coming for? Going to be an English teacher?"

"No sir. I am just on a vacation, taking some time off before starting work."

"Damn fine idea," said Jan. "You're going to be chained in the rat race soon enough. Might as well take the opportunity to see the world and sow some wild oats first."

"Well, I am kinda interested in that last part, sowing some wild oats, I mean," Nate admitted with a chuckle. "I'm kinda excited about that."

"I bet you are!" responded Chuck. "If I'd come here when I was your age, young dumb, and full of cum, well, I don't think I ever would've left."

"Well, I mean I couldn't help but overhearing you. You two seem to have some experience in Thailand. Do you live there?"

Both men laughed. "In our dreams! No, we don't. Jan and I work together in Phoenix. We've got families and kids, who we love dearly, I might add. But this is our annual 'fishing trip' that we take together." Chuck used his fingers to make imaginary quote signs when he said "fishing trip."

Jan leaned over to chime in, "Yea, fishing trip for girls! Oh, we go out once on the sea to get some pics to show the family and all, but most of our 'fishing' is done at night in the bars."

"So how do you find them, girls I mean? I read on the internet about Patpong Road, but how do you know where to go there?"

"Patpong?" Chuck snorted with disdain. "Patpong is for tourists. You don't want that, do you?"

Nate thought for a second. Well, he was a tourist, wasn't he? But he didn't want to look foolish. "Oh, no sir!"

"Forget Bangkok altogether. Get thee down to Pattaya! The girls are hotter and the beer colder, and both are cheaper."

"I read about Pattaya, too. But I have a free room in Bangkok at the Holiday Inn. My dad had some points with their frequent guest program, so he gave them to me to get six free nights." He barely hesitated over that little lie, not the free room, but that his dad had given him the points.

"Hey, not a bad dad there! Well, if you got to stay in Bangkok, steer away from Patpong. It's too commercial, and it's a rip-off joint. You can go to Nana Plaza or Soi Cowboy."

"OK, but how do you know where to go? I mean what places have girls who, well, you know?"

"You mean what places have girls who'll fuck you silly?"

Nate jerked at Chuck's blatant language. He looked around, but no one seemed to be able to overhear them over the ambient noise of the plane. "Well, yes. That's what I mean."

"Young Nate, you are going to see that every single place has girls, working girls. Every single girl in every single bar in Nana or Soi Cowboy will ride you until you cry for mercy. They'll beat you down. And do you know why?"

Nate swallowed hard. "No sir."

"Because they are money-grubbing bitches. Oh, don't get me wrong. I love them all. But they are whores, and don't you forget that. They know how to treat you right. They give you the best GFE, and that means 'Girl Friend Experience' to newbies like you, that money can buy. It's great. But never, ever forget that this is a business for them. They all got Thai boyfriends, and most have a couple kids to feed. So don't listen to their bullshit. Don't pay for their water buffalo. Just fuck them and leave them." Chuck settled back in his seat and took a sip of his drink while Jan nodded in agreement.

At school, and during his five weeks with the Marines, Nate had of course been introduced to swearing and earthy language, but around his house, adults pretty much refrained from it. So he was uncomfortably shocked by Chuck's profanity. He wasn't sure what to say next. Grasping for some sort of response, he could only blurt out "Water buffaloes?"

Both men laughed. "Yea, water buffaloes. You see, these girls will wring every drop of cum out of you, then they'll wring every penny out of you. That's what they do. They extract things from you. You meet little Miss Noi, and she treats you like a god. She says she loves you and wants to be with you forever. She tells you she is quitting the bar and is saving herself for you. She writes to you after you leave, and you start remembering her hot little body smoking your pole, and you want more. But then, she writes to you that she has an emergency. Her family has a water buffalo to farm the property, but the buffalo is sick and is going to die unless it gets to a vet. But they don't have any money to do that since she had to quit the bar for you. But if you could only send some money, they could take the buffalo to the vet, and the family will be saved. And, of course, she will be so grateful to you later when you're together again."

Jan added, "Of course, it is all BS. She never left the bar, and she's got 10 *farang* on her list, and all are getting the same e-mails."

"*Farang?*"

"Yea, that's what they call us. White boys are '*farang*' and our black brothers are 'black *farang*.' And no matter what, we are never going to be as good as them. Oh, they like our money…"

"And big cocks!" interjected Chuck again, gesturing wildly, drink in hand, a little of the Jack Daniels splashing out.

Jan laughed, "Yea, that too. But when the money dries up, they're going to drop you like a hot potato."

"OK, I got that. I'm just here for a good vacation. I am not going to fall in love."

"Ah, the folly of youth. You say that now, but when you've got cute little Noi, as Chuck says, it might be hard to resist. Just remember our conversation here."

"I'll remember. But I still don't understand. If I go into one of these bars, how do I get a girl to say yes? I couldn't find anywhere online which gave instructions."

Chuck downed his drink in one gulp. His voice seemed to be getting a little sloppy. "There's no 'instructions' as you say, 'cause no one needs them. Look, you go into a bar. You pick who you want to fuck. You buy her a drink, pay her bar fine, then take her back to your room and fuck her. Pay the bitch. Kick her ass out. Period." He reached over to grab the passing flight attendant to ask for another Jack.

"You pay the bar fine, but then you pay her?"

"Man, you really are a newbie! Look, I'll explain it once to you. You go into the bar and pick your girl. You gotta pay the bar for her 'cause she won't be working at the bar any more that night if you long-time her. Depending on the bar, it might be 400 or 500 baht. Then you take her back to your hotel. If you want to pay her short time, give her 1,000 baht. Don't pay more! She's going to ask for it." He paused while the flight attendant came back and handed him his drink. He took another swallow. "Look, she's going to ask for more, but they ain't worth it. So don't screw it up for the rest of us by paying more. If you want to long-time her, you can give her 1,500 baht. No more." His previously friendly tone seemed a little harsher. He leaned back in his seat and took another sip of his drink.

Nate had more questions, but he was feeling uncomfortable. Over Chuck's head, Jan shrugged and imitated taking a drink, then pointing to Chuck. Nate just nodded and leaned back in his own seat, waiting for the plane to land in Bangkok.

Chapter 4

Nate stepped through customs and out into the airport arrival lobby. He was both physically exhausted and mentally excited at the same time. He was actually here in Thailand!

"Taxi sir?" A smartly dressed young woman holding a clipboard looked at him hopefully. Nate had read about this little scam on the internet, though. He knew he should just go to the taxi line outside the terminal.

"No thanks." He started to walk past her.

"Where do you go, sir? We have the official taxi for you." She started to pace him.

"I have friends here. They're going to pick me up." He didn't slow down and tried to walk past her with what he hoped was a purposeful stride. She shrugged and turned to find her next target.

He was in a square, open area right outside of customs. On either side of this area were two means of exit, two passages cordoned off by rails. Hanging on the rails and behind them two or three deep were literally hundreds of people. On the Discovery Channel the other night, Nate had seen a show about livestock, and part of that had been about livestock auctions. This reminded him of that, but from the steer's perspective. He smiled as he suddenly felt a degree of kinship with that steer, in a pen with people surrounding it, people examining him, judging him, evaluating his worth.

He hitched up his back pack and chose the right-hand exit. Along the very front of the rail were mostly well-dressed men with placards from various hotels or with neatly printed names of people. "Mr. Niimoto." "Mr. Andress." "Mr. Choi." "The Oriental Hotel." "The Shangrila Hotel." "The Sukothai Hotel." No Holiday Inn, though. Behind these men were more casually dressed people scanning the faces of the people entering the arrivals lobby.

Entering the chute-like exit which ran a few hundred feet before the rails quit, he thought again to the show. This was rather like the chutes which led the cows to be slaughtered. Nate chuckled a little to himself. He hoped that analogy was not too accurate. Along these rails were more people, some with crudely handwritten signs with names on them, but most simply watching for what he assumed to be familiar faces.

Two men with shaved heads and orange robes leaned up against the rail in front of him, casually chatting. Nate recognized them as monks from the Thai websites he had surfed before leaving. It struck him as odd that they should seem, well, so normal. He obviously knew monks couldn't spend all their time chanting in the lotus position, but he wondered who they were waiting for. Do monks go on foreign vacations? To where would a monk be flying?

As he neared the end of the rails where they opened up to the terminal proper, a young girl gave a squeal of delight and rushed past him to a middle-aged man pulling two roller bags. She jumped up to hug him around his neck, her feet off the ground as he hugged her back. Nate stared at her ass in her tight jeans for a moment before feeling suddenly guilty. She was this guy's girlfriend, after all. He quickly turned back and walked towards the exit. He noticed quite a few women waiting. Some were dressed quite demurely with nice day dresses, others were, well, looking rather more provocative. One girl with extremely low-cut blue jeans had half of a huge dragon tattoo visible above the jeans, the other half disappearing down her backside. He wondered if it was possible that they were all waiting for foreigners. It would have been kind of nice if there had been someone eagerly awaiting his arrival.

He stopped at a currency exchange booth and gave the attendant two worn $100 bills. The attendant checked them over carefully, holding them up to the light. Nate knew the bills were good, but he still felt somehow guilty. He tried to look nonchalant as the attendant marked the bills with some sort of invisible ink, then grudgingly counted out the Thai baht. He slipped a paper under the plexiglass between them, pointing to a signature line. Nate signed on the line, and the man slipped him the baht.

He took the baht, shoving the bills into his pocket before continuing. Moving through the huge revolving door that led outside, the hot and humid night air hit him with an almost physical force. It was after midnight, but the heat was still oppressive, to say the least. The taxi line was right there in front of him, but that didn't stop two more touts from trying to land him. He ignored them and walked up to the dispatcher, giving her the name of his hotel. Moments later, he was in the blessedly air-conditioned cab and off and running.

Nate settled back in his seat as the cab sped down the highway. He glanced out the window, but he really couldn't see anything in the darkness.

"First time Thailand?"

Nate looked up to see the driver looking at him in the rear-view mirror. "Yes, this is my first time."

The driver gave him a thumbs up. "Very good! My country, Thailand, very good!" He smiled broadly. "Thank you to ever visit my country!"

He reached over to turn on the radio. Atonal music filled the cab. "You like Thai music?"

"Uh, sure. It's very nice." Nate didn't really know if he liked it, but being polite never hurt.

"Good, good. You good farang." He turned his attention back to the road, head bobbing to the music.

They turned off the highway and onto a surface road which traced underneath it. At the first red light, they stopped and waited. And waited. A signal counting down the time until the light changed started at 220 seconds. No cars were coming from the cross street, but motorcycles would slide past the taxi, slow down, then scoot across against the red light. Nate was shocked at the blatant disregard for traffic rules, but the driver didn't seem to notice. Finally, the light turned green, and they resumed driving.

After a good 20 minutes, the driver turned down what seemed to be a side road, the traffic slowly moving along. Nate was a little nervous. On one website, a forum about Thailand, some people warned of scams being pulled by taxi drivers. But this driver seemed like a pretty nice guy, so he hoped his concerned was misplaced. After awhile, the street widened out some and the taxi driver pointed to the left.

"Soi Cowboy," he said, somewhat subdued.

Nate had read about Soi Cowboy, and the two guys on the plane had recommended it, so he looked over with interest. Between a line of taxis and tuk-tuks, he saw a fairly small street brightly lit with neon. Despite the hour, it seemed crowded with women and foreign men. Nate was only able to take in a quick glance before his taxi drove past and turned right onto a main road. If that was Soi Cowboy, one of the main bar areas, then this road had to be Sukhumvit, the main business and entertainment road in Bangkok.

Nate had spent a good deal of time online reading about Sukhumvit, so he looked out the window of his cab with interest. Even at close to 1:00 AM, the road was jammed. Taxis jostled with cars, shifting from one lane to the other. Above the road stretched the tracks for the BTS, or elevated train. Small food booths lined the sidewalks.

Once again, the driver indicated over to the left at one intersection crowded with pedestrians, "Nana." He didn't seem to be too enthusiastic about it.

Nate looked down the small side street, but he couldn't see much. Nana

Plaza was also one of the regular haunts of foreigners, according to what he had read.

The taxi veered to the right around the center median and started going down the wrong lane. Nate's heart jumped into his throat as he grabbed the seat back in front of him before he realized that other cars were doing the same. A few minutes later, the taxi pulled into the courtyard in front of the Holiday Inn. The driver's smile was back in force as he jumped out to open the trunk. A man in hotel livery opened the door with a crisp "Welcome to the Holiday Inn." Nate paid the driver, gave him a 100 baht tip, and followed the doorman inside.

Nate had stayed at a few Holiday Inns before, but that had not prepared him for this one. The entry was stunningly beautiful in a stark, minimalistic kind of way. He walked up the steps and into the lobby. A bellhop took his bag and put it on a cart, then motioned to the reception desk straight ahead. Nate walked up to the desk and stood in front of a woman who was standing on the other side, but bent over some paperwork. He waited, not knowing if he should say anything when she looked up and saw him standing there. She quickly brought her hands together in a praying-type position up high on her chest and bowed her head. (Nate had seen images of this online—this was what was called a "wai.") She then looked up and broke out into a huge smile.

"I am so sorry, sir! I didn't see you there. Are you checking in?"

Nate was speechless. The woman before him was simply gorgeous. Her long green dress hugged tightly around her small waist and hips, and the high austere neckline only set off her perfect oval face and long elegant neck. Her hair was in a bun on top of her head. The skin on her face was flawless. He had heard the phrase before that a girl's smile "brightened up the room," but he had thought that sort of corny, not something that really happened. But now, he realized, it was true. Her smile did that for him.

"Do you speak English, sir?' She looked up at him with concern.

Nate realized he was still standing there with his mouth hanging open. "Oh, yes, yes, I'm sorry. Yes, I'm checking in," he managed to stammer out.

"Welcome to the Holiday Inn! May I see your passport, please?" She reached out a delicate hand expectantly.

Nate slung his pack off his back, opened up top pocket, and got out his passport. She took it and bent over the computer. Nate just stood there and stared, mouth agape.

"Ah, yes, I have you here, sir. Mr. Foster. We have you here for 6 nights, and, let me see…," she paused for a moment. "Yes, Mr. Foster, as a preferred guest, we have been able to upgrade your room." She punched in some numbers on a small machine looking like a credit card terminal, then ran a plastic card though a slot on it. Sliding the card into a small paper envelope, she wrote a number on the card and showed it to him.

"You are in room 1204." She handed the card to a bellhop who had quickly come up alongside of him. "Mr. Somsak will show you to your room. Welcome to Thailand, and if there is anything we can do to be of assistance, please let us know."

Nate wanted to say something, but he really didn't know what. He looked at the nametag on her dress. The single name "Pamonrat" was printed there.

"Thank you, Miss Pamo, Pama.., uh, Pamon..."

She laughed with a musical trill. "Thai names are difficult to pronounce. You can call me 'Nok.' It means 'bird' in Thai."

"Well, thank you, Nok. Thanks for your help." He turned around to follow the bellhop who was waiting expectantly at the elevators. Just before he reached them, he turned around to look once more at Nok. Nok was watching him, and she smiled and waved.

Feeling embarrassed, he smiled and waved back, then stepped into the waiting elevator. As the elevator started to rise, the bellhop asked with a smile, "This is your first time in Thailand?"

"Yes. My dad has been here, but this is my first time."

"Welcome to Thailand, sir!" The elevator came to a stop, and the bellhop stepped out holding his arm out to the left to indicate the direction down the hall to the room. As they approached the room, he held out his hand. "May I have the key, sir?"

Nate handed it over, and the bellhop slid the card through the door reader. A green light flashed on, and he opened the door. Nate followed him in.

The room was impressive, better than any hotel room he had ever stayed in before. He only half-listened to the bellhop explaining the room features as he drank it all in. The bed was calling his name after the long and tiring flight, but he was in Bangkok! He could sleep any time!

The bellhop finally finished the room tour and stood there expectantly. Nate wondered why he was doing that when realization hit him. He hurriedly dug into his pocket and pulled out a handful of bills. Picking out a hundred-baht bill, he handed it over to him.

With a smile, the bellhop accepted the bill and wai'ed. "If you need anything, Mr. Foster, please call me and I will help." He backed through the door and closed it.

Nate looked around the room. He wanted to get out on the town. Lifting his right arm, he took a sniff of his armpit and grimaced. Perhaps a shower was called for first. He opened his backpack and pulled out a wrinkled shirt and pants, sniffing them as well. They seemed OK.

He stepped into the bathroom, shucking off his clothes. There were several different bars of soap on the sink. Two had the word "Facial" printed on the wrapper, one had "Body." "Body" it was, then. He stepped into the shower. Much to his surprise, there were two shower heads there, one belly height, and the other overhead. Nate could not figure out how to control them with the two knobs on the wall, so he just turned one and was jolted with a cold blast of water hitting him in the stomach. He yelped and jumped out of the shower, almost slipping and falling. With a little experimentation, he was able to get the water warm, but he still couldn't figure out how to get water flowing through the upper showerhead. He gave up, stepped back into the shower to clean up.

Ten minutes later and feeling much fresher, Nate stepped off the elevator into the lobby. Looking at the reception desk, he was somehow relieved when Nok was not in sight. He quickly walked to the front door, thanking the doorman for opening it, and stepped out into the muggy night.

Since his taxi had come to the hotel from the left, Nate turned that way and began to walk, waving off the waiting taxi drivers offering him a ride. It wasn't that far, as he remembered it. His feeling of freshness quickly began to fade as he began to sweat. He looked at his watch. 1:15 in the morning, and it was still uncomfortably hot. Oh well, that would only make the beer seem colder. He picked up the pace and continued down the sidewalk.

Fifteen minutes later, he was still walking. It hadn't seemed that far when he was in the taxi. The sweat now soaked the back of his shirt making it stick to his shoulder blades. Finally, he saw a busier intersection. There was a McDonald's there, the landmark he noted when the taxi driver pointed out Nana Plaza. He crossed the street and walked down a smaller side road crowded with cars. On the left sidewalk were wall-to-wall stands from which a veritable smorgasbord of smells reflected the wide variety of food being cooked. Nate joined the press of people walking. Many, if not most of the people, were attractive young ladies, something which did not escape his attention. One girl walking in front of him has on a pair of impossibly tight shorts. He tried to be inconspicuous as he watch her butt sway as she walked. He didn't want people to see him gawking. But not gawking was hard to do.

"Welcome sir! Come inside!" A high lilting voice called off from his left. He looked up to a smiling young lady holding what was probably a drink menu in an open-bar. There was no front wall on the place—it opened right to the sidewalk. Nate felt an embarrassed flush creep over him as he hastily looked away and kept walking.

A few steps beyond, there was a small road on the left which led into a large square. The arch over the small street with the words "NANA PLAZA" left no doubt that Nate had reached his destination. Walking through the arch, he entered a square, surrounded on all sides by three stories of bars. He felt like a gladiator entering the Roman Coliseum. Or maybe he should be feeling like one of the Christians being shoved out onto the Coliseum arena, instead. Music blared from each of the bars, making a cacophony which blurred everything into a single dull roar.

Despite his determination not to act like a tourist, he stopped dead in his tracks and gawked. It was almost too much for his senses. He was suddenly shoved from the back and stumbled forward. He looked around to see two young girls brushing past him, neither one of them deigning to notice the boy they had just pushed.

Nate didn't know how to pick a place to go in and sit down, so he looked to the left and just picked one at random—the Red Lips, the sign proclaimed it to be. A slightly-built man saw him approaching and lifted the curtain covering the entrance.

"Welcome sir, welcome!" he said with a huge smile.

Nate nodded and entered. Right in front of him was a raised, long, narrow dance platform with about 6 girls in bikinis dancing on it. Poles rose from the floor to the ceiling. The bar was surrounded by bar stools, half of them filled by a variety of men. To the left was another long dance floor up against the wall. To the right were a number of booths, some occupied by men and attendant women.

Two slightly heavy-set young women jumped up as he entered, smiling and motioning him to sit up at one of the seats right at the edge of the center dance platform. He hurriedly looked at the dancers, but feeling awkward, he didn't really stare. Ignoring the two girls, he looked around the darkness and found an empty spot in the corner, back away a bit from the dance stages. He slid behind the seat and sat down facing the dancers. He could see both dance floors from his perspective. Immediately a short, somewhat stocky girl came up and asked him what he wanted to drink. He hesitated a moment. He was still underage, after all.

"Beer, please," he said with a small amount of trepidation.

He needn't have worried. Without batting an eye, the waitress asked "Singha?"

"Sure, that'll be fine." He watched her leave, then focused his attention back on the stage. The six girls on the near stage, the one in the center of the room, and the three girls on the far stage were dancing with various degrees of enthusiasm. All the dancers were dressed alike in silver metallic bikinis with long frills hanging from both the tops and the hips. Two girls were not dancing at all, but hanging on a pole while bending down to talk with a young man sitting in front of them at the edge of the stage. Another girl was slowly gyrating her hips and bending her knees, but her attention was on her reflection in the full length mirror along the side wall. She seemed oblivious to the scattering of men in the bar.

One girl was actually making a game attempt at dancing. Extremely slender, she moved aggressively with the music, lifting her knees up with the beat, swinging her long hair. Her small ass barely seemed to swell beyond the width of her narrow hips. She moved well, and Nate was attracted to that, but she was so thin that he wondered if she was healthy. Was it possible that she had HIV? He had read on the internet that the bargirls were tested for diseases, but he was worried about that none-the-less.

The other dancers were not really doing what could be called dancing, unless shifting their weight from one foot to the other could be construed as that. One kept glancing at her watch as if anxious to leave the stage.

The waitress brought him his beer. She put the bill in a small tubular vase-like container on his table. He started to get out his wallet, but she walked away. Nate picked up the beer and took a large swallow. The coldness of the beer hit him hard. It felt great. Nate didn't actually like the taste of beer so much, but he loved the feel of it hitting the back of his throat. He took a second big swig and looked back up on the stage.

The second girl away from him looked in his direction and suddenly blew him a kiss. Flustered, Nate quickly took another swallow, then looked back up at her. She smiled and blew him another kiss.

It was hard to tell height while they were on stage with their heels, but this girl seemed a little taller than the rest. She was also a little heavier. Her belly was slightly overlapping her bikini bottom, but the swell of her breasts nicely filled out her top. She leaned over to give him a view of her cleavage, then covered her mouth with one hand and laughed while moving to the back of the closest dancer, hands on that girl's shoulder. The second girl, the one now in front, motioned with her hand, pointing at the first one and then to Nate, repeating the motion several times. The first girl remained behind her, hand covering her mouth, but her laughter was still visible.

Nate flushed and looked down to take another sip of the beer. He looked up, but at the dancers more to his left, not really at those two. As his eyes involuntarily looked back at them, the second girl started her hand gestures again, nodding her head, eyes questioning.

Well, she certainly is pretty enough. Screwing up his courage, he gave the second girl a quick nod. The first one, still hiding partially behind her friend, broke into a huge smile, then hurried to the edge of the stage, climbed down the steps, and came over to Nate. She gave him a wai.

"May I sit with you?" her soft, lilting voice was almost lost in the music.

"Sure, please." Nate felt his face flushing as he scooted over to give her plenty of room to sit.

He needn't have bothered with giving her too much room as she sat down right next to him, her bare leg in full contact with his leg. She smiled again, then covered her mouth. Up close, Nate had a hard time not focusing on her swelling breasts.

She reached out a dainty hand. "I am Nok. What is your name?" Each word was carefully enunciated, what he might imagine an English class would be like.

Nok? Wasn't that the same name as the girl back at the hotel? "I'm Nate," he stammered out. At a loss for what to say next, he said the first thin that came to his mind. "'Nok' means 'bird,' right?"

Nok squealed with delight and clapped her hands. "Oh, you speak Thai!"

"Oh no, I just know that. And I read '*Sawadi ka*' and *krup khun ka'* on the internet."

She giggled at that. "OK, *mai pen rai.* Never mind. Where you from?" She leaned forward, her breast now pressing against his right forearm.

To say Nate was acutely aware of that breast against his arm would be an understatement to the word "acutely." Trying to focus, he answered back, "America. I'm from the US."

"Ah, good. I like American. My auntie, she marry farang America. She live At-a-lan-ta. You know?"

"Uh, sure I know. That is on the other side of the country. I'm in California."

"At-a-lan-ta very good, right?" She shifted her position and hugged his arm, forcing her breast even tighter into him.

Nate merely nodded. He lost his battle of the wills and looked down openly to stare at her breast, seeing how it seem to curve around his arm. She didn't seem to notice his attention.

"How old are you?"

Nate had planned on being 21 in case it was ever brought up, but his mind was otherwise focused, so the truth came out. "Nineteen."

"Oh, baby! You just baby!" She laughed.

Nate wondered if he had blown it when she called out in Thai to her friend still dancing on the stage, but after her friend laughed and gave him a thumbs up, Nok moved even closer, if that was even possible. One of her hands dropped to his thigh.

"You here for holiday?"

"Yes." He took a sip of his beer, eyes dropping to look at her breast against his arm.

"Where you stay?"

"I'm at the Holiday Inn."

"Oh, very nice. Expensive *mak mak!*"

Nate wasn't quite sure what *mak mak* meant, but he could guess from her intonation.

"No, I get the room for free."

She seemed to ignore his response and looked idly to the stage for a few moments, lost in her thought. Then as if suddenly remembering he was there, she gave his arm another squeeze and asked "you buy me drink, OK?"

He looked up at her face. Was this one going to be "the one?" She certainly had his attention, and she felt good clinging to him. He had read on the internet that most of the "ladies' drinks" were little more than colored soda water, but he didn't hesitate.

"Of course," he tried to say in a casual voice. He wasn't so sure it came out that way. She didn't seem to notice anything though and raised her arm to catch the attention of one of the waitresses who was sitting in the back talking to the others.

The waitress finally noticed and came over to take Nok's order. Nate looked back onstage and caught the eye of the second dancer, the one Nok had hid behind. She gave him a big thumb's up, then made a motion with her clenched hand up and down in front of her mouth, pushing her tongue up against the inside of her cheek repeatedly, then pointing at Nok and laughing. Nate had never seen anything quite so blatant before, but it wasn't hard to catch her meaning. He felt a flush creep over his face as he looked away, but he was excited all the same.

The waitress came back with Nok's drink and put another piece of paper in the little cylinder in front of him. Nok lifted up her glass in a toast. Nate hurriedly lifted up his glass and clinked it with hers before taking a big swallow of the still cold beer.

They sat there, side-by-side, not saying much. The dancers on the stage seemed to be getting less energetic. Except for Miss Mirror, who still kept dancing and watching her reflected image, most seemed to be barely moving as they stood and talked to each to each other. The two who had been talking to the young man at the bar were now ignoring him.

A petite girl with closely cut hair emerged from a room in the back wearing blue jeans and a yellow t-shirt. She went up to an older, heavyset man dressed in brown shorts and a white button-down shirt who had been sitting alone in the booth two down from Nate. She nodded at the man, and he eagerly got up. She took his arm, waved towards the dancers on stage, and escorted him out the door. She looked about half the man's weight, but she was doing the leading. Nate suddenly realized that he had witnessed a transaction. That girl had been a dancer, and now she was going with that man back to his hotel room.

Nate had made up his mind. He wanted Nok to come back to his room with him. But he still wasn't sure how to make that happen. He sat there, mulling over his choice of words. He had just mustered up the courage to ask if Nok was doing anything later when the lights of the bar came up. He blinked in confusion.

Nok stood up, drained her glass and leaned over to kiss Nate on the cheek. "You come here tomorrow, OK?" She spun around and strode off purposely to the back of the bar and disappeared through a door there.

Nate watched her dumbfounded. *What has just happened here?* Some of the men in the bar stood up to evidently leave while others didn't pause in their drinking and conversation. The waitress came over and picked up Nate's little cylinder, removed the slips of paper, and after a short period of seemingly intense concentration, told him "225 baht please, sir."

She stood there expectantly as Nate dug out three 100 baht bills, checking carefully their denomination, and put them on the tray in her hands. She did a sort of head-bob-curtsy thing, then walked off to the cashier in the back.

He felt rather awkward sitting there, not really knowing what was going on. He continued to sip at his beer, watching as some of the dancers came out of the back room with their street clothes on. After a few minutes, his waitress came back with his change. He waved it off and she did her head- bob-curtsy thing again and started to walk away until Nate called out to her.

"Is this place closed?" He looked at his watch, which he had set to Thai time at the airport. It was only 2:00 AM.

"Yes, sir. Closed. Two o'clock. You come back tomorrow, *ka*." She walked off.

He felt deflated. From being quite excited, mentally and physically, now he felt as if the rug had been pulled out from beneath him. He took one last swallow of beer and stood up. A few earnest men seemed deep in conversation, but there was general drift of patrons out the door where they merged with other streams of patrons leaving the many bars in the plaza. He looked out the door. With the neon lights off, Nana Plaza looked different. The harsh white lighting gave it a more naked air, a more authentic feeling.

Still inside the Red Lips, a few men sat in small groups nursing their final drinks, and a few women seemed intent on negotiating rates with a few men for a night's entertainment, but there wasn't the vitality which was present even 45 minutes ago as he came in. He turned an exited the bar and joined the slow movement to the entrance of the plaza, making his way past street stalls of grilling chicken legs and skewers of meet chunks. A skinny bare-chested young boy in filthy shorts held out his hand as he passed, a vacant look in his eyes as he pointed to his stomach. Nate pushed by the boy and out into the street.

In front of him, in the parking lot of what the sign proclaimed as the Nana Hotel, a handful of women scanned the passing men with forlorn hope in their eyes. One caught Nate's eyes and smiled broadly at him, using her finger to motion between them, asking if she could join him. Tempted for a moment, he took in her rather thin frame and worn face, and thoughts of HIV kept intruding. She scared him, to be frank. He shook his head and turned right, walking to Sukhumvit, ignoring the tuk-tuk drivers trying to catch his attention. Several of the other men walking alongside of him had women on their arms, and Nate looked on them with a degree of jealousy.

As he hit the main drag, he was surprised to see Nok, the girl from the Red Lips, walking a few paces over to his right. He started to push his way through the people between them when Nok stopped beside a motorcycle, said something to the young, bored-looking man who was leaning against it, put on the helmet which had been sitting on the seat, and got on the bike. The man stubbed out his cigarette and threw it on the ground, put on his own helmet, and got on as well, kick-starting the bike to life. He slowly wove the bike through the walking people until he pulled out on Sukhumvit and sped off.

Nate stared after the receding taillight, then shook his head. The sweat was already starting to build up again as he hitched his pants and started walking back to his waiting bed for the night.

Chapter 5

Nate glanced over at the clock next to his bed. The red LEDs lit the edge of the nightstand with the time: 6:18. Only 4 minutes had passed since the last time he looked? He had been exhausted when he finally hit the rack, but after what turned out to be only a couple hours of sleep, he woke up and could not return to his slumber. He looked back up and stared at the growing lightness which crept in through the almost closed curtains.

With a sigh, he finally gave up and sat up in his bed. Picking up the remote, he turned on the television. The screen came to life, welcoming him to the Holiday Inn and offering him his choice of pay-for-view movies or broadcast television. He picked broadcast, not even tempted to watch a movie which would increase his room charges. Flipping through the channels, he found Al Jazeerah television. With a guilty start, he stopped to watch it. Wasn't this the propaganda tool for Islamic extremists? The report was on some sort of trash-to-power generation project in Kenya. It looked just like something CNN would broadcast. This was followed by a series of rather mundane reports, even a short piece on the US president's trip to Mexico. This certainly didn't seem like the propaganda he was led to believe was the standard Al Jazeerah fare.

Bored, he switched channels, but nothing caught his interest. He perked up when he switched to ESPN, but the SportsCenter was only covering soccer in Europe. Sliding out of bed and standing up, he wondered what he should do.

He realized he felt like exerting himself. He needed to get some exercise. Nate had never been a person much on working out, but his short time at boot camp had got him into the habit of morning exercise. He hated it each morning when he was forced to do it, but now, well, it seemed like a good idea. He had read on the hotel brochure that there was a gym for the guests, so now might be a good time to try it out seeing as how he couldn't sleep.

He hadn't really packed with exercise in mind, so he rummaged through his bag to see what he could wear. A pair of walking shorts and a t-shirt would do, and he slid on his Nikes. He had worn Nike for several years, not for exercise, but for the swoosh and comfort. But they were designed for exercise, so they should serve him well now.

He left his room, almost forgetting his room keycard and took the elevator down to the small so-called "gym." The gym was a cramped space with a handful of exercise machines and a rack of some smallish dumbbells. An older man in perhaps his 50's was sitting on a bench doing curls with a set of dumbbells. He had on dark blue running tights and an oversized tanktop. The top of his bald head glistened in sweat and caught the morning sunlight streaming in through the windows. Nate nodded to him and looked around, not sure what to do. At bootcamp, the recruits were led in the Daily Seven by one of their drill instructors. Here, it was up to him.

Nate looked at the various machines, and while he could recognize a stationary bike, of course, he felt a little unsure of himself getting on it with the other man in the room. He didn't want to look like an idiot. So he got on the Universal instead, lying down on the bench for a bench press. Nate had lifted some free weights as part of his high school weight training for football, but he had never really used a Universal before. So he left the pin in the stack where it was and benched the bars ten times. He sat up, looked around, and moved to the pull-down bars. He awkwardly kneeled, mimicking the instructional image posted alongside the vertical frame and pulled down ten times there as well.

"You don't do this much, do you?"

Nate startled, then looked up to see the other man sitting on his bench looking at him quizzically.

"Uh, no sir, not really."

"Didn't think so." He smiled. "I mean, you're as strong as an ox, but you don't have any form. I know what I'm doing, and I struggled with that stack earlier, but you lifted it without a problem."

Nate looked at him, unsure what to say, unsure if he was being played for some reason.

"Excuse me, I guess I should introduce myself." The man pulled the glove off his right hand and stuck it out. "Tom Amirault. Pleased to meet you."

He drove his hand deep into Nate's, getting a firm grip and squeezing hard, but not bone-crushingly so.

"Nate Foster, sir."

"That's two 'sirs' in two sentences. You military, son?"

"Yes sir, Marines." He felt surge of guilt sweep over him. He wasn't a Marine anymore, so he shouldn't claim that distinction.

"Thought so. I spent 30 years in the Navy myself. Now I'm with Microsoft. That's why I'm here now, in fact, but as usual, jet lag and the time shift has me up early."

"Yea, I couldn't sleep, either. Is that normal?"

"Sure is Nate—you did say your name was Nate, right?" When Nate nodded, he continued. "You never really get used to it. I normally work out before dinner, but on these Asian trips, I'm always up early, so I work out then."

"You come to Thailand often?"

"Well, about two or three times a year, I guess. I go to Korea more. Excuse me, I've got one more set to go."

He bent down and picked up the dumbbells. Nate could see they were 20 kg each, but he didn't know how much that was in pounds. Tom slowly and smoothly brought the weights up into a curl, alternating each one. His biceps bulged with each curl, and the chords of muscles in his shoulders shifted with each movement.

"You see Nate, you need to keep your body still and only use the muscles you're working right then. You're a big strong kid, but your jerking and reliance on Uncle Mo keep you from getting your full work out."

"Uncle Mo?"

"Momentum, Nate, momentum. See?" He changed his curls so that he jerked each dumbbell up, swaying with his whole body. "Now I'm using momentum and my whole body when I should just be using my biceps for this." He slowed down and kept his body still again as he had been doing previously, his elbow seemingly pinned in place against his side. "See?"

"Ah, I get it!" And he did get it. When he played football in high school, no one had really paid much attention to him, not that he had ever done anything to stand out. And no one had ever trained him in how to lift weights. But Tom's one little piece of advice really did make sense.

"Well, I've got to get going. Shower and breakfast, then fighting the Bangkok traffic to my meeting." He took off his glove again and stuck out his hand. "Good to meet you Nate. Enjoy your leave here."

Nate shook Tom's hand and watched him leave the small exercise room. He moved over and sat on the bench, picking up the weights Tom had left there. Concentrating, he slowly curled each arm in turn. There was mirror on the wall, and he looked at his reflection in it, trying to keep his body and arm as still as possible. It felt pretty good, and he could see his muscles play under his skin.

He went to each of the stations on the Universal and tried to mimic the images representing the exercise at the stations and showing which muscle group that specific exercise worked. He tried to keep his body still while performing each exercise. After he finished the last station, he looked over at the stationary bikes, but he decided he had had enough for the morning. Vowing to look up proper exercise techniques on the internet, he went back up to his room to shower.

An hour later, after a hot shower and then stuffing himself on the breakfast buffet—he had never had noodles nor salad for breakfast before, but along with the more traditional eggs, bacon, and pancakes, they tasted pretty good together—he stepped out the front door and into the hot morning sun.

The driveway into the Holiday Inn was shared with another large hotel, the Intercontinental. Even though the Holiday Inn was the nicest hotel at which Nate had ever stayed, the Intercontinental looked even higher scale to him, if that was possible. He had an urge to walk across the drive and look around the lobby, but looking at his shorts and t-shirt, he thought he might be out-of-place. So he turned left instead and went back to Sukhumvit. Without a firm destination, he started following the same path he walked the night before.

Bangkok at 8:30 in the morning was much different than at 2:00 in the morning. Men, both Thai and foreign, walked purposefully by in suits. Women in professional-type clothing walked alone or in small groups, hurrying to their jobs. A few street vendors had set up small food stands, serving what looked to be dim sum or noodle dishes. Several of these had smartly-dressed men, briefcases between their legs as they sat in small plastic chairs, eating their breakfast. An older man on a small bicycle cart pedaled against the traffic with what looked to be a hundred or more hand-made brooms. He thumbed a small bell periodically, but the traffic was so heavy that the cars facing him were essentially stopped.

He passed a McDonald's and had an urge to go in, but he really wasn't hungry after the breakfast buffet, so he had the discipline to walk on by. As he walked, the complexion of the people walking around him changed. There were still Thais hurrying to wherever they were headed, but there cropped up some men in Arab dress, and then some black men speaking English loudly, but with an unfamiliar accent. Nate wondered if they were African, but he didn't have the nerve to stop one of them to ask. As he arrived at the intersection where Nana Plaza was, a man in a white Arab-type robe walked by, followed by three women completely covered in black robes. Each woman had some sort of metal shield over her nose. Nate stopped to stare as they walked by; they ignored him.

Weaving through the stopped cars in the road, he walked kitty-corner across the intersection and down the road leading to Nana Plaza. As he approached the open bar which marked the entrance to the plaza, he could see it was empty save one young woman wiping down the tables. He walked around the corner and into the plaza proper.

What a difference a few hours made! Without the flashing lights and hordes of people, the plaza was a rather dingy, sad-looking place. Bags of trash were outside most of the bars. A forlorn, dirty tan-colored dog nosed one, hoping to find a morsel to eat. Outside the first bar on the left, a young woman sat on a barstool, head down on her arms on the bar, sleeping away. Her head was slightly tilted back, her mouth open. Nate could hear her snores emanate across the 20 feet or so separating them.

With nothing there to see, Nate turned around quickly, almost running down a small, elderly woman who looked up at him, hand stretched out. Her ragged and filthy clothes hung loosely on her thin frame. She gestured with her other hand towards her mouth. Poverty like this frankly scared Nate, and he quickly stepped around the woman and hurried back to the main street. He glanced back to see her standing at the entrance to the plaza, watching him. Shaking his head and shoulders as if he was a horse twitching off a fly, he turned and started walking down Sukhumvit.

Already getting bored, but not wanting to admit it, Nate was wondering what to do as he approached the Holiday Inn again. He thought about the pool there, so he re-crossed the street again and went into the lobby, feeling the rush or the cool air against his sweaty skin. Glancing at the reception desk at the back, he was surprised to see Nok there, talking on the phone. Hadn't she been there only 8 hours ago? Before he knew what was happening, his legs took him right up to the desk to stand in front of her. She looked up and broke into a huge smile as she put the phone back down on the receiver.

"Good morning Mr. Foster! How are you today?"

"I'm fine, Nok," he managed to stammer out.

"Good. I hope you had a good sleep. I think so," she smiled. "Our SimplySmart bed is very lovely, don't you think?"

Nate wasn't quite sure what the SimplySmart bed was, and he really hadn't slept well given the jetlag, but he was afraid to disagree, fearing anything that might put a damper on her beaming smile. So he simply nodded.

"Yes, I think so."

They stood there for a few moments, neither one saying anything. Nate forced out a question.

"You were just on duty when I came in. How come you're back again so soon?

"Ah, thank you for your concern. But today is shift change. I work daytime shift this week. Last week, I worked afternoon shift."

Nate stood there, almost transfixed by the lyrical quality of her voice.

"What will you do today, Mr. Foster?"

"Please, call me Nate. My name is Nate."

"OK, *Khun* Nate. Please to meet you." She brought her hands together in a *wai*, then held one hand out western-style over the desk, giggling as she did so.

Nate tried a clumsy *wai* of his own, then reached out to briefly grasp the offered hand. The hand felt awfully small in his, cool to the touch.

"Pleased to meet you too, Miss Nok." He smiled back.

"So what will you do today, *Khun* Nate?" She brought her hand back down in front of her.

"I don't really know. I didn't make any plans."

"Oh, you should go to the Grand Palace. It is very beautiful, the old home of our king, and you will like it very much. Yes, I think so."

Thoughts of going for a swim vanished from his mind. "OK, that sounds great! How do I get there?"

"Oh, all taxis know where it is." She looked at his shorts. "But you must change to long pants. Short pants are not allowed."

"Sure, I can do that." He stared at her as she looked expectantly at him. "Well, I guess I better go change." He took a step back, looked at her for a second again, then wheeled off to go back to his room.

"Have a good time, *Khun* Nate," Nok said to his retreating back.

Chapter 6

Two hours later, Nate handed the driver 150 baht and stepped out of the cab at the Grand Palace. The drive over from the hotel had been long and tortuous—traffic was very heavy, and the air conditioning in the cab was erratic. Stretching his body to get out the kinks, he looked up a tall stone wall stretching from just to his left to out-of-sight on the right along the entire length of the street. He could see the tops of some elaborate buildings over the top of the wall.

Not quite sure exactly where was the entrance, he started walking with the flow of the wide variety of tourists moving towards the corner of the wall. A heavy-set Thai man in a pair of dark blue slacks and a nice button-down tan shirt broke into a smile and came up to him.

"You come to see Palace?" He held out his hand to be shook.

Nate rather thought that was obvious, but he took the hand and replied in the affirmative.

"Ah, sorry, but Grand Palace is closed this morning for royal ceremony." The man kept Nate's hand grasped in his.

Nate looked at him with confusion. Why hadn't Nok told him the Palace would be closed? You would think that a big hotel would know things like that. "Closed?" he asked lamely. "When will it open?"

"Oh, one o'clock, mister, It open one o'clock. Sorry you come early." Still grasping Nate's hand, he looked around a moment as if considering something. "What is your name? I am Wun."

"Nate. I'm Nate," he answered warily.

"You first time Thailand?"

"Yea, this is my first time here."

"OK, I want you like Thailand. I take you on tour for free. Then I take you back here one o'clock, then you see Palace no problem."

A heavy feeling of misgiving came over him. Free? Nothing in life was for free. He looked over at a soldier guarding a closed gate in the wall a few yards away. The soldier merely looked back, no expression on his face. Well, the soldier would say something if there was anything wrong, right? And a free tour for a couple hours was not a bad idea.

"Free? Are you sure?" he asked the man.

"Yes, yes, free." Wun started pulling Nate across the street to a large open park. Nate resisted, pulling back.

"Don't worry, free. You can trust me. Over there my tuk-tuk. See? Over there." He pointed at a parked tuk-tuk under the shade of a tree lining the park.

Nate let himself be led across the street and up to the tuk-tuk. Wun pulled out a set of keys and hopped on the driver's seat, looking back expectantly at him.

Nate still hesitated. "For free, right? I won't have to pay, right?"

"Yes, yes, for free. No pay. Come, I take you on tour."

Making his decision, Nate climbed onboard the vehicle. Sitting down on the vinyl seat, his head brushed the plastic fabric which served as a roof for the passenger compartment. The plastic was stretched over a frame which covered the top of the tuk-tuk and curved down a foot or so on the sides. Even with the open sides of the tuk-tuk, this overhang was low enough that Nate couldn't really see much as they scooted off into the traffic except for the road they were on and the bottoms of cars next to them. He tried to scrunch down somewhat so he could see more of where they were going, but it didn't do much good. He held onto one of the vertical supports holding up the overhead cover as the tuk-tuk wove its way through the traffic.

"Where are you from?" asked Wun, shouting over his shoulder and the clatter of the two-stroke engine.

"America," he replied tersely, wondering if he had made a mistake in accepting the ride.

"Ah, America! Go Broncos!"

It took a second for him to realize what Wun had said. "I'm from San Diego. I'm a Charger fan."

"Yes, yes. Go Broncos!" He looked back over his shoulder, shifting his none-too-small bulk so he could look back at Nate, a huge smile on his face. Nate decided to let it go as the guy obviously had just picked up the phrase from someone not knowing anything about the NFL.

Wun pulled around some cars at an intersection, moved right up to the curb, then squeezed between the curb and some cars before picking up speed again. He pointed off to his left, "Khao San Road. Good place for disco, for meet girls, for drink."

Nate tried to scrunch down so he could see, but all he saw was a sidewalk and ordinary-looking buildings. He had read about Khao San on the internet, and he wanted to check it out sometime.

They continued in the traffic, then started driving around a round-about. Wun looked back and told him simply "Democracy Monument." Nate tried to look, but all he could really see was the massive base of something. The cover over his head kept him from seeing the monument proper.

Wun attempted to say a few more things while they drove along, but the noise of the engine kept drowning out his words, so he pretty much gave up. The route took them to a more shaded, green area. Nate began to wonder just where they were heading. His anxiety level began to rise, his pulse quickening. He was debating on whether he should just jump out at the next stop, when Wun entered a driveway and stopped the engine. He jumped off his seat and motioned for Nate to get out.

Nate extracted himself from the back of the tuk-tuk and looked up to see a rather nice-looking courtyard. Wide glass doors flanked by a neat guard dressed in a blue uniform led under a sign that proclaimed the building to be the Royal Gemology Museum. Through the glass doors, he could see a middle-aged man in a suit and several young women in smart-looking tan and turquoise uniforms.

Wun took Nate by the arm and started leading him up to the glass doors. "This very good museum. Royal museum. You see, and I wait you here."

Nate was still a little apprehensive despite the nice appearance of the place. An older foreign couple had gotten out of their cab as Nate was getting out of the tuk-tuk, and now they walked up the steps of the museum, the guard grandly opening the door for them.

"You're gonna wait here?" Nate asked Wun.

"Yes, yes, not worry. I wait here for you." He motioned towards the door.

Nate slowly walked up the steps, looking back over his shoulder as Wun moved over to join a small group of men standing near the courtyard's front wall, smoking and talking. The guard at the door opened it for Nate.

"Welcome, sir," he said with a beaming smile.

"Thank you." Nate walked in and the man in the suit hurried up to him.

"Welcome to the Royal Gemology Museum. We have a tour starting in a few moments, so please, come this way." He indicated a small group of couches and chairs off to the side where the couple who had preceded him in were already seated along with a young couple sitting hand-in-hand and two women, pretty obviously mother and daughter, given their similar looks. Nate sat down as an older Thai woman in a white uniform came up to him with a tray of what looked like cola, orange soda, and water. Nate took the cola, thanking the woman.

Nate looked at the young couple. They spoke what might be German together. The girl was really quite stunning. With long blonde hair, she had on a pair of tan shorts which revealed a nice expanse of leg. But more to Nate's interest, she had on a thin green cotton top which plunged remarkably low, and it was evident that she was not wearing a bra. As she leaned forward, putting her forearm on the knee of her companion, Nate could almost glimpse her nipple. He tried to look without seeming to look, but he couldn't see much more across the seating area. Nate briefly took in the guy—good-looking, probably tall (it was hard to tell with him sitting), and with an air of confidence about him. It merely confirmed that if she had a guy like that, she was out of Nate's league.

The mother-and-daughter pair was chatting away about shopping. The mother was fairly fat, and the daughter was on her way to getting there as well. They also had on tan shorts of a shade only slightly darker than the blonde girl was wearing, but Nate was not as interested in what those shorts revealed. They both had pretty impressive breasts, though. Even completely covered up with white smock-like shirts, Nate did wonder what they would look like, what they would feel like. The two women had American accents and seemed oblivious to anyone else sitting there.

Nate looked away, afraid that his wandering thoughts might lead to a physical reaction that others might notice when he stood up. He shifted his attention to the last couple when a very pretty young Thai lady in the tan and turquoise uniform came up to them.

"Hello! My name is Poungkaew, but you can call me Kaew for short." She began to hand out a clipboard with a paper to each group. "I will be your tour guide today, but before you go, please fill out our visitor's form." She smiled as she handed Nate his form, the last one left.

"Today, I will show you how we make gems and jewelry in Thailand. Thailand is one of the world's most important and expert jewelry centers." She went on in that vein as Nate started filling out the form.

He could understand some of the question on the form, such as name, citizenship, and such, but he wondered why they needed to know his income. Not wanting to admit he was unemployed, he checked the box for $50,000 and up. He finished up his form at about the same time as the others and handed it up to the waiting Kaew. She gave the forms to the man in the suit who began to go over them.

"Please, if you follow me, we will begin our tour." She held out her arm in the direction of two swinging doors.

They entered a large room where a number of people seemed to be sorting small stones. Kaew started to explain about gem selection, but Nate's mind was wandering. His interest was more attuned to the blonde girl, who was much shorter than he had imagined while she was sitting down. She kept her arm firmly locked in her companion's, her other hand crossing her chest and holding his arm as well. That unfortunately kept her blouse pressed closed so that Nate could not get a peek at anything.

The group followed the guide towards a line of windows. Behind those windows, technicians were grinding gems on small wheels. Since the blonde was still holding her companion's arm tightly, Nate let his attention wander to the others in the group. The mother and daughter team oohed and aahed at the gems being ground, and Nate's eyes were once again drawn to both of their huge breasts. Looking at the younger girl as she leaned forward to look through the window, her right breast pressed against her blouse, effectively getting outlined. This stirred something inside of Nate, yet he was somehow embarrassed by that. Was it OK to be turned on by a fat girl? He knew what the guys at Oceanside High would say about that, much less what his fellow recruits would. But the fact of the matter was that he was rather intrigued by what he saw.

Turning back to Kaew, the tour guide, he felt more at ease. Now this is someone about whom it was OK to fantasize. She had a very pretty almond-shaped face, rather fair-skin, and was nicely made-up. Her tan one-piece uniform highlighted her slim physique, and the bright turquoise scarf and belt drew his eyes to her flat belly and delicate neck. She was quite a bit shorter than him despite her high heels, and he wondered what it would be like to slow dance with her. Where would her face be if they were dancing close? As she led them to the next room, he walked next to her and tried to gauge just where that would be.

"Here is where we turn our fine gems into beautiful jewelry. Our experienced jewelers have won many international awards for their designs and work."

The mother and daughter rushed up to one of the men who was putting the finishing touches on what looked to be a bracelet. They chattered their amazement and appreciation. The guide stopped talking for a few minutes while they watched. The mother pulled out a small camera and told her daughter, Melody, it turned out was her name, to pose next to the jeweler. Melody put her chubby arm around the jeweler who with good grace, turned away from his work and towards the camera for the photo. Then Melody motioned for her mother to switch places, and then she took her mother's picture. Melody told her mother to stay there, and looking around, she glanced at Nate briefly before catching the eye of the older man there with his wife.

"Can you please take our pic?"

The man looked at his wife before looking back at Melody. "Sure, I reckon I can do that," he responded with what might have been an Australian accent to Nate's untrained ear. At least it sounded sort of like the Crocodile Hunter on the Discovery Channel.

Melody rushed back to her mother, and together, they flanked the slender jeweler, dwarfing him. They looked up at the camera with huge grins on their faces.

"OK! One, two, three!" There was a slight pause, then the flash went off. "Hold on, one more time."

He shifted his position slightly coming closer by about a foot. "One, two, three!"

Again the flash went off and the two women hurried back to retrieve the camera, turning it around so they could see the photo.

"Oh, that is great," squealed Melody. "Look, Momma!"

As she moved to show her mother, she jumped up and down a little, making her massive breasts shift up and down in counter point. Nate was mesmerized.

"Thank you so much, sir!" Melody looked back at the camera, her unabashed pleasure actually refreshing to see.

The tour guide looked around at the others. "Does anyone else want to take a photograph?" When no one stepped up to say yes, she continued, "OK, that ends our tour. Please follow me to the show room." She turned and walked through another set of doors.

That was the tour? Nate wondered how long it has been, certainly no more than 10 minutes total. But he dutifully followed Kaew into a large room with a number of desks and people standing evidently waiting for their arrival. A very petite young girl in the same tan-and-turquoise uniform came up to him and introduced herself.

"My name is Ae. I am pleased to meet you." Her English was good, but a little more stilted and forced than Kaew's rather fluent English. "Would you please sit down here?" she motioned to a seat against a small desk as she sat down behind it.

Another older woman in white came back with a single glass of Coke on a tray, offering it to him. He took it, thanked her, and took a sip.

"So, did you like our tour?" She looked up at him expectantly.

It wasn't much of a tour, but trying to be polite, Nate said, "Yes, it was very interesting."

"I am so happy you liked it. Have you thought about what you might like to take home?"

Take home? It took Nate a minute to realize she was trying to sell him some jewelry.

"Yes, but we want something OUR man made, the man in our photo," Melody's mom almost shouted eagerly as Melody fumbled with her camera to show the young man attending them.

Nate watched them at the next desk over from him, using that as an excuse to delay. He didn't have any money to buy jewelry, and he didn't even want anything. But he was afraid to say that.

"What do you like the most?" Ae asked helpfully.

"Uh, they are all, um, I mean they are all nice, but I really don't need any jewelry now," he at last managed to stumble out, face growing red.

"You don't like our jewelry?" She sounded hurt, a woeful expression coming over her face.

"No, no! They are beautiful. I just don't need any now."

"What about your wife? Don't you think she would like this?" She reached under the desk and pulled out a pair of earrings.

"I'm not married."

"Oh, then how about your girlfriend. You are so handsome and young, I know your girlfriend loves you very much."

"No, no girlfriend." He eyed the exit, wishing he could make his escape.

She gave it another try, putting down the earrings and picking up a necklace, a thin silver chain with a red gem hanging from it. "Well, then everyone has a mother. Think of what she will say when her son gives her this?"

The mention of his mother give Nate a sudden feeling of fortitude. "My mother is dead. And I want to leave now." He stood up.

Ae put the necklace down and motioned to the man in the suit who quickly came over. Ae spoke a few quick words to him.

The man looked to Nate. "So you do not want to buy any jewelry?

"No, sir, I don't." He looked down and met the man's eyes.

"If you don't want to buy any jewelry, why did you come here?"

"The driver, the Thai guy, he took me here. I didn't know where we were going."

The man looked at Nate for a moment, seemed to come to a decision, then shrugged. "Then you are welcome to leave." He stepped back and motioned to the exit door.

Nate, in uncharacteristic defiance, reached over and drained his glass of Coke, then turned and walked across the room and out the door. As he stepped out, Wun looked up and hurried over from the small group of other men he had joined. He asked the guard something in Thai and got a response back.

He got up to Nate. "You no like this place?"

"No, and I want to leave. I am not buying anything here." He looked over at where three tuk-tuks were parked, trying to remember which one was theirs.

Wun motioned him to the middle tuk-tuk and waited as Nate climbed aboard. He looked back "You want different place? Better place, better price?"

Nate felt a little anger take over him. "No! Just take me back now!" Although nervous for taking a stand and confronting Wun, he also felt a bit empowered, and that was a unique and rather pleasurable feeling for him.

Wun stared back at him for a moment, then shrugged, kick-starting the tuk-tuk and pulling out of the courtyard and into the traffic. Not a word was said as he negotiated the route, finally pulling up against the Palace wall. Nate got out and looked around. Wun moved in front of him, hand out.

"200 baht," he demanded.

"What? You said it was for free!" Nate felt a little more anger seep into his soul.

"I take you long way, You no buy anything. I waste time. You give me 200 baht." He held his hand out defiantly, staring up into Nate's eyes with a determined expression on his face.

Nate's anger momentarily fled to be replaced with fear. Was Wun going to attack him? He started to reach into his pocket to pay him, but something stopped the motion of his hand. "No," he simply said, and turned to walk off. For one of the few times in his life, Nate had stood his ground. As he walked off, he listened with a sense of dread for Wun's footsteps coming after him. He almost turned back to give the man the 200 baht, he was so concerned. But he made it to the corner without a confrontation. He quickly glanced back before he walked around the corner of the wall and saw Wun with two new tourists, a big smile on his face.

"Ah, sorry for you, but Palace is closed. Royal ceremony," Nate could barely make out.

He gave a huge sigh of relief, then the shaking started. He felt dizzy. Moving around the corner, he backed up against the wall, sliding down it into a sitting position. He held out his hands which trembled uncontrollably.

How stupid was that? he thought. *I could have gotten killed over 200 baht!*

He sat there for five full minutes, calming his breath as tourists and Thai schoolchildren walked past him. Finally, feeling a little more in control, he looked up to get his bearings. Down about 50 yards was a line of people, so that probably was the entrance to the Palace. He looked at his watch. 12:35. So he had 25 more minutes until the Palace re-opened. He staggered upright, then walked down to the entrance to get in line.

As he joined the line, he saw that it was moving, that people were getting tickets and entering the Palace grounds. He looked at his watch again. 12:37. He frowned in confusion. Alongside the line going in was an intermittent stream of people seemingly coming out. A family of five, two adults and three children came towards him, evidently from inside the Palace. Uncharacteristically for Nate, who normally shied away from strangers, he stepped out a little from his own line and stopped the father.

"Excuse me, sir. But are you coming from inside the Palace?"

The man gave him a puzzled look. "Uh, yes, this is the Palace, and yes, we are leaving it." His eyebrows scrunched together as he seemed to try to figure out Nate's game.

"But isn't the Palace closed for some royal ceremony?"

"Sorry son, if there was a royal ceremony, we never saw it. And the grounds have been open all morning." With his daughter in tow, he stepped around Nate and went on his way.

Nate stepped back into his place in line. So the Grand Palace was never closed today. It had all been a scam by Wun. And the soldier standing right there never said a word. He shook his head, more than a little bit pissed-off.

With the line moving quickly forward, he paid for his ticket. To his right, he saw a foreign couple. The woman was being given a blouse to put over her tube top. Nate was glad Nok had told him about the dress code. He moved forward and entered the grounds of the Grand Palace.

Chapter 7

Nate's jaw literally dropped open. Looking over the heads of a group of older Thai women in front of him, and past a small enclave, a huge building rose up, resplendent in the afternoon sun. Bright white columns supported a layered roof, looking like three roofs had been laid on top of each other, each one a little smaller than the one below it. The top of the roof was a bright orangish red with a surrounding green and then white border. But the front apex of the roof was intricately carved in gold-painted wood. To say it was impressive would be putting it mildly.

Nate followed the crowd past some statues and boxes of sand in which people had placed burning incense sticks, their slightly cinnamony smell permeating the air. He made his way up the steps to the building. A sign proclaimed it as Wat Phra Kaew, home of the Emerald Buddha. People packed the steps, so Nate worked his way up to the top. Shoes were lying everywhere, and people were either in the process of putting on or taking off theirs. Nate reached down and slipped off his Nikes, heedless of untying the laces. He shoved his shoes under a bench, then entered the temple.

As his eyes adjusted to the lower level of light inside, he could see easily a hundred people kneeling on the floor in front of him, most with hands clasped together. Some seemed to be quietly chanting. And the object of their attention was in front of them. In a very ornate pavilion, and high on a gold throne, sat a dark green Buddha. The Buddha looked to be about two feet high, and it was wearing a bright gold hat and some gold straps. But the jade green color was evident. Nate stared at the image, wondering how many people had sat before it and prayed. Millions and millions, he guessed.

Nate took out his camera before noticing a sign with an image of a camera and a slash through it. Too bad, he would have loved to get a photo of it.

On the walls of the structure was a series of very intricate murals. Nate wandered over to the wall on the right and looked closely. He was amazed at the amount of detail in the paintings. It seemed like every inch of it had a figure involved in some activity. Nate didn't know much about Buddhism or Thai history, but the murals reminded him of some Indian paintings he had seen while on a school trip to the San Diego Art Museum.

Nate looked back at the Buddha. He had an urge to join the people praying, but he had no idea on what their reaction would be. What would they think of a foreigner joining him? He decided not to chance it.

With one last look at the Buddha, he moved to the entrance and stepped out, blinking in the bright sunlight. It took him a moment to find his shoes. He tried to put them on while standing up, but after almost falling, he just sat on the ground, having to untie them before he could get them on.

"And in front of you is Wat Phra Kaew. This famous wat houses the Emerald Buddha, perhaps the most famous Buddha in Thailand,"

Nate looked up to see a well-dressed middle-aged Thai woman leading a group of ten or twelve tourists. Her group looked up at the building with interest.

"The Emerald Buddha was first discovered in 1434 in Chiang Mai. What is interesting about the Buddha is that it was then covered in plaster. It wasn't until much later that an abbot, seeing some plaster flake off the Buddha's nose, discovered the jade beneath. The theory is that Thai monks covered the Buddha in plaster to protect it from being looted by foreign soldiers." She started up the steps. "Please take off your shoes before entering the wat."

Nate watched them take off their shoes and enter the wat. He was glad he had overheard the tour guide. Covering a jade Buddha in plaster to make it look less valuable tickled his sense of fancy. He could picture some young monk trying to convince the senior monks to do it, probably getting a lot of grief for that. But it sure paid off in the long run. Now the Buddha was intact and available for everyone to see it.

It was hot out there in the sun, so Nate moved into the shade of a covered wall which ran the length of the compound and looked to continue in the distance around the corner. He looked closer to see another mural on the wall, this one huge in scope. It was aged and somewhat faded, but as with the murals in the other building, the detail was incredible. As he slowly walked along the wall, he saw village scenes, war scenes, many with what looked like monkey-men fighting, palace scenes, monsters, bare-breasted women, children playing, fishermen fishing and farmers farming. He wondered about the people who made it. Did some long ago artist, after working all day, come home to tell his wife that he had painted a whole section of fighting monkeys, only to have his supervisor tell him to paint it over, that his monkeys were not good enough? He rather doubted that the artists had a union back then. He took photos of the mural every few feet, thinking he might want to put them all together in some sort of panoramic view.

Nate wandered where his feet took him. At every turn was something new to see. One building, well, structure, to be more accurate, looked like nothing more than a huge gold hand bell turned upside down. A small sign in front of it proclaimed it to be the Phra Si Rattana Chedi, a stupa erected by King Rama IV in 1855. Nate really didn't know what a stupa was, but he overheard a young Thai woman tell an equally young white guy that there were Buddhist relics inside. Nate wanted to interrupt her to find out just what kind of relics there were, but he couldn't get up the nerve to do so. He just snapped some more photos and hoped to ask someone later.

The buildings really caught his attention. He was impressed at how intricate everything was, the carvings, the paintings. Nate had seen a few old churches back at home, and while some had some fairly detailed stone work, none of them could compare to the detail in the Thai buildings. Again he wondered how long it took to make them, how many people were involved.

Interspaced among the structures were a number of large, 20-foot tall monster men holding swords. Nate figured that they had to be some sort of guards. They looked pretty fearsome, at least, especially the one with a red face. Nate spent quite a bit of time taking their photos, trying to make what he thought might be artistic viewpoints. When he reviewed them on the small camera screen, they didn't actually look that artistic, but maybe they would look better on a computer.

Tour groups, school groups, and groups of monks wandered the grounds. It seemed a little incongruous to see orange-robed monks snapping away with cameras. He thought monks didn't own anything. He wanted to take some photos of them, but he didn't know how to ask. So he took a few photos of the various structures with the monks in the background, instead.

About half of the visitors seemed to be foreign, from small groups of backpackers and families to large, organized tour groups. Nate didn't speak Chinese, but it sounded to him like Chinese was the language of the majority of the tours.

There were also a good number of couples where the men were older and white, with one black guy, and the women were young Thais. One 50's something guy was so red-faced and puffing that Nate thought he was going to collapse.

The Thais seemed to be of all types, although except for the school groups, older people seemed to out-number the younger. The older ones walked slowly, sitting on benches to rest and chatting with others.

Nate wandered back-and-forth, taking photos and drinking in the atmosphere. He eventually found himself in a newer section where huge buildings became prevalent, fronted by nice green lawns. Ceremonial guards in white jackets stood watch. These buildings seemed to be in use. While this area was still interesting, Nate rather liked the older area better.

It was brutally hot, and Nate needed a drink. So reluctantly, he made his way back to the gate. Leaving the grounds, Nate felt that he had really seen Thailand. He vowed to look up more of the history of the country when he next got access to the internet. As he stood on the sidewalk wondering what to do next, his stomach let out a complaining growl. He realized he was starving as well as being thirsty.

He remembered from his internet search that Khao San Road had quite a few places to eat, and since he had passed it on the way to the jewelry store, he knew it was close by. Asking directions, he was pointed across the huge park next to the Palace grounds, so he crossed the road and headed in that direction. Stopping to ask a few more times, he eventually came to the head of the road. There was a Burger King at the top of the intersection of Khao San and the connecting street, and Nate was almost tempted to go inside, but he wanted to try some real Thai food. So he turned left to walk down the Khao San proper.

Khao San was flanked on the sidewalks by numerous vendors selling everything from t-shirts to bikinis to jewelry to handicrafts. Walking between the vendors and the actual store buildings on the narrow path left on the sidewalk was slow going because of the number of tourists ambling around, stopping to look at goods. A very pale-looking girl sat on a chair in a small space beside a booth, a Thai girl braiding her brown hair into very tight braids and incorporating colorful beads every inch or so. The Thai girl's dark hands were in sharp contrast to her customer's pale face.

The press of people pushed Nate past them and further along the sidewalk. To his right, he saw a money exchange. Glancing at the rate for US dollars, he was surprised that it was almost three baht better than what he had gotten at the hotel that morning. He had to remember that for next time.

Feeling a bump in front of him, he looked down to see a very short woman in some sort of native dress, mostly dark blue with some colorful accents and lots of silver. She looked up hopefully at him, holding a carved wooden frog. The frog had some raised bumps along the back, and as the woman ran a wooden stick over the bumps, it made a sound vaguely reminiscent of a real frog's croaking. Nate smiled but shook his head no and sidestepped around her.

The narrow pathway opened up a bit to a restaurant with tables outside. The restaurant had no front, so even inside, it was open to the air. An attractive young lady in a very tight yellow blouse and skirt looked up at Nate and smiled.

"Would you like to have lunch, sir?" She motioned with her arm to an open table.

Well, he was hungry and looking for something to eat, and she was quite pretty, so Nate nodded and sat down at the proffered seat.

"What would you like to drink, sir?" she asked, in a singsong and delicate voice.

Nate looked at her, taking in her slim figure, then noticing that her dress was actually some sort of uniform, albeit a sexy one, for Singha beer. "I'll have a Singha, thank you," he answered right away.

She smiled and walked off to get it. As his stomach growled again, Nate wondered how he could order food. He sat back down to wait to ask the Singha girl for a menu when another girl, a little heavier, but with a very cute smile walked up and gave him the menu. She stood there, pad of paper in hand, ready to take his order.

With her standing there, he felt a little pressured to make his order, but he wasn't familiar with the menu, so he needed to study it.

Nate had had Thai food before, of course, back at home. But was only familiar with the limited menus in the few Thai restaurants to which he went with any degree of regularity. Looking at this menu, which was thankfully written in English as well as transliterated Thai, he scanned it for any of the dishes he had eaten back in California.

Most of the first page had dishes he didn't recognize. The second page had mostly western dishes like burgers, sandwiches, and spaghetti. That was a little disappointing. He could get those back at Denny's in Oceanside. Finally, on the third page, he saw what was labeled as "Thai Dishes."

Partway down the list was "Garlic and Pepper Pork." Nate knew what that was, and he liked it. The transliterated Thai proclaimed it to be *Moo kratiem.* He was hungry, so he wanted more, but the waitress still quietly standing there made him a little nervous, so he picked a noodle dish at random.

He looked up at the waitress, then held the menu out for her, his finger pointing at his first choice. *"Moo katam, kratim,* uh …," he gave up. "Number 32, please." He pushed the menu closer to her, and she wrote it down.

"And, number 64, please," he pointed at the noodle dish.

She nodded. *"Pad see eiw,"* she intoned.

"That's all for now."

She nodded again and walked towards the back as the Singha girl came up with his beer. She placed it on the table in front of Nate, put a slip of paper in the small square box on his table, smiled, then moved off towards the sidewalk, obviously looking for more customers. Nate took a sip of his beer and looked around at the other tables.

When the internet described Khao San Road as a backpacker's destination, it wasn't fooling. Most of the tables had two or more young people of various appearances sitting at them, and fully five of the groups had backpacks on the floor beside them. Nate could hear at least three distinctive languages being spoken, although as one bearded guy motioned to the waitress, he changed languages and asked for his check in accented English.

To his right were two girls, both in shorts and rather small tops. The one furthest from him was quite pretty with red hair and a splash of freckles across her nose. Both were sipping a red, icy looking drink. It looked pretty good to him. He looked back and caught his waitress' eye, motioning her over.

When she got to him, he pointed to the drinks. "Can I have one of those, please?"

She looked over. "Watermelon shake, OK." She noted that on her pad and walked back.

Nate was feeling a little sleepy as he leaned back to watch the people walk by on the sidewalk. He guessed that jet-lag was catching up to him. He looked at his watch.

What time was it back in Oceanside? He wasn't sure if he was supposed to add or subtract. No matter, it was night time back there.

The waitress brought over his watermelon shake, then added her piece of paper to the little box on the table. Nate reached over and took a big sip through the straw. He actually smiled in delight. This was good! He pushed his beer further away from him on his table and replaced its former position with the shake. He probably wouldn't admit it to his friends back home, but he actually liked it better than beer. He looked over at the two girls, wanting to raise his glass in a silent toast of thanks, but they took no notice of him, and he couldn't catch their eyes.

Slowly sipping his shake, he waited until his food came. Looking down at the plates, the pork dish looked similar to what he had had in the States, but the noodle dish was new to him. It consisted of flat brown noodles, some green vegetable, a few small pieces of what looked to be pork, and some egg. He hesitated for a moment. Thai food was supposed to be spicy, so he took a small bit of noodle on his fork and put it in his mouth. Not spicy at all, the noodle had a rich, savory flavor. He took a large bite, this time getting in some of the greens and the pork as well. As with the shake, he was quite pleasantly surprised.

Switching plates, he took a bite of the pork. This was a little different than what he had eaten in California. Where that garlic/pepper pork had tended to be a little dry and very garlicky, this was moister with more sauce and less of a garlic taste. Both styles were good, but this Thai version felt more satisfying than what he remembered getting back home.

In only a few minutes, Nate had scarfed both dishes down. He considered getting another, but looking at his watch, he knew he would be eating dinner before too long. He caught the eye of his waitress and mimed writing a check with his hand. He figured she would just bring it over with her.

Instead, she came over and asked, "You want your check?"

He thought he had been clear on that, but he just responded, "Yes, please."

She reached over to the little box on his table and took out the three pieces of paper there. Her brow furrowed as she looked at the numbers on them in obvious concentration. At the bottom of one, she wrote down some numbers, put that paper in a small tray, then handed it to him.

"Two hundred eighty baht."

She had written the same, of course, on the paper. Nate could see above the 280 two entries in Thai with the number 70 beside one and 60 beside the other. Nate took three 100-baht bills and placed them on the tray.

"Thank you. It was delicious!"

She wai'ed to him and walked back. Nate stood up, stretched, and took a last sip, emptying his shake glass. His beer glass was still half full, but he left it there and walked out.

The Singha girl called out "Thank you for coming sir. See you next time!"

Nate nodded and re-joined the pedestrian flow. Mostly satiated, he let out a contented burp, then looked about in alarm to see if anyone had heard him. No one was paying him the slightest attention, so he just patted his belly and walked on, taking in the atmosphere.

"Sir, fine suits here. Ready in only one day!"

Nate looked up to see an Indian-looking guy standing in front of a tailor shop. The man looked up hopefully at him, but he just smiled and walked on. Two young girls in extremely short shorts were going through a tray of jewelry, excitedly speaking in another language, maybe Japanese, he thought. The girls sort of looked like the jarukan girls he had seen in the videos, at least.

An enticing smell hit his senses. Looking over at the source of the aroma, he saw an older woman grilling pieces of meat on skewers on a cart. He could see chicken and what might have been pork. It really did smell good, but just having eaten, he decided to wait until dinner before eating again.

The entire left side of Khao San Road was now in the shade as the sun moved further to the west. That was a welcome relief from the heat, not that it was really cool in the shade. Just not quite so blistering hot.

"Massage sir?"

Three 20's-something women, each a little stocky and in matching white tops and black drawstring pants stood outside a massage parlor with what looked like menus in their hands. Although he had been determined to ignore all the entreaties coming his way, he was too intrigued not to look. The plastic-covered "menus" were lists of various massages and prices.

"Welcome sir, please have a massage," pleaded the shortest girl, a rather cute girl if a little pudgy. Nate felt trapped. He had made direct eye contact with her, and now he either had to break off or give in. But the idea of a massage was a little exciting. He had read about some massage parlors, and knew they gave "happy endings," and the price of 250 baht for an hour was pretty reasonable.

Taking a deep breath, he made up his mind.

"OK, yes, I want a massage." He pointed to the line on the card for the oil massage. "One hour, please."

She smiled and took his arm in hers, escorting him into the shop. Her head barely came up to his chest. An older girl was reading a newspaper in back of a high counter. She put down the paper as they walked up. The short girl said something in Thai, and the older girl nodded.

"Two hundred-fifty baht, please, one hour," she told him.

Nate took out the money and gave it to her. She put it in a drawer and picked up her newspaper.

"Come with me, please, sir," his masseuse directed. She led him up a rickety stairway to a small open area on the next floor. She motioned for him to sit down on a well-worn wooden bench. Nate sat and watched her bustling about in a counter, then going over to a sink. He was a little nervous, not knowing what to do. Another girl popped her head out of a small room, saw Nate and smiled, then popped back in the room. He could hear a television on inside as the door closed.

His masseuse returned with a basin of water and knelt in front of him. She motioned for his feet, then took off each shoe and sock, placing them neatly under the bench. Then taking each foot in turn, she washed them in the basin. The water was cold, and the brush she used half-way tickled, but Nate had never had his foot washed since maybe when he was a baby, and it felt pretty good.

After she dried his second foot, she took him by the hand and into the adjoining room. Pulling aside a curtain revealing a small, flat floor pad, she motioned him inside.

"Take off your clothes, please, then lay down."

She closed the curtain on him. Nate looked down at the pad. Outside the shop, this sounded pretty exciting, but now that he had to undress, he felt apprehensive; still a little excited, but more on the apprehensive side. He took off his shirt and hung it on a nail sticking out of the wall. Looking around to make sure no one could see him, he took off his jeans. Standing there in his underwear, he wondered if she had meant completely naked or not. He decided to keep on his boxers. He slowly lay face down on the pad, pulling the folded towel and placing it over his butt.

He lay there for several minutes, wondering what was going to happen next. Finally, he could hear approaching footsteps, and a voice called out.

"Are you ready?"

"Uh, yes," he croaked, his voice catching.

Face down, he couldn't see her enter, but he could hear the curtain close again, and he could feel the floor pad give as she walked on it. She placed a towel over his butt and legs, then knelt beside him, her knee touching his side. He could hear something squirt, then hands touching his shoulders.

"You like hard or soft?"

Nate considered. He really didn't know which he preferred, but since his masseuse was so small, she probably was not too strong. Hard made more sense, then.

"Hard, please."

Her hands increased the pressure, As she pushed down between his shoulder blades, the air was forced out of him in a huff. She was much stronger than she looked.

Nate was extremely aware of her hands on him. A girl's hands on his naked back, skin to skin. He started to get an erection, but lying on his stomach, it was not free to spring up. Embarrassed, Nate was glad he was on his stomach.

"What is your name, sir?" she asked, hands steady in their strokes.

"Nate."

"Pleased to meet you Nate. I am Gaey."

She didn't say anything more, and Nate didn't know what to say, so he just lay there in silence, feeling her hands. She pulled down the towel off his butt a bit, then his underwear, tucking the edge of the towel inside the boxer's elastic band. Nate's erection grew even more rigid. It was painful in that position, but Nate was not going to reach under to move it into a more comfortable aspect.

Gaey's rhythmic hands lulled Nate into a deep sense of relaxation. This really felt good. His neck was uncomfortable as he was face-down without a pillow, but despite this, he felt himself drifting off.

"OK, turn over please."

Nate woke up with a start, a little bit of drool hanging outside his mouth. He couldn't believe it. He had fallen asleep. He could feel the oil residue on his back and legs, so he must have slept for some time.

"Turn over please," she repeated.

Gaey was holding the towel up in between them, blocking her view as he turned over. He was glad his erection was gone, even if he had his boxers on and if Gaey placed the towel over his waist after he was on his back.

She picked up his left arm, placing his hand in her lap as she started to work the muscles in it. Nate was very, very aware of the proximity to her crotch that this placed his hand. His erections started to spring up again. Quickly glancing down, he could see a small tent forming with the towel, his erection being the tent's center-pole.

"You are very big. Make me no power," she laughed.

Grateful for the interruption, he responded, "Oh, you have plenty of power. You are very strong."

"You like?"

"Yes, very much."

"Good. You are from America?" She didn't pause in her work.

"Yes. From California."

"Yes, yes, I know California. Some day I will go California. See Sea World! Shamu!"

"Ah, Sea World is near my home!"

"Really? Maybe I stay with you then!" she laughed.

She moved to his hand, cracking each knuckle, then massaging his palm and each finger. It really did feel good, he thought.

She took a small towel and wiped down his arm, removing most of the oil. Then she shifted position and moved the towel exposing all of his left leg, rolling up the edge of his boxers as well. She tucked the edge of the towel and underwear under his penis, moving it slightly. Nate almost jumped up, but forced himself to lie still. She had to have noticed his erection, but she said nothing.

She started to work on his leg, making long sweeping strokes up his thighs. Nate's erection grew harder, throbbing in time with his heart beat. She didn't seem to notice. Nate could feel his face get red, even if he couldn't see it. She moved down to his lower leg, and then, mercifully, at last to his foot. Nate risked a look down, and he could see Gaey's rounded butt as she knelt facing away from him. He looked back up at the ceiling, then closed his eyes.

She shifted to his right leg and started the same routine. Nate was torn between the pleasurable sensation of her hands, his excitement, and embarrassment. He wanted the massage to last longer, but at the same time, he wanted it over.

Finishing with his leg, she moved to the bottom of the pad and brought his two feet together. Alternating between pushing on his toes and pulling, she stretched out his calf muscles. Then she walked up his legs with her hands, placing them right in the crease between his thighs and groin, pressing down. He could feel that press the towel tightly against his erection, but she said nothing. She held that position for at least 20 seconds—Nate could feel his femoral pulse start to pound as it had nowhere to go. Suddenly, she released the pressure, and he thought he could actually feel the blood rush back into his legs.

Moving to his right arm, she mirrored what she had done to his left. Her strong hands searched for tight spots in his muscles. Once again, Nate was very aware of where his hand was, once slightly brushing her breast, and once laying on her inner thigh as she worked.

With the arm done, she moved to his torso. With broad, horizontal strokes, she pressed strongly against his stomach. On one stroke, her hands caught the towel, pulling it over, releasing his erection from constraints, although it was still thankfully covered by his boxers. Gaey calmly took the towel, slid the edge of it beneath his erection, then folded the rest of the towel back over and down his groin. She moved up to his chest pressing down hard, forcing his breath out with each push.

Finally, she told him to sit up. She moved around behind him, sat down, and told him to lie back down, his head in her lap. She took his head and proceeded to massage it. In some ways, this was the best, most enjoyable part of the massage. Nate really didn't want her to stop when she told him to sit up.

Bearing down on his back, she compressed his spine, then stretched it back out. She twisted his arms in a few positions, then lightly hit his back a number of times. The final hit was a little harder than the rest.

"OK, finished!"

She stood up and walked to the front.

"You get dressed now, then come outside."

Nate looked around the now empty space. He was both disappointed and relieved. What about the "happy ending" he had read about? He could imagine her strong hands giving him relief. On the other hand, he had been pretty embarrassed, and he was at least a little glad that it was all over. He got dressed and walked out of the space and back to where his shoes were.

Gaey came out with a cup of tea for him. He sipped it as she took his shoes and put them on him. She didn't quite get the socks smooth enough for him, but he decided to fix that after he left. He stood up, and reaching into his pocket, he pulled out a 100-baht note and gave it to her. She wai'ed and thanked him before escorting him back down the stairs and out into the street.

"See you next time!" she told him with a smile.

He looked at his watch. It was already after five o'clock. He should get back to his hotel. Walking back to the head of Khao San, he was quickly accosted by several tuk-tuk drivers. Picking the one nearest to him, he told him to take him to the Holiday Inn, clamored aboard, and leaned back for the traffic-clogged ride.

Chapter 8

Nate walked into the refreshing coolness of the hotel lobby. Despite the massage, he felt grimy from the sweat and road dust. Checking the reception desk before heading to the elevators, he was happy to see Nok still on duty. He walked slowly up to the desk and stood there for a moment until she looked up from some papers.

"Ah, Khun Nate!" A huge smile broke over her face. "Did you enjoy the Grand Palace? Yes, I think so."

"Yes, it was very beautiful."

Not as beautiful as you, though, he thought.

"I am happy you liked it."

She looked at Nate with that huge smile never wavering. Nate felt awkward, at a loss for something to say. He grinned back stupidly at her. He felt a small degree of panic starting to creep over him.

"Well, I think I need to go to my room now. I need a shower."

"OK, Khun Nate. Have a good night."

She looked back down to her papers as Nate hurriedly turned and walked back, his heart rate racing a little. He made it to the elevators without tripping, a major accomplishment, he thought, and went up to his room.

He hadn't only used the shower as an excuse to leave the reception desk. He positively reeked. Slipping off his clothes, (and leaving them in a pile on the floor) he stepped into the shower, luxuriating in the hot needles of water. This really was some shower!

After a long 15 minutes, he stepped out and toweled off. Dropping his towel on the floor, he eased himself down on the bed. He glanced at the clock: 5:36. He didn't want to sleep this early, knowing that was a good way for him to wake up again at zero-dark-thirty. Grabbing the remote, he turned over and turned on the television. Flipping through the channels, his attention was caught on *The Biggest Loser*. Kind of surprised to see that on Thai television, he pulled the pillow down and under his head and settled back to watch. Although not really overweight himself, he had always had some empathy for the contestants on the show, he felt somehow in the same boat with them. His mind started to wander a bit as the red team discussed their workout strategy, and…

…a knocking on the door woke him up.

"Sir, turn you bed down?" came the voice through the door.

He looked up at the clock. 10:48. Crap! He'd slept for five hours. Still naked from the shower, he struggled to a sitting position.

"Uh, no thanks! Not now," he managed to shout out.

"Very good sir."

He looked back up at the clock, willing it to be earlier, but it defiantly stayed the same. Sleep dragged at him, trying to pull him back down. But he knew that would be the kiss of death. He would sleep like the damned, but wake up again at 2:00 or 3:00 AM ready to go, bright-eyed and bushy-tailed. Besides, he was in Thailand! He could sleep when he got back home.

Pulling himself out of bed, he stumbled over to the bathroom where he took a leak, then splashed water on his face. He blearily checked his reflection in the mirror. He guessed he would do. Walking back to the bedroom, he picked up his underwear off the floor and gave them a sniff. Well, maybe he should wear cleans ones. Dropping them back on the floor, he got a fresh pair out of his suitcase, then pulled on a pair of shorts and a t-shirt. He took a few thousand baht out of his wallet and put them in his pocket, then opened his safe and locked his wallet away. He read horror stories about men being robbed of their wallets, not just on the street or the bars, but also in their rooms. He had read online that in Hong Kong a few months ago, two Filipina hookers drugged their American clients in order to rob them, but they had given the men too much of the drug, and both Americans actually died.

Nate looked at the mirror over the dresser, tucking his shirt in, then pulling it out again, wondering which way looked best. Doing this several times, he finally decided on out. Giving the short stubble on his head a stroke with his hand, he nodded, then left the room.

Getting off the elevator, he peeked around the portioning walls to the reception desk to see if Nok was there. Feeling relief that she wasn't, he quickly walked out the doors, and waving off the waiting taxis, he turned left again for his walk to Nana Plaza.

An elevated train rumbled past over his head. Nate knew the BTS, as it was called, would take him right to Nana in two stops, but he was a little nervous at trying to navigate the process of buying a ticket, so walking seemed easier.

Traffic was heavy, albeit not quite as heavy as the night before. Then again, it was late Sunday night, so it made sense that traffic would be lighter. After 20 minutes of walking, Nate came up to the intersection with Soi Nana and Sukhumvit. Looking further down Sukhumvit, Nate could see a dense line of booths and stalls lining the sidewalks. He was somewhat intrigued by them, but he was more interested on what waited for him inside Nana Plaza, and he really didn't want to get caught short like he was the night before. So wiping his brow with his arm, he joined the mass of people slowly crossing the intersection. Walking directly behind two young girls wearing extremely tight white shorts, he felt his excitement level rising. Was tonight the night?

Several girls called out to him as he made his way past the open-walled bar and entered Nana Plaza, but he wanted Nok from the night before. As he approached the Red Lips, a girl started to ask him to come in, but when she saw his determined walk, she just quit her spiel with a smile and held open the curtain closing off the doorway. Nate entered the bar and stood for a moment trying to get his bearings. Several girls held out their arms indicating tables for him, but as the table at which he sat yesterday was free, he chose to sit there, ordering a Singha from the waitress.

Peering at the dancers on the stage, he tried to find Nok.

Was that her in the back?

Nate wasn't quite sure. He wasn't great with faces, and that could be her. When she glanced at him, he smiled and waved. She smiled back. Satisfied that that was in fact Nok, he settled back a little in his chair and took a sip of the beer the waitress has just placed before him.

So he was a little startled when two arms came around his neck and a voice said in his ear, "Hello Nate! You come back!"

He turned within the grasp to see Nok standing there behind him. He quickly brought his hands together in front of him in a wai.

"*Sawadi kha.* I wanted to see you again, so I came back."

"*Sawadi kha,* Khun Nate," she wai'ed back with a small bow of her head.

Nate was little embarrassed that he had mistaken the dancer for Nok, and as Nok slid down beside him in the bench seat, he caught the eye of the dancer. She frowned over-dramatically at him, using a finger held up to the corner of her eye to mime that she was crying. Feeling doubly bad for a moment, he was relieved when the dancer broke out into a laugh.

He forgot about the dancer as Nok grabbed his arm with both of hers, pulling it into her, up against her breasts, her small black bikini top not offering them much protection. She leaned over to give him a kiss on his cheek.

"Welcome back. I miss you *mak mak!*"

She had on a wrap of some sort which covered what was probably the same type of bikini bottom the other dancers on stage were wearing. But she still had quite a bit of naked thigh, and as she scooted closer to him, her right leg was pressed up against his left leg, skin-to-skin.

"You buy me drink, OK?" She dropped one hand from his arm to give his thigh a squeeze.

At his assent, she motioned over the waitress and ordered something in Thai. Waiting for the drink, she stroked his bicep.

"You very strong man. Big."

She held up her own arm in a flexed bicep position, then laughed. She squeezed her own bicep, then squeezed his again in comparison.

"Maybe everything big!" she said, quickly patting his crotch.

His erection had been pretty rampant from the moment she sat down, so she could clearly feel it.

"Oh, your little brother very happy!" she laughed again, then saying something in Thai to the waitress who was bringing up her drink at that moment.

The waitress laughed, then said, "Strong man!"

Nate felt both mortified and excited at the same time, if that was possible. He didn't know what to say, so he was relieved when Nok picked up her drink and offered it for a toast.

"Cheers!"

Nate clinked her glass with his bottle, then took a sip. Nok took a few rather robust sips, draining half of her glass.

She pulled Nate's arm in closer to her breasts, then watched the dancers for a few moments. Not sure how to proceed, Nate watched them, too. The girl dancing directly in front of him wasn't dancing the night before, he was sure. While he wasn't always good with faces, her body was something he would have remembered. She had a very flat belly and extremely small waist, but her breasts swelled rather spectacularly, lushly filling out her bikini top. She danced slowly, ignoring the men while watching her reflection on the mirrors along the wall. Nate had a hard time keeping his eyes off of her.

"Many beautiful girls here. You like?" Nok indicated the dancers with a sweep of one arm.

Nate felt guilty for a moment, ogling a dancer with Nok right beside him. "They aren't so pretty. I like you the best."

"Oh, sweet lips. *Kop khun kha!*" She managed to wai with her arms on either side of his arm.

The song being played ended, and the girls milled around the stage for a few moments, several of them clumping together to talk before *One Night in Bangkok* came over the speakers. Most of the girls clapped and squealed, moving into a half-assed line and doing the same dance together. A couple of the waitresses started moving in place as well, not so much doing the steps, but doing the same arm movements along with the dancers. This was obviously a popular song, one with its own dance steps.

Nate's father had told him once that the song was really about a chess tournament in Bangkok and that it rather demeaned the bar scene. He looked around the bar and wondered if any of the other patrons knew the real meaning of the song. The dancers certainly didn't seem to realize they were actually the brunt of the criticism in the lyrics. They had bigger smiles and danced with more energy than with the previous couple of songs being played. They looked like they were actually having fun.

Nok nudged him and pointed at her empty glass, eyebrows raised in an unspoken question. Nate nodded, and Nok quickly got the attention of their waitress, raising her glass with one hand and pointing to it with the other. By raising her hand, her arm drove Nate's arm deeper into her breast. He could feel her bare skin above her top on the bare skin of his arm.

They watched the dancers in silence until her second drink arrived. She lifted it up for a toast, then after clinking drinks with him, she again drained half of the pale blue liquid in the glass with her first swallow. Putting the glass down, she stood up and leaned over to kiss him on the cheek.

"I go dance now."

A little disappointed, he watched her leave, but instead of going directly to the stage, she went to a table in the corner where a bald man seemingly deep into his cups sat. She scooted around the table top to sit beside him, giving him a kiss on the cheek before lifting a glass there up in a toast. It was hard to tell in the dimness of the bar away from the stage, but the man didn't look too happy. He did, however, lift his bottle of beer up to clink with her glass.

Nate was rather confused and slightly upset, truth-be-told. He craned his neck around to watch the two of them, wondering what he should do.

"You don't want to be messing with her, mate," a voice intruded from his left.

Nate looked over to see two men in the adjoining table, the nearest one leaning towards him, a bottle of beer in his hand. He lifted it up in a small salute, then took a sip.

"Excuse me?"

"Nok. That bird. You don't need to be messing with her." The man used the beer bottle as a pointer, indicating Nok.

The man was very skinny and probably short, but he had an air of toughness about him. He spoke in what Nate thought was an English accent.

"What do you mean?"

"Nok's just a tease. She doesn't shag anyone. A young lad like you, I know what you want. And Nok isn't going to give it to you." He winked before taking another swig from his bottle.

One Night in Bangkok finally stopped, and the dancers on stage began to file off of it. Other girls stood up and began to move to the stage. Nok was one of them, and she blew Nate a kiss as she walked past him.

"But, I thought, I mean…"

"Yea, I know what you thought. And most of these girls, sure, they're up for it, but not Nok. She just gets lads to buy her ladies' drinks." He scooted over a bit along the bench seat to get a little closer to Nate.

Nate watched Nok climb the steps up to the stage. He really wanted her. But if this guy was right, then he wasn't going to get her.

The man stuck out his hand. "Name's James," he said with a smile.

Nate took the hand. "Nate, sir. My name's Nate."

"Well, 'Natesir,' you want to get laid, right?"

"Just Nate, not 'Natesir'"

James rolled his eyes. "I bloody well know that. I'm just pissing with you."

"Oh sorry, sir."

"Just James, not sir. Well, do you bloody well want to get banged or not?"

Nate was a little embarrassed by his directness. On the other hand, having someone else take charge seemed like it might make things easier.

"Yea, I want to get laid."

"Of course you do, lad. That is why we come to LOS after all, isn't it?" He pronounced "LOS" as "El Oh Ess."

Nate knew that "LOS" meant "Land of Smiles," but having only read it online, he didn't know how it was pronounced.

"Take my advice, lad. You want a good time? You want a stunner who'll full-on take care of you? Then take An. She's that short-haired bird who just sat down over there."

Using his beer bottle as a pointer again, he indicated a slender girl who had just sat down a couple of tables away. Nate realized that she was the same girl he had seen last night, at closing time.

"Is she good?" he asked.

"Is she good?" James repeated, with an exaggerated American accent. "Hey smeghead!" he shouted at the other man at his table, a rather tall, rotund man with a bright-white shock of hair.

He looked over the head of the smaller Thai girl who was sitting next to him with a bored look on her face.

"This is my new mate Nate. He needs to get shagged, and he wants to know if An is any good."

"Smeghead" merely looked over and gave Nate a thumbs up.

"See, what'd I tell you? All these Thai birds are slappers, but An is the full monty. They don't come any better. Just trust your Uncle James."

He started waving his arms to get her attention. One of the other girls saw him and touched An's arm, then pointing at James. He motioned her over.

A little embarrassed at how this was turning out, Nate never-the-less liked what he saw of An's slender body as she walked over. Her short hair was somewhat boyish, but there was no mistaking the sway of her hips as she walked. She made it to Nate's table and wai'ed.

"An darling, this is my mate Nate. He's a …." He looked over at him. "You a Yank, Nate?"

"Yea, from California."

"A Yank , a Yank with a crank, and he needs someone to take care of him tonight. Be a doll and do what you do best."

An smiled and slid on the seat beside Nate, holding out her hand.

"Pleased to meet you, Nate," she said, with only a light trace of accent.

Nate took her hand in his. It seemed small and fragile to him,

"*Sawadi kha*," Nate said, trying to wai while sitting behind the table.

An smiled and started to say something when James broke out laughing. "You a nancy boy Nate? Maybe we got you the wrong kind of date tonight."

Nate wasn't 100% sure what a "nancy boy" was, but he could guess. "No, I like girls. Why did you ask me that?"

"You said '*sawadi kha*.'"

"Yes, so what?"

"Only girls and ladyboys, say 'kha' after a word. Men say '*krup*.' Men say '*Sawadi krup. Kop khun krup.*'"

Nate felt his face going red. *Was that true?* He looked to An who smiled.

"*Mai pen rai*. Never mind," she said.

So it was true. He felt mortified.

"I'm just pissing with you." He slapped Nate on the shoulder. "You just have a good time tonight, and you can buy me a pint tomorrow." He winked and scooted back over to his own table.

An scooted as well, moving closer to Nate. She seemed so small sitting there. He wondered just how much she weighed.

"Welcome to Thailand, Nate. Are you here on your holiday?"

"Yes," he replied simply, trying not to look too closely at her small but firm breasts.

"How long will you be here?" She didn't seem to notice his wandering eyes.

"Um, I am not sure. Maybe a month."

"Oh, that is very good. You can have a good time here. Maybe with me," she laughed, putting her arm on his.

"Maybe."

She laughed at him. "I am just teasing you , Khun Nate. You are young and strong. I think you are a butterfly." She looked up at his face, really sizing him up for the first time. "You really are young. How old are you?"

"I'm 19." He had planned on saying he was 21, but the truth blurted out again.

"Oh my goodness. You are a baby!" she laughed again.

Nate didn't know how to respond to that, so he picked up his bottle and took a swig. A voice in Thai seemed to be directed at him from the stage. Nok had moved over and was directly opposite him, and she was angrily saying something in Thai to An. An responded back. This went back and forth a few times until An flipped her hand at Nok, like she was brushing off a fly.

"Is everything OK?" asked Nate worriedly.

"*Mai pen rai*, Khun Nate. Never mind." She squeezed his arm.

"But she seems pretty pissed."

"She is a bitch. She is mad because you are with me now." She suddenly looked up to him with a questioning look. "Do you like me?"

"Yes, yes, I do. I like you."

"OK, then. No problem."

She leaned her head to lay it on his upper arm. They sat like that for a few moments. Nate wondered what he was supposed to do next.

"An, do you want a drink?"

"Oh thank you Khun Nate." She smiled and scooted up so she could give his cheek a peck.

She motioned to the waitress and made her order.

"I think you are a very nice man, Khun Nate. I want to make you happy tonight."

Nate was pretty sure what she meant, and he could feel a quantum leap in his excitement level. It looked like tonight would be a night to remember.

An's drink arrived, a bright yellow liquid in a glass with ice. An thanked the waitress and took a sip, grimacing.

"Oh, this is very strong," she said, shaking her head. "Here, you try it." She held the glass up to his mouth.

Nate hesitated. He wasn't sure how he would handle something too strong, and he didn't want to cough or choke in front of her. But he really couldn't back down now. So he hesitantly took a small sip.

Of water. Nothing more.

He looked down on her with a confused expression. She was smiling broadly and broke out into a laugh.

"The joke is for you! It is just water."

"I don't get it."

"Khun Nate, we all use colored water for ladydrinks. So we don't get drunk." She put her hand up to her face, flicking her forefinger against her cheek. "Some girls get real drinks, but then they are drunk and can't get more drinks. Can't…" she leaned closer to him and lowered her voice. "…can't boom boom good." She laughed again.

Nate must still have look confused as she added, "Khun Nate, Baby Nate. We get one half of ladydrinks. If you pay 150 baht, we get 75 baht for our salary. So we need to be able to drink many drinks. If we drink many drinks, we make many money. No wait, we make much money, right? Much money, not many money."

Nate laughed. He just realized that he was sitting with a bikini clad "stunner," as James had described her, an apt a description as Nate had ever heard, and he was in the midst of an English lesson.

"Why did you laugh? Did I make a mistake?"

"No, no. I just like you, and I'm happy I'm here." He felt a moment of courage and slipped his arm around her.

"OK, good. I am glad you like me."

"And now you've given me all your trade secrets. Now I know the truth about ladydrinks," he teased.

"I am a bar girl, but I am honest. I want you to buy me drink, but I do not lie to you." She seemed earnest.

"I know, and I appreciate that."

He leaned back. She felt good under his arm. She was tiny, but firm. He was getting pretty excited. He wondered how he was supposed to get to the next step, because without a doubt, he wanted her.

"An, you said you wanted to make me happy," he stammered out. "Um, well uh, how do we do that?"

"Do you want me to go to your hotel with you?" she asked as if she was asking about the time or commenting on the weather.

"Yes," he said simply.

"Do you know about the bar fine?"

"I read about it, but I have never done this before."

"So I am your first Thai girl? Thank you! For me to go with you, you pay the bar first 500 baht. Then I will go with you, and you pay me. Do you want long time or short time?"

Nate only hesitated second. She was really pretty spectacular, and getting prettier by the minute. "Long time."

"For long time, you pay me 2500 baht. And I leave at 6:00 AM. That OK with you?"

Nate tried to remember what the guy on the plane had said. *Was it 1,500 baht for a long time?*

He was tempted to ask for a lower price, but really, he didn't care. "That's fine."

She smiled and kissed him on his cheek again. "Do you want to go now, or do you want to stay here?"

"I want to go now," he managed to get out.

She smiled again. "I thought so."

She motioned to the waitress who started totaling up the bill. With the bar fine, it came to almost 1,000 baht. Nate paid it.

"OK, Khun Nate, I will go change my clothes."

She stood up, her head barely higher than Nate's as he sat there. She gave him another kiss, then walked towards the back of the bar, her small butt swaying alluringly. Nate couldn't believe that in a short time, he would have that butt, naked, in front of him.

He sat back down to wait, and the minutes stretched on. Nok was still dancing, taking every opportunity she could to stare daggers at him. Not wanting to catch her eye, he stopped looking at all of the dancers.

"Well my mate Nate. What'd I tell you?" James asked from his table.

"Yea, she is pretty good."

"Pretty good he says," he said, turning to Mr. Smeghead. He looked back at Nate. "She is full-on hot!"

"OK, yea, she's pretty hot," he said sheepishly.

"Bloody right. Speaking of which, here comes your bride," he indicated over Nate's shoulder where An was returning.

An had changed into a pair of jeans and a white casual top. Carrying her purse, she looked a pretty far stretch from a bargirl. She smiled at Nate and tilted her head to the door in a question.

"Yes, let's go."

Nate stood up, let her take his hand, and started walking out. James put his left hand over his chest and held up his right in a priestly benediction pose.

"Go forth, my son, and sin some more," he intoned.

An reached over to give him a smack on his shoulder.

"Ah, my child, you wound me!"

"I will wound more of you, Khun James!" she laughed.

"Is that a promise?"

She pulled Nate along and out the door. Nana Plaza was still busy, the smells of stale beer, grilling chicken, and cheap perfume intermixed into a heady miasma of blatant vice. Nate breathed in and could feel his excitement level creep up a notch.

"What hotel are you at?" she asked.

"Holiday Inn," he replied, looking down at her as she grasped his arm. The way she clung to it made him feel protective.

"Which one?"

"The one right down the road here, across from the Intercontinental."

"OK, I know that one."

She released his arm and leaned down to speak into the open window of a cab on the street in front of the Nana Plaza entrance. She evidently came to an agreement as she looked back at Nate and gestured for him to get in. He ducked his head and slid into the seat the best he could, and she followed him, scrunching up close so that her legs were pressed up against his. The taxi crept up a few feet to wait for the light to change. Nate was surprised that there were so many cars still on the road at this hour.

The light finally turned green, and the taxi pulled onto Sukhumvit. Traffic opened up, and in a surprisingly short time, perhaps two minutes or so, they were pulling into the hotel drive. Nate paid the driver and got out. He felt guilty, but the doorman didn't blink an eye.

"Welcome back, sir," he said, pulling the large door open for the two of them.

They entered the lobby. Nate kept his head down as he moved to the far left, anxious to stay as much out of sight as possible as he went to the elevators. As he made it past the partition, he let his breath out, not realizing that he had been holding it. He turned back to An and was shocked to see her marching up the reception desk, bold as can be.

He hurried after her, panic raising a lump in his throat. She reached the counter and handed over her ID. She looked up at Nate.

"Which room," she asked.

He was tempted for a second to make up a room, but he answered her truthfully, "1204."

The receptionist typed something into the computer, gave An back her ID card, then smiled.

"Have a nice night, Mr. Foster."

An took his arm and started walking to the elevators. He let himself be pulled along. The doorman hurried over from the front doors and pushed the elevator up button.

"Have a good night, sir," he said cheerfully, as the door opened and they stepped inside.

The doors closed, and Nate got his voice under control.

"Why did you do that?"

"Do what, dear?" she asked.

"Go up to the desk like that, give them your ID."

She looked perplexed for a moment. "That is rules of hotel. All girls must register. Then they know who is here. It protects the men. Some street girls are not so good, you know."

Nate still felt embarrassed. He didn't want anyone to know he was with a prostitute. What if they reported it to the US embassy? What would happen when he got back to the US?

An mistook his hesitation. "But you do not worry. I am a good girl for you. I am not a bad girl."

The door opened and An stepped out with Nate in tow, immediately turning to the right without bothering to read the little signs directing guests to the room numbers. They got to his door, and Nate swiped the keycard, having to do it four times before his hand was steady enough for it to be read. The indicator light finally turned green, and they entered the room. He took the "Do Not Disturb" sign and hung it outside the door.

An stepped in, slipped off her shoes, then walked over to the bed and sat down on it. She stretched lazily, like a cat. Nate came over to sit beside her, not sure how to proceed.

"Do you have a condom?" she asked matter-of-factly.

"Uh, yes, I do. He stood up and went to his suitcase, feeling beneath the bottom plate where he had stuffed his condoms so they could not be seen by anyone looking in his luggage. It was a little difficult to get his fingers into the small opening, but he was able to snag the edge of a condom and pull it out. He held it up for An to see, then sat down beside her again.

"You want to take your shower now?" she asked.

Nate hadn't realized that a shower was necessary, but if it was, he had no qualms.

"Sure, I'll take mine now."

He stood up, looked around the room as if not knowing what to do, then went into the bathroom. He considered, then closed the door partway, leaving it open a good two or three inches. He hurriedly brushed his teeth, then slipped off his shorts and shirt. As his shorts and underwear came off, his cock stood up at rampant attention. He turned on the water, and after it warmed up, he jumped in, quickly lathering himself up with the sweet-smelling soap. As he was rinsing off, he thought he heard something and pulled the curtain back to reveal An demurely sitting on the toilet like a princess, but a princess stark naked. He gulped and reflexively started to duck back behind the curtain, but then he realized that looking was OK now, so he gave a goofy grin instead.

An looked up at him and smiled, so she wasn't upset that he could see her. She reached for the butt spray thing alongside the toilet. It looked just like a sprayer on the kitchen sink at home, but it didn't take a genius to figure out its use. She put the sprayer head between her legs for a second. Then put it back and stood up.

Nate gulped again. Standing not two feet away from him was a completely naked woman. Her hair was very short, shorter than he had ever really seen on a girl, but it seemed to frame her cherubic face. But it wasn't her face which drew Nate's attention.

Very petite, she never-the-less had well shaped, if small breasts. Their shape could not have been better, in Nate's excited opinion, and each had a rather large, protruding dark nipple. Below her breasts, her waist shrunk to the point that Nate figured he could span it with his hands. And then, below that, he could just see a few tufts of pubic hair peeking out at him.

She let him take her in for a moment before she stepped into the shower to join him. Nate hurriedly stepped back to give them both some room.

"Oh, too hot!" she exclaimed, moving to lower the water temperature. Nate liked it hot, but she could have changed it to an ice mist, for all he could care.

She fiddled with the shower knob for a few moments before nodding with satisfaction and turning toward Nate. Taking the soap, she lathered up her hands, then reached up to start soaping down his chest.

The massage he had gotten also had a girl touching his chest, but this was different. This was electrifying. She rubbed his chest in slow circles, spreading the soap further and further. She motioned for him to turn around, and after he complied, she did the same for his back.

She stepped away for a second, and Nate looked back to see her soaping up her breasts. She turned Nate back around and pushed her body up against his, rubbing her soapy breasts against his lower back and butt. Her hands grasped his hips to enable her to put pressure as she rubbed against him. To say he liked that was rather an understatement.

Nate was acutely aware of his erection, but she seemed oblivious to it. He was both embarrassed and proud of it at the same time, if that was possible.

His senses seemed on overload. He could feel her soapy hands rubbing his back, and the warm needles of water hitting him.

"Turn around, please," she directed him.

He complied and looked down at her small body. Her hair was now plastered to her skull, and the water flowed down off her shoulders and over her breasts, water streaming off her nipples. She soaped up her hands again, then reached out and took his penis in her hands, soaping it up as well. Nate groaned, in pleasure or pain, he really wasn't quite sure. She used her foot to kick the inside of his foot, indicating for him to spread his legs. He did, and she reached under his scrotum and ran her soapy hands along his anus. Nate had never felt anything like that before.

His pulse was hammering as she moved back to his cock, rubbing it with her soapy hands. In a panic, Nate could feel himself quickly coming to the brink of release. He started to step back, but he hesitated, and that was enough. As her hands cleaned up and down his shaft, he exploded in a rush. The rush of water from the shower head was no competition as his ejaculate burst upwards, part of it hitting An's chest and face.

An didn't seem to notice for a moment, then she jumped back, almost slipping in the shower.

"*Chok rai,*" she exclaimed, as she grabbed Nate's arms to keep upright.

Nate was mortified. He could see his sperm on her chest where the water hadn't rinsed it away yet.

"What,...why did you do that?" she asked, if not angrily, then in something close to that.

"I'm sorry! I didn't mean to. I just, well, I've nev..., I mean, I've never had a woman touch me like that, and I, well,..." he trailed off.

She looked up at him for a second before understanding seem to come over her face. "You mean, you are a virgin?"

Nate felt a familiar feeling of inferiority come over him. He was 19 years old and still a virgin. Some of his friends had gotten laid when they were 13 or 14. Most of his friends back in San Diego had had sex, but the closest Nate had ever gotten is when he and Rick Patterson had felt up Susan Throndson behind her garage one night, and that was over her clothes. He has never touched the naked skin of a woman, much less had sex. And now An knew the truth. He was pretty much a failure in the girl department. He looked at her, wondering how she would react.

She stared at him for a second, then to his surprise, she broke into a laugh—not laughing at him, but with him, as they say.

"You should have told me that. No wonder 'you horny *mak mak*,'" she said, using a very exaggerated accent for that last part.

She gave him a big hug, squeezing him tight. He could feel his still somewhat rampant cock press up against her stomach, almost reaching her breasts. She leaned back a bit so she could look up at him.

"Don't worry. We have more time, and you will have more power soon. You are young, so we will fix this soon."

She casually ran her hand over the last bit of sperm still clinging above her right breast. Bending down to pick up the soap where she had dropped it, she soaped up her hands again, and started washing him.

As she started to wash his penis once more, she bent over as if addressing a child, one finger wagging. "This time, you wait until your big brother is ready."

She handed Nate the soap and turned around, offering him her back. He took the hint, glad to get his mind off of his premature accident. Soaping his hands, he rubbed her back. And it felt good doing so.

An had very little fat, and her back felt firm and hard. But as he got lower, and past her waist, her butt flared out some, and Nate was surprised at the softness of her cheeks. Each cheek seemed to move beneath his hands. She shifted her legs apart a bit, so Nate hesitantly took the hint and bent down so he could run his soapy hands between her legs. This was the first time that he had ever touched a woman's genitelia since he made that first trip at birth, and he tried to savor the touch. But with the soap, he really could not distinguish much. He moved back up, and An turned around. She lifted her arms, and Nate started soaping her chest. Her breasts were small, but they still felt wonderful. Nate marveled at the contrast between her slightly hard nipples and the softness of the breasts themselves.

An took the soap out of his hands. "Thank you Nate. You go dry off, and I will meet you in the bed, OK?"

Nate would have been happy to do some more cleaning, but he stepped out of the shower and dried off, wrapping the towel around his waist and going back into the bedroom. The television was on now, turned to a Thai show, so Nate left it as is and laid back on the bed. He waited, listening for An to leave the bathroom.

She came out at last, towel wrapped around her as she took a corner of it to rub her short hair. She smiled at him, then clamored on the bed to lay beside him. She moved to her side and put one arm over his stomach.

Lifting up the edge of his towel, she looked in an exaggerated manner and asked," You ready yet?"

Nate laughed. "Almost, I think!"

"Yes, I think he will be ready fast."

Nate was trying to think of something to say. He felt awkward just lying there. Excited, true, but still awkward.

"An, you speak very good English. Where did you learn it?"

She hesitated a moment before answering. "I studied English for one year at Khon Kaen University. After that I had a Canadian boyfriend, and so I learned English," she said with a degree of finality.

She unwrapped her towel, exposing her body, then leaned into Nate, putting her top leg over his waist, and her arm on his chest. Nate took the opportunity to put his arm around her. She felt warm in his embrace. He looked down at her face leaning against his side. In the lights of the room, her face looked a little older than he had thought in both the dim lights of the Red Lips and with the shower water cascading over her. Not that she was old, but she had the beginnings of a few crinkles at the corner of her eyes, and her skin was not quite as smooth and unblemished as he had first thought. He had figured her to be about his age when he first saw her; now he figured she was in her mid-twenties.

His hand seemed to have a mind of its own as it began to explore her body. He touched her belly, the left half being exposed to him while the right half was hidden against his hip. In the bedroom light, he noticed a few faint traces of faint lines there. Like very faded and thin tiger stripes. He leaned forward a bit to get a better look.

An noticed his attention and grabbed the towel, bringing it to cover her belly.

"That is from my baby," she said quietly.

"Your baby?" Nate was surprised. Somehow, he never thought of bargirls having babies.

"Yes, my baby boy." There was a pause. "Do you want to see him?"

Nate didn't really, but he wasn't that much of a social dunce. "Sure, I'd like that.

An jumped up, the towel falling off of her. She hopped to the dresser and fished her phone out of her purse. Hitting a few buttons, she jumped back into bed, her small breasts bouncing. She held up the phone to show Nate a photo of a serious-looking boy in front of what looked to be a temple. Nate was not great with kids' ages, but the boy looked to be at least 8 or 9 years old.

"He's a handsome boy," he dutifully told her. "How old is he?"

She turned the phone so she could see the photo. "He is 13 years old," she said proudly.

"Thirteen? How could that be," he blurted out. "How old were you when you had him?"

"How old do you think I am?" she asked.

"I dunno, maybe 25?"

"Ah, *pakwan*, Khun Nate." She wai'ed, phone still in hand. "You are very sweet, but I am 33 years old."

"Thirty-three? Are you sure?" Nate couldn't believe it.

She laughed. "Yes, I know my own age."

"OK, but wow, you don't look it."

"You can call me 'Grandmother An,' if you want."

"Ah, no, I think I will call you 'Sexy An,'" he replied. He couldn't believe he was flirting like that. Maybe being in bed with a naked girl did things for him.

"So where is his father, if I can ask?" Nate was curious now.

An shrugged. "In Canada, I guess."

"Canada? Your ex-boyfriend?"

"Yes. When he found out I was pregnant, he left me. He found another girl," she said stoically.

"I'm sorry." Nate really didn't know what to say.

"*Mai pen rai.*" She seemed to gather herself a bit. "And when my university found out, I had to leave. "

"You had to leave school just because you were pregnant? In my high school, we had two girls who were pregnant at our graduation. And we had a couple of girls with babies already."

"Well, in Thailand, you have to leave. So I left school and tried to work in Khon Kaen. But I couldn't make enough money for my baby and me, so I left him with his grandmother, and I came to Bangkok."

"And that's when you started working in the bar?" he prompted.

"No, I tried to work at a farang restaurant. I spoke English, so they needed me. But the salary was bad, and then one customer liked me, and I went to Phuket with him. After he went back to Australia, I went home. He sent me money for almost a year, but then he stopped. So I had no money again. I went back to Bangkok, but I didn't want to work in a restaurant. So I started as a waitress at a bar, then I changed to dancer."

She recited this with out too much emotion one way or the other. She sighed, then suddenly reached under his towel and grabbed his penis.

"No more sad stories. I think he is ready again to play!"

She started stroking him, and he began to respond.

"See, I told you. I am always right!"

She took the towel off his waist and moved down, licking his belly. He could feel the head of his cock touch her cheek as it got harder. She kept one hand on it, then lifted it up, licking his belly under it. Shifting position, she went lower, slowly licking his balls, then gently taking them one-at-a-time into her mouth.

She moved back up and positioned herself, putting the tip of his erection into her mouth. She hesitated, then looked up at him.

"You don't cum in my mouth, OK?"

Nate merely nodded. She went back and slowly took him into her mouth, going the full length of his shaft. He looked down to see the top of her head moving rhythmically. Reaching down to touch her shoulder, he was astonished at how good this felt, how much better it was than he had ever imagined it would be. Suddenly, he felt the rush again of an impending explosion.

"Stop, stop," he cried out, taking her head in his hands and lifting it up. "I'm gonna cum!"

She laughed, wiping her mouth. "So fast again, baby."

She took the condom which Nate had gotten out earlier and opened it. Putting it into her mouth, she moved back and went down on him. She moved up and down a few times, and when she sat back up, the condom was on him already.

Wow! That was pretty cool!

She turned to face him, licked the fingers of her right hand, then rubbed them between her legs. Straddling him, she raised herself up, then grabbing his erection, she slowly lowered herself on him, eyes closed.

Nate could feel himself slide into her.

This is it! I'm no longer a virgin!

Nate looked up from his prone position, taking in her small body. She put her hands on his chest as she settled all the way down. Then she started moving back and forth in a rocking motion, the muscles in her stomach shifting with each stroke. Nate hesitantly reached up to hold her breasts. She moved one hand off his chest to cover one of his hands, squeezing.

Nate felt like he wanted to be in this position forever, but the rising tension let him know different. His vision began to constrict, his breathing began to shorten. With a violent spasm, both his head and his feet came off the bed as he convulsed in ecstasy.

An began to rock harder, but after his orgasm, the sensation became too strong, bordering on painful. He grabbed her waist and stopped her.

She gave out a little girl laugh. "OK, Khun Nate, you are a man now!"

He sat up, still inside of her. Even with her astride him, his head was higher than hers. He pulled her in close, her head against his shoulder. They sat there, him gathering his wind and her just waiting.

After a long few minutes, Nate slowly lay down. An just as slowly raised herself, coming free of him. His cock, flopped back on his belly.

"Wait a minute baby," An told him, moving off to the bathroom.

Nate could hear the water running. An came back a few moments later, wet towel in hand. She reached over and slowly took the condom off, inspecting the reservoir tip before wrapping the entire thing in a piece of toilet paper. She took his penis in one hand and started to wipe it down with the warm wet towel.

"You OK baby?"

Nate smiled. "Yes, very OK. Thank you."

She finished cleaning him, then went to the bathroom again. Nate could hear the water running again. He felt lazy, satisfied, and happy. His mind started to drift again, and he didn't quite remember An getting back into bed with him.

He wanted to stay awake, to do it again, but the lassitude creeping over him and the still present jet lag worked their tandem conspiracy against him. He lost the battle.

He came to sometime later. An was dressed and was gently shaking him. He looked at the clock beside the bed. 6:02 AM.

"Huh?" was the best response he could manage.

"I have to go now, baby." She held out his wallet to him.

It took him a moment to gather his thoughts and to realize what she was doing.

"Oh, sorry." He took the wallet out and opened it. He didn't have 2,500 baht in exact change, so he just gave three 1,000 baht bills before closing the wallet and letting it drop on the bed.

"Thank you, Khun Nate," she wai'ed to him. Then she leaned down to kiss his cheek.

Nate wanted to get up to escort her to the door, but he was pretty dead to the world. She put the money in her purse and walked out. Nate could hear the door close behind her and he drifted off again.

Just before going completely out, the phone rang. Nate looked up in confusion, realized what was happening, and picked up the receiver.

"Hello?"

"Mr. Foster. This is the front desk. Miss An is leaving now. Is everything OK?"

"Uh, yes, sure, everything's fine," he mumbled.

"Thank you, sir. Have a nice day."

Nate barely got the receiver back on the cradle before he was out cold.

Chapter 9

Opening his eyes took some time, but they finally made it as the sunlight was streaming into the room. He stretched, feeling contented, but for a moment, not really realizing why. Then he remembered. An!

He looked over to the left side of the bed. He could almost make out a depression there. Leaning over, he could smell her faint scent still lingering on the sheets.

I am now a man, he thought, with a sense of satisfaction. That thought sounded a little corny even to him, but that was the only way he could describe it.

He turned back over to lay on his back, staring at the ceiling. In his glow of satisfaction, he thought back to the night before, savoring the memory. He did feel a little bit of remorse when he thought of her story, how she started working that way. But she enjoyed it, too, right? She wasn't really forced to do anything, right?

He looked at the clock: 12:36 PM. Felling guilty, he jumped up. How could he have slept so late? But then he chuckled at his reaction. He was on vacation in Thailand, so who cared how late he slept?

Purposely taking his time, he meandered through his morning ablutions. It was almost 45 minutes later before he came down to the lobby, hunger being perhaps the biggest motivator. Coming out the elevator doors, though, the two internet computers set up for guests' use caught his eye. He hadn't been online since he left, and he knew he should check his e-mail.

With more than a little bit of foreboding, he sat down, pulled up hotmail, and logged in. There were only two new e-mails waiting for him in his in-box. Nate stared at the in-box for a moment before clicking on it. Both were from oohrah8@hotmail.com: his father. His right finger hovered over the mouse to open them, but he logged out instead and stood up. He wasn't ready to read them yet.

Walking out to the lobby, he looked over to the reception desk and saw Nok helping another guest. He really didn't have anything to say to her, but he waited until she was finished, then walked up. She looked up and smiled, the corners of her eyes crinkling up adorably.

"Khun Nate I hope you had a great night!"

He hesitated a second. Did she know what he had done?

"Oh, yes," he faltered. "I slept very well."

"So you like our SimplySmart bed? Yes, I think so," she said with almost a giggle.

"Yes, they're very nice." His stomach chose that second to rumble loud enough for Nok to hear it.

This time she laughed out loud, a sweet, trilling laugh. "Oh Khun Nate, you must eat! Your stomach is very loud!"

"I know! I'm very hungry!" he responded with his own laugh, a little embarrassed but captivated by hers. He wanted to prolong their conversation, but he wasn't sure how to do it. "Maybe you can recommend someplace for me to eat?"

"We have a very fine restaurant here," she pointed behind him off to the left.

Nate knew from reading in an online forum that the restaurant food in Bangkok tended to be more expensive than that found outside the hotels, and he wanted to husband his money as much as possible. So he needed an excuse to not take her up on that recommendation.

"Well, Nok, I sorta wanted to try real Thai food, not the tourist food. Where can I do that?"

She thought for a moment, then her face lit up. "You should try MBK!"

Nate knew that MBK was a huge shopping mall, so he was surprised at her suggestion. Nok could read the confusion on his face.

"On the 6th floor, the food court. There are many food stalls, and they have English, and the food is very *aroi mak mak*! Very delicious! You can try many things"

That actually sounded good to Nate. He leaned over the desk. "Can you write that in Thai for me for the taxi?"

"Oh, take the Skytrain! The traffic is bad for the taxi. The Skytrain is only 20 baht, and it is fast. Go outside to the station, then go to the direction of Mo Chit. Go one stop, then change to the Skytrain to National Stadium. It is only one stop. That is at MBK"

Nate felt his apprehension level rise. He didn't think he could manage that, but he didn't want Nok to think he was incompetent. So he swallowed his growing stress and merely said "Thanks, that does sound better," instead.

He stood there for a second, not knowing what else to say, then feeling uncomfortable, he wheeled around and walked out.

The BTS station was only a short walk away. Riding up the escalator, he entered the station. People were rushing by him, all with places to be and things to do. He felt lost. There was a support structure in front of him with what looked to be vending machines on the walls. Hesitantly moving over to them, he studied the BTS map on one of the machines. To his surprise, it was really pretty self-evident. He could see the National Stadium stop at the end of one line, with a "2" designated beside it. On the other lines, he could see that number getting larger the further away it was from the his station. There were several "2's" before some "3's" took their place. The highest number was a "6." Beside the square push button for "2," 20 baht was printed, so Nate put the baht in the coin slot, then pushed the "2" button. His fare card came out a slot at the bottom of the machine.

Joining the line of people going through the turnstiles, he slid his card into the slot at the front of the entry. It buzzed in his hand, then came back out. He tried to feed it in again, and it buzzed again. A man in a uniform hurried over and held his hand out for the card. Embarrassed once again, Nate handed it to him. The man held it up and pointed to a small arrow on the card corner, and with exaggerated motions, fed the card in, arrow first. The card was accepted and popped out another slot a foot or so away. The man smiled at Nate and motioned him through. Nate grabbed his card, and the plastic barriers blocking his way slid into the structures, leaving it clear for him to proceed.

Past the entryways, Nate looked up, not sure of where to go. One sign indicated On Nut. The other, Mo Chit. Mo Chit it was. Moving up the escalator, he joined a fairly large number of people on the platform. Within a minute, a sleek-looking train came up, doors whispering open. Passengers pushed out while the oncoming passengers waited for the doorways to clear. He joined the throng getting onboard, and he was a little surprised to see how clean and modern it looked. It was a far cry from the graffiti-laden subway cars he had seen while he was in New York.

The train took off with a small lurch, and Nate had to grab suddenly for the straps dangling in his face to keep from falling. Within minutes, the train came to a stop, and Nate got off with what seemed to be about half of the other passengers.

Now where? he wondered.

But there, right in front of him, was a sign for National Stadium, and by the time he walked the few steps to get over there, another train was pulling in. Hurrying onboard, he found an empty seat and sat down. This train was not nearly as crowded as the other one.

Sitting down, he could see out the window. Tall buildings flanked the elevated tracks, making it seem as if the train were going through a canyon. After an extremely short ride, however, the canyon opened up to a broad intersection below them, and on the other side was an immense building with a huge "MBK" emblazoned on the side. The train came to a stop, and Nate got off along with everyone else; this was the end of the line.

Following everyone, he crossed a walkway and entered into a department store, which to his surprise, looked pretty much like any department store at the Carlsbad Mall or North County Fair back at home. Still following the herd, he exited the department store and passed by a number of shops selling a myriad of gold chains. Business looked good.

For the last couple of years, Nate had acquired an odd habit in shopping malls. At the Carlsbad Mall one day, he was with a group of guys from school, and they were girl-watching, which was a fairly normal pastime. Josh Haden, one of his, well, not quite friend, but acquaintance, was talking about if he was king, he could just order any of the girls walking by into his bed. That led to some debate among the five of them as to just whom they would so order, if they were in fact King of the USA. As each of them had different tastes in girls, they decided each of them had to select five girls, one for each of them, and to tell the others why he had selected each girl. That led to a lively 30 minutes with some intense debate.

Since then, every time Nate entered a mall, he had to select five girls to bed. Not four, and he couldn't select six. It had to be five. And considering that he never talked to any of his selections, that he knew it was all fantasy, he was serious in his task, acting in many ways as if he really had those kingly powers.

Coming into MBK, Nate was using up his five pretty quickly. First, in the department store, there was the extremely pretty store clerk with the tight fitting uniform. Then there was the tall blonde girl with the bare midrift and generous cleavage. She was speaking in some unfamiliar language to a shorter, brown-haired companion, and Nate almost added the companion as well before deciding that her butt was slightly too big. Almost immediately, he graced his selection on a girl in tight jeans with a tiny, tiny waist. Her long hair swung gently, seductively with each step. He had been in the mall for only two minutes, and he had already chosen three girls. He had to slow down before he used up his quota.

Nok had said the food court was on the sixth floor, so Nate continued on, looking for some escalators. Suddenly, the mall opened up, and Nate could see seven floors surrounding an empty center. This place was huge!

Spying the escalators, he started up. The escalators did not feed into each other, as they did in the US. After reaching one floor, he had to walk around to the other side again to take the next one up instead of merely turning around and getting on the next one. One floor seemed to have nothing but small cell phone booths, and even though he was starving, Nate took a few minutes to look around. The press of people, mostly young, attractive women, was distracting, but the array of cell phones was amazing. Nate hadn't realized that so many different types of phones even existed. It was a far cry from the handful of phone models available at his local Cingular shop.

He wanted to wander around more, but his stomach was making a nuisance of itself. He continued up to the sixth floor, and a wide sign proclaiming itself to be the Food Court guided him to the right spot.

The food court at MBK consisted of a large number of food stalls situated mostly around the walls and with a few in the center. Menus in Thai and English listed what each stall offered, but while Nate could read the words, he really didn't know what the dishes were. He walked up and down the line of stalls, not knowing what to get until his complaining stomach forced him to make a choice. Spaghetti with garlic, chili, and pork sounded interesting. The woman behind the counter pointed to him, so he pointed at the sample dish she had behind a glass cabinet.

"*Spaghetti kee mao moo sap*" she told one of the two cooks standing above the woks along the booth wall.

One man nodded, and put some oil in the wok while the woman put together a plate with spaghetti and some greens and handed it to him. With a deft touch, the cook used a long-handled spatula to throw various ingredients into the wok: ground pork, what looked to be spices, and liquids. A large fan kept drawing the smoke away, but Nate thought he could make out the aromas of the sizzling dish, and his mouth was watering. In went the greens, and a few minutes later, the spaghetti noodles followed. A couple more partial spatula-fulls of spices, and the cook scooped the mixture on a plate and put it up on the counter.

The woman informed him in English "Thirty-five."

Nate dug into his pocket and took out a 100-baht note. He held it out to her, but she refused to take it.

"No, coupon," she exclaimed.

Nate was confused. He looked at the note again, wondering if he had mistaken it for something smaller. No, it was a 100. He held it out again.

She looked at him with an exasperated expression. "No! Coupon!" She pointed over Nate's head.

Nate turned around wondering what he was supposed to be looking at.

"Excuse me, sir," a soft voice said beside him.

Nate looked down to see a tall, slender girl in one of the Roman Catholic schoolgirl-like uniforms prevalent among the girls walking around Bangkok. She caught his eyes.

"They don't take cash money here. You must use a coupon." She saw the confusion in his eyes, so she added, "Here, let me show you."

She started walking off, hand held out to indicate a direction. Nate looked back at the food vendor, then back at the young lady who was now a few steps away, but stopped and looked back at him. He shrugged and followed her.

They walked through the many tables in the middle of the food court and up to a booth where two women sat behind a plexi-glass partition. His guide stepped up to the opening before looking back to Nate.

"How much coupon do you want?"

Nate still wasn't sure exactly what was going on. "Well, my food was 35 baht, I think."

"OK, you give her 200 baht." She stepped to the side letting Nate come up to the slot in the plexi-glass.

Nate handed the woman two 100 baht bills. She pulled out a packet of paper coupons, flipped through them, then handed them to him. Nate took a look. They seemed to be slips of paper stapled together, each one designated with a number between 5 and 20. Now it was making a little more sense.

The girl next to him nodded. "*Ba*! OK, you can pay for food now."

She led him back to the booth where his meal was still sitting. He separated a 20, a 10, and a 5, handing them to the vendor. She smiled and indicated his food, letting him know he could take it. Nate looked back down at the girl.

"Thanks for your help. I don't know if I would've ever figured that out."

"OK, no problem. You can eat now." She turned back to the counter and made her own order.

Nate wasn't sure if he should say anything else. She wasn't extremely attractive, but she was female, and that was Nate's prime requirement. But while he considered saying something else to her, he knew that he really didn't have the courage to pursue anything.

Most of the tables seemed full, so he stood there feeling uncomfortable, tray in hand. Out of the corner of his eye, he saw a group of three people stand up, so he rushed over to take their seat. The people had left their trays on the table, so Nate just pushed them off to the side and sat down.

Across two more tables, there was an obvious fruit drink stall, so leaving his tray there, he went over and studied the menu. Another watermelon shake would be great, but the passionfruit shake looked good, too, so he ordered that instead. The girl behind the counter took a clear container and put ice in it, then put in a ladleful of some clear liquid, and at last a tiny spoonful of what looked like salt. She reached into a small refrigerator and took out a pitcher full of what must be passionfruit juice and poured out some into first a small measuring cup, which she then poured into the container. She put the container on a VitaMix, which surprised him. He loved going to the Del Mar Fair each year, and in the commercial pavilions, there were two booths always selling VitaMixes. While extolling the wonders of this blender, they made smoothies, sorbets, salsa, and even hot soup and gave them out to the crowds. While he had never bought one, the free food was worth waiting through the demonstrations, and he had sat through enough to have the machines attributes engraved into his mind.

The drink was handed to him, and he gave her 40 baht's worth of tickets. His drink cost more than his food, he realized. At his table, a woman was clearing it, and Nate rushed to make sure his lunch was still there. But the lady was merely removing the dirty dishes, leaving his alone.

Sitting down, he took a sip of his passionfruit shake. Cold and tart, it was pretty darn good. He studied the spaghetti. He had spaghetti with only olive oil and garlic once, but usually, his spaghetti came covered in a tomato sauce. He twirled his fork in it and took a taste. Well, it was certainly different. He wasn't sure if he liked it or not. It was rather spicy, but the taste was just odd to him. Garlicky, chili-type hot, and a meaty taste underneath it all. He took another tentative bite and decided that yes, maybe he did like it.

"Excuse me, sir."

Nate looked up to see his guide of a few moments ago standing next to his table, tray in hand.

"May I sit here?" she asked, looking decidedly nervous.

"Oh, sure, please!" Nate jumped up to pull out her seat, which was foolish as each seat was attached to an arm under each table. He ended up just pointing to the seat, as if she hadn't the brains to see it herself. Something about girls just made him pretty much always disengage his mind.

They both sat down and looked at each other, minds racing on what to say. They both finally opened their mouths in unison, then stopped as they realized the other was talking. Which, of course, made it silent again.

"Uh, thanks for helping me. I don't think I would've ever figured it out."

She gave him an abbreviated wai. "You are welcome, but I am sure you would be OK."

"No, I think I would've starved to death first," he replied.

She seemed to think abut this for a second, translating his words. He knew when his meaning became clear when she broke into a smile and laughed.

"Good joke, right?" she asked.

"Yes, joke."

They both seem to visibly relax. She put her spoon in the soup she had chosen and slowly twirled it, but did not actually take a spoonful to eat.

"Are you on holiday?" Her voice was very feminine, but not as light as An's from the night before. It was appealing, none-the-less.

"Yes," he answered. Then when she didn't respond, "Are you a student?" he asked he asked, anxious for anything to say.

She looked at him a little oddly. "Yes." She gestured at her white blouse. "This is the uniform for Chulalongkorn University."

She seemed to expect a response back from him, and although he knew nothing about that school, he just said, "Wow! That's great."

She nodded with a smile. "I study sociology, and I take English classes, too."

Nate knew the word, of course, but he didn't really quite understand what sociology entailed. But English classes, that was different.

"So that's why your English is so good!"

A huge smile broke over her face. "You are too kind," she said, each word carefully enunciated.

They slowly ate and talked, the conversation meandering back and forth wherever it wanted to go. Nate spent quite a bit of the time just observing her. While they were standing, he noted that she was a tall girl, the top of her head even with his chin. That made her somewhat unique, certainly different from An—well from most of the girls Nate had ever met, for that matter. And that made her pretty attractive to him.

Her face was plain, but pretty enough, framed by long, straight hair. Her bright turquoise glasses were a bit distracting, though. Nate had initially thought her quite slender, but that was only in proportion to her height. She actually had some substance on her bones. As she moved, her tightly buttoned blouse gaped a little around her breasts, and Nate got several peeks of the side of a plain white bra cup. He had to admit that he was pretty attracted to her.

Nate was not too open about himself, but Rattana-- that was her name— seemed more than happy to discuss herself and her life. A Bangkok girl, she lived at home. This was her first year at Chulalongkorn, which, according to her, at least, was the finest school in Thailand. She liked her classes, but was concerned about English. To him, though, her English was pretty good, if accented (of course this was from a guy who never earned more than a C in any English class.)

She had been to the US once, to the Orlando theme parks and Washington D.C., and she had been to Japan and Australia, but she mostly traveled out-of-the-country to Singapore and Hong Kong with her mother on shopping trips.

Nate had long finished his lunch and was listening to her with the appropriate grunts and "uh-huhs" thrown in when she suddenly looked at her watch.

"My goodness, I have to return to the university." She stood up suddenly, and for a moment seemed to be considering something. She took a deep breath and looked somewhere over his left shoulder.

"Nate, can I meet you on Friday? I would like to practice my English with you." Her eyes swung forward to lock onto his.

"Sure, Rattana. I would love that." Nate couldn't believe that someone was asking him out on a real date.

She smiled and pulled a small piece of paper out of her purse. Taking a pink pen with a Mickey Mouse doll attached to the end, she quickly wrote on it, then gave it to him.

"This is my phone number. Please call me so we can meet."

Nate nodded. "OK, I'll call you on Thursday, if that's all right."

She smiled again. "That would be most fine. I will wait for your call. *Ba!*" She wai'ed and turned suddenly to walk off.

Nate watched her walk off, rather intrigued by her swaying hips. Come to think of it, Roman Catholic schoolgirls never wore school uniforms with skirts that tight or that short. As she walked away, he decided to bestow on her the number four selection on his whom-to-bed list.

On a real-life note, he had a date. He couldn't believe his luck. An last night, and now Rattana? What was happening with the universe? Whatever it was he rather liked it.

He got up and followed the footsteps decaled on the ground leading him up to the refund counter where Rattana had told him he could cash in his unused coupons. He received his 125 baht, then started to wander around the mall. The sixth floor had a wide variety of stands, most selling Thai handicrafts, t-shirts, what Nate called beach pants (cotton pants with a draw-string instead of zippers and belt loops) and various souvenirs. Nate poked around the offerings, but disappointed each upturned hopeful face of the vendors when he moved on.

Although he had intended to withhold his final bedmate selection, he had to give that to an extremely petite girl who could not have been over 4'8" tall. She was tiny, like a doll, but a pretty curvaceous doll. A real-life Asian Barbie. The girl actually looked up and caught his eye as he was awarding her with his selection, and he quickly looked away in embarrassment as if she could read his thoughts. He realized the foolishness of that as he walked away, ruefully chuckling at himself.

Nate slowly wandered down the different floors, from the sixth to the furniture on the 5th (where he didn't linger long), to the 4th with all the cell phones. Interspaced with the phones were a number of booths selling DVDs, and at 100 baht apiece, they seemed to be a great deal. On this floor, Nate saw two more girls who made him wish he had left slots open for them, but rules were rules, and he couldn't change his mind now.

On the next floor now, his attention was caught by a selection of spy cams. Some were in clocks, some in pens, some without a disguise but small enough to hide most anywhere. At around 6,000 baht, they were pretty tempting, but unsure how long his money would hold out, he decided against splurging. He didn't know what he would do with one, anyway.

He wandered around for about an hour. Surprisingly, a number of girls smiled at him when their eyes connected. Nate said nothing to them, and none of them approached him, but he felt just the slightest swelling of pride in his chest. And that was a very unique feeling. The idea that he might be attractive to girls was a completely foreign concept.

His feet were getting a little sore, so he made his way to where he thought was the BTS, only to find out he was on the opposite side of the mall. So he hiked back the other way and found the train. A short 20 minutes later, he was back at the lobby, waving to Nok behind the reception counter before heading up to his room for a nap.

Chapter 10

Nate had gotten engrossed in a show about chimpanzee rescues on television, so he was a little later than he wanted to go out for the evening. But he was on vacation, so time wasn't a big concern. He put on a clean t-shirt and the same shorts he had worn earlier to go to MBK, then left the room.

Peaking around the partition in the lobby, he didn't see Nok at the counter, so he hurried out the door. He considered taking the BTS to Nana, but walking was no problem, so hoofing it it was. Traffic seemed much heavier. The cars going the opposite way were in complete gridlock. Nothing was moving. Nate was pretty glad he wasn't stuck there.

As normal, Nate was sweating by the time he reached the Nana intersection. There was the McDonald's there, and even though he had just eaten at one at the airport a few days before, he decided a Big Mac might be in order. He crossed the street and went inside. The lines were long—it seemed like every foreigner in Bangkok was there. Most of the men were quite a bit older than him, and most had a young Thai companion in tow. One older, rather fat guy sat at a table, his generous ass overlapping the seat. His face was bright red as he kept yelling what he wanted to a rather frustrated young girl at the front of the line. She kept looking back at him, then to the cashier as the man continually berated her.

"You dumb bitch! I said 'Angus Burger, no lettuce, no mustard. Only ketchup,'" he shouted with a heavy accent.

She looked back at the cashier, not saying anything, then back at the man. The next man in line looked up and rolled his eyes, then moved forward. He nodded at the girl, then told the cashier what the man wanted. The girl looked up at him with obvious relief.

"*Kop khun ka*," she said very quietly, nodding her head to him slightly. He merely gave her a sympathetic smile.

Eventually, Nate made it to the front of the line and ordered his Big Mac set with a large fries and a coke. Within a minute, he was served. Along with his order, he received two very small round white plastic dishes. He wondered what those were for, but as he went to get some ketchup at the dispenser, a Thai girl was there filling the little dishes with it. He waited his turn and pressed the handle to get some. It looked almost orange, though, not the normal red. He was about to take a small taste when he saw an image of a red chili on that dispenser. A tomato was on the other one, so he filled his other dish with that. The deep red color proclaimed it to be the ketchup he wanted.

Walking to a table, he passed the red-faced fat man and his girl. The man was ignoring her, but he found the time to reach out and take some of her fries despite still having his own in front of him. Nate shuddered and hoped that wouldn't be him in 40 years.

Nate wasn't in Thailand for the McDonald's, so he slammed his Big Mac and fries down before draining his coke. He gave a satisfied belch and got up to go to his real destination. Crossing the busy soi, he brushed past vendors, bargirls, and men and into Nana, heading straight for the Red Lips.

The girls were all dancing in leopard-print bikinis this evening. Nate peered into the dim light to scan them, trying to find An when an arm clasped around his waist. He jumped, then looked down to see An's upturned smiling face.

"Are you happy today?" she asked.

He gave her a hug back, vitally aware of her firm body. "Yea, I'm happy!"

Several of the waitresses were motioning for him to take their tables. He just picked the nearest one and sat with An beside him. Immediately, one of the waitresses came up to him, pad of paper in hand.

He wasn't quite in the mood for a beer yet. "Can I just have a water?" he asked.

She nodded, then looked pointedly at An who just as pointedly was looking elsewhere. Nate only hesitated a second before nodding. An immediately looked back and made her order in Thai.

She squeezed Nate's arm. "I am happy to see you tonight."

"Me, too."

Over on the stage, below the dancers, a girl was sitting with several men crowded in front of her. Nate craned his neck to see what they were doing. It looked like her legs were spread. Even a couple of the dancers had stopped dancing and were leaning over her to look.

"What're they doing?" he asked An.

She laughed. "Go see."

He got up and looked back at her, but she indicated that she would stay there. So he walked over and looked over the heads of the men there. With her back to the stage, her front was in the shadows, but she had her underwear off and short skirt hiked up to expose her pussy. Nate's mouth dropped open. He had seen them on the internet before, of course, and while he had been in An's last night, so-to-speak, he had never really gotten a good look at it, if that made sense. So this was the first real pussy he had ever seen like that. He stared for a few moments. One man was speaking to her, and he reached out to touch it, even spreading her lips a bit.

Nate shook his head in amazement, then left the group and returned to An.

"She's showing everything up there," he exclaimed excitedly.

"Are you sure," she asked, a wry grin on her face.

"Yes, yes, I saw it." He looked back over at the group of men still gawking.

"Well, it is brand new, so she is proud of it."

"Oh," Nate intoned knowingly. Then he looked confused. "Brand new? What do you mean?"

"Well, Cherry is a ladyboy, and she just got her pussy made at Yanhee Hospital. She just came back tonight to show everyone."

"You mean, they...he had... I mean they cut..."

An made a scissors motion with her fingers, moving them down to Nate's crotch. "Yes, cut, cut!"

"Ohmigosh! But it looked so real. I mean he looks like a girl!" He looked back at Cherry and her entourage.

"Yes, the doctors at Yanhee are very good! Maybe you want to do it?"

Nate crossed his legs and put his hands in a protective shield over his crotch. "No, I think I'll keep what I have, thank you very much!"

"Yes, I like what you have. It makes me feel very good." She leaned up against him.

They sat together for a few moments, watching the dancers and Nate sending a few more glances Cherry's way. An suddenly sat up.

"Your friend James, he asked me to give you this." She reached inside her bikini top and took out a piece of folded paper.

Nate laughed and mimed kissing it, earning a playful punch in his shoulder. He had meant it merely as a joke, but as he kissed it, he thought he could smell An on the paper. He unfolded it, and tried to find some light. Finally, he was able to get enough stage light to fall on it to be able to read the scribbled writing.

My Matenate,
    You owe me a pint. We are at the Longgun at Soi
Cowboy. Get your ass over here.

                                                James

An looked up at him. "So you must go?"

Nate laughed. "Oh, you read my secret letter!"

"Me no understand English, mister!" she said in an over-the-top atrociously accented English.

He laughed again. Although his thoughts on An were rather carnally oriented, he actually liked her as a person, too. He wouldn't mind having a real girlfriend like her.

"And of course I believe you! But yea, I think I gotta go to meet him."

An put an exaggerated frown on her face and then rubbed her fists under her eyes as if drying away the tears. His water arrived in a bottle along with An's drink. He grabbed the bill before the waitress could put it in the little container on his table, counted out the baht, and gave it to her.

He picked up the bottle of water without opening it and stood up. An stood up too and put her arms around his neck, pulling him down to her so she could kiss his cheek.

"Will you come back tonight?"

"I'll try," he replied.

"OK, see you soon." She released her hold on his neck and sat back down.

For a second, Nate considered staying there with her, but he did owe James a beer, and he wanted to see some other bars. So he turned and walked out, giving one last glance at Cherry still displaying her new hardware.

Quite a few people were coming into Nana Plaza as he was trying to get out. He felt like a salmon fighting the rapids. As he made the soi, the hopeful girls standing in front of the Nana Hotels parking lot were the grizzly bears, anxious to scoop out a salmon or two of their own. Nate managed to defeat the rapids, avoid the bears and reach the Sukhumvit sidewalk. He knew Soi Cowboy was further down the road, so he turned right.

The path on the sidewalk was claustrophobically narrow with vendors on the street side of the sidewalk and others on the building side. He had to slow down as a group of three heavily robed women slowly walked in front of him. There wasn't room for him to pass on the side. The stalls on the right ceased at a bus stop, but the number of people waiting there made it almost as bad. Most of the people waited facing the street, waiting for their bus. But a number of girls, some being cute and a few looking, well masculine, were facing the pedestrians. A few caught Nate's eyes and either nodded or made kissing motions with their lips. Remembering Cherry, Nate wondered if each of them was what they seemed to be.

The juxtaposition of the three Arabic women in front of him walking by revealingly clad working girls seemed surreal to Nate as he walked. He took the momentary opening in the crush to move past the three women and move on.

Nate was not particularly claustrophobic, but the constricted sidewalk with the vendors and the people walking up and down were making him uncomfortable. Sweat started to flow a little heavier than normal. Even the smells began their assault on his senses.

On the other hand, the visual assault was more interesting. Several vendors were signing across the cacophony. Nate did not know how to sign, but their motions were noticeably different from what he had seen before on television or in real life. He couldn't say exactly how they were different, just that they were.

He passed a middle-aged dwarf sitting on a stool outside a small bar entrance. Wearing a cheap green vest, he looked like a tired version of someone's idea of a leprechaun. Nate wondered if he was supposed to be a bouncer, and if so, how could he do it.

A very tall girl in tight shorts caught his attention. She was in earnest conversation with two young tourists, haggling over some t-shirts, calculator in hand.

"No, 100 baht. That's the most I can pay!" insisted the shorter, blonde haired guy, his heavyset companion nodding, her hands around his biceps, jerking him forward a bit in emphasis.

As Nate got even with them, he turned to see the girl. He was shocked to see that the girl was a guy. He was in heavy make-up, and his bra straps could be clearly seen peeking out of his white top, but there was no mistaking that she was a he.

A little shocked, and a little ashamed as he had been thinking a few carnal thoughts about him as he approached, he quickly jerked his gaze away and strode forward. What did it mean if he had been attracted to someone, then found out that someone was a guy? He didn't want to think about that.

On all sides of him, an abundance of things were for sale. Thai carvings. DVD's. Cigarette lighters. Knives of every shape and size. Sunglasses. There was a table with half-a-dozen boxes of Cialis and half-a-dozen of Viagra sitting neatly on it with no one obviously attending to them. Another table without an obvious attendant simply had a hand-written note stating "PORN DVD." Shirts, blouses, pants, and shorts. Sandals. Paintings, some rather nice, in Nate's opinion. Some rather stunning photos of monks, elephants, temples, and other traditional Thai images. Wallets in a myriad of colors, designs, and sizes. Purses, Music cds.

As some pedestrians stopped to look at the wares and haggle, they pretty much blocked the narrow passage in the middle, and Nate had to either wait for them to move, or he had to sidle past them, which he couldn't do without touching them. Twice, a person pushing a loaded cart came down the center of the passageway. They shouted out their approach, and it was up to the people to jump aside or essentially in a stall to give the cart room to proceed.

At each street corner, men leaned back against the buildings, jumping up as Nate or other single men approached.

"Massage sir? Girl, sir?" they asked hopefully, flashing post-card sized photos of 20 or 30 girls in an adult version of a class photo. Nate wanted to take a closer look at the photos, but he was frankly afraid of making eye contact with the men.

Interspaced throughout the confusion were small food stalls with orange juice, coconuts with straws sticking out of them, small grills with sizzling pork-on-a-stick, hot dogs with the ends sliced and spread open (looking like so many small, round squids), real squids, meats too foreign for him to determine what they were, and fruit. There were also small areas with a handful of plastic tables being served by a mobile cart cooking with a wide array of ingredients. The mixture of smells was at first enticing, but then became a little nauseating, a little too much

A rather large African lady in a bright yellow buba dress and matching head wrap blocked most of the passage as she fingered some small wooden carvings. Her rather generous posterior was an obstacle that Nate wasn't sure he could transverse without coming into close contact, more contact than he really wanted at the moment. He hesitated, looking for a way around her, but the stalls were packed too tightly for him to make it to the street. A young boy squeezed past her coming towards Nate, barely slowing down as he maneuvered around her bulk.

Nate decided to go for it. He sucked in his gut and tried to slide around her, hopping up a little into the stall behind her as he went past. He almost made it, too, but he lost his balance and began to fall forward. There was nothing else to do but put out his hands to arrest his fall—both hands landing squarely on the upper curve of her butt. In panic mode, Nate shoved off her in an attempt to get free of her, and that shove pushed her forward, her almost as equally generous belly hitting the table with the carvings, tipping a number of them over with a crash.

The woman gave an inarticulate cry, then turned towards her assailant, but Nate was already darting off. There was no way he was going to face her.

Despite his horror, a small part of his mind was a little titillated. He never considered himself to be a chubby chaser, but the feel of her huge ass under his hands was, well, intriguing. He couldn't help it when images of her formed in his mind, images of her naked, her huge butt in front of him, looking over her shoulder at him with an inviting leer. The image was both frightening and enticing at the same time.

He literally shook his head, trying to forget the image, so he was not paying too much attention to where he was going, and he almost stepped on the legless man.

Flat on the ground in front of him was a prone man in the filthiest clothes Nate had ever seen. The man had a bowl in front of him. His pants, which might have once been white or tan, maybe, flopped loosely below the knees where his lower legs used to be. The man reached forward, and just like the terminator in the first movie, after he lost his skin and legs and was only a partial exo-skeleton, pulled himself forward with his arms. That put the begging bowl under his chin, so he reached for it, pushed it forward, then repeated the pulling up of his body. And also like the terminator, he seemed mechanical, oblivious to the world around him, just a mindless automatron.

Nate hurriedly stepped to the side so the man could continue his progress. Nate wasn't much on giving to beggars, but he reached into his pocket, blindly pulling out a 50-baht bill. He dropped it in the man's bowl. The man didn't acknowledge it. He just kept his slow movement forward.

Nate stood still as the man made his slow progression. As he passed him, Nate stared at the empty pants legs, filthy and tattered. He looked at his own legs and tried to imagine himself without them. He couldn't really get his mind around that.

The crush of people on the sidewalk eased up a bit as the buildings on the left gave way to a Robinsons shopping center with a large McDonald's facing the street. There were no stalls on the sidewalk in front of it, so it was a breath of fresh air (well, fresh Bangkok city air) to be able to walk at a normal speed. Escalators rose up to the Asoke BTS station, so Nate knew he was getting closer to Soi Cowboy.

Alongside and under the BTS station, there weren't many stalls, just a few push carts with orange juice or grilled meats. A number of women with children in tow were begging for money, and a young, fit-looking man was kneeling on a piece of cardboard, looked forlornly at the wet, dead body of a puppy laid out in front of him, begging bowl beside the pup. Nate looked away in discomfort, and it wasn't until he walked passed the man that he came to the conclusion that the man had drowned the puppy to elicit sympathy and, more importantly, money from soft-hearted passersby.

He turned back to look at the man, filled with disgust, but not willing to confront anyone, he turned back to walk on.

He came to the large intersection that he knew must be Asoke. Soi Cowboy had to be right across the intersection. After a long wait, he crossed and turned left, wending his way past a few sidewalk restaurants before the crush of taxis ahead of him clued him to Soi Cowboy's location. A few drivers perked up when he approached, offering their services, but Nate ignored them and turned down the soi. Even without the arch over the soi with the large letters "SOI COWBOY," there would be no mistaking the place. It looked to be about a hundred yards long, and each side was lined with wall-to-wall bars, bright neon lights promising good times inside. A bevy of girls stood outside each bar, smiles and welcomes trying to entice men to enter. Men, mostly in groups of two or three, wandered up and down the road, smiling, laughing, and in the mood for wine, women, and song.

Nate hesitated for a moment, not sure where the bar was where he was supposed to meet James. He took a few steps into the bustle and saw the Longgun almost immediately off to the right. Several girls came out to greet him and ask him to come inside as he got closer, but when they saw his purposeful walk, they just smiled and stepped back, holding open the curtain which served as a door. Their job was done without even having to open their mouths.

Stepping inside, his attention was drawn to the 10 or so girls dancing on the stage. Even without taking time to really examine them, it was obvious that these girls were much better looking, and that they were doing an actual choreographed dance, not the individual semi-dance the girls at the Red Lips were doing.

Several waitresses clamored for his attention, offering various seats from where he could watch the dancers. Nate ignored them as he searched for James.

The dance stage was long and narrow, running the length of the bar right in the center. Two rows of tables, the back one higher than the front one, lined the walls on both sides. Around the stage itself were bar stools, so patrons could get a close-up look at the dancers while enjoying their drinks. Nate walked down the left side, but could not see James. Turning the corner of the stage, he started coming back up the other side. Possibly because his attention may have wandered to the girls dancing away in fringed bikini tops and tight white shorts, he walked right past James. A waitress hurried up to him, pulling on his arm to get his attention, then pointing to James sitting right in the middle of the upper level. He had one young lady under one arm and Smeghead sitting on the other side of her. He waved a bottle of beer in a beckoning motion to him. Nate apologized as he brushed by a half-naked girl sitting at the table below, then sat down next to Smeghead.

"Close your mouth, lad. You are drooling all over the floor," laughed James.

Nate automatically wiped his mouth, only hesitating when he realized there was no drool. He sat back as the waitress came up for his order. He was pretty thirsty from the walk over, and despite having already drunk his bottle of water from the Red Lips, he still really wanted something cold and non-alcoholic with which to start.

"Can I have an ice water?" he asked.

"Core! What was that, you poof?" James leaned forward, his arm around her neck forcing the girl sitting next to him forward as well. He looked at the waitress. "The lad will have a Heinie." He looked back at Nate. "And you're paying for this one, too," he said, waving his half-empty bottle.

The waitress looked back at Nate. He took the easy way out and nodded.

"Yea, I'll have a Heineken."

Smeghead tipped his bottle to Nate in a bar salute. Curiosity overcame him, and although he was usually too shy to ask a personal question, he had to ask. "Is your name really "Smeghead"

He got a puzzled look in return, so he added, "Yesterday, James called you 'Smeghead.'"

That brought a smile, and in a deep, quiet voice, he replied, "James is a berk. The name's Dennis." He stuck out his pudgy hand and gave Nate a deep, almost crushing shake.

The music stopped as the DJ got a new track ready. The dancers removed their shorts to reveal very skimpy string bikini bottoms. Nate settled back a bit to get a better view.

At Red Lips, the dancers were average-looking, with a few really pretty girls. Here, almost each girl was really quite beautiful. A few were slender, a few were tall, a few were short, a few were curvy. But all were attractive. They faced out on each side of the stage, and as the music started, they began a choreographed dance. The girls facing Nate's side of the bar were pretty, but Nate's attention was on the butts of the girls facing the other way. With the string bikinis, those butts all looked pretty fantastic. All thoughts of the African woman on the sidewalk vanished from his mind like faint wisps of smoke on a windy day.

"My Matenate, you hearing me?" Nate realized James was leaning over again, shouting above the music to be heard. "I asked you, how was An? She treat you right?" As he shouted, he still had an arm around the girl, one hand on her breast as she seemingly watched the dancers.

Nate gave him a wide grin and a thumbs up.

"Yea, that's my girl. She's a good 'un." He turned to an older, rather fat man sitting next to him and made a comment, then pointed to Nate.

The man nodded to Nate, who hadn't realized that he was part of their group. He seemed a little overdressed for the crowd, with a nice white buttoned-down shirt and what looked to be some dark slacks showing high on his waist and above the line of the low table holding the drinks. His white beard and receding hairline along with his girth reminded Nate as nothing so much as Santa Claus. He wondered if ole' Santa ever got a vacation from his workshop, and if he did, would he come to Thailand? The thought made him laugh, almost choking on his beer.

Dennis gave him a slap on his back. "Easy, there, mate. You don't wanna kill yourself."

Santa heaved himself up to his feet and laboriously made his way down the floor, then up to the other side of the table to sit down next to Nate. The seat under Nate lifted as Santa sat down. He held out his hand to Nate.

"Brian Best," he introduced himself, holding out his hand. "James over there told me you were a newly arrived compatriot, so I wanted to welcome you to the Land of Smiles." His breath was heavily laded with booze as he made his welcome.

Nate struggled to hear him over the music, and he wasn't 100% sure what "compatriot" meant, but he held his tongue.

"So where're you from?"

"I'm an American," Nate answered.

"Yes, I know you're an American. But from where?"

"Oh, I'm from Oceanside, from San Diego."

"Oceanside? And short hair like that? Are you a Marine?"

Nate could feel his face flush. "No, I'm not. My dad is."

Brian observed Nate's flustered response. "I guess that's a sensitive subject. I'll leave that one alone. Well, I am formerly from the great state of Iowa, now a happy denizen of Siam."

Nate was really more interested in watching the dancers rather than talking to some old stranger, but that piqued his interest. "Really, you live here?"

"That I do, that I do."

"So, how do you live? What do you do for work?" Nate had read in a Thaivisa.com, a Thai-related forum he found, several threads about working in Thailand, and how hard it was. He had toyed with the idea of teaching English for while so he wouldn't have to go back home.

A break in the music enabled James to overhear the question. "Work? The professor work? You've got the wrong bloke there, my lad. The professor don't work." He laughed loudly, the kissed the girl's head. She hadn't seemed to move since Nate arrived.

"You don't work?"

"No, I am afraid my astute friend there is 'spot on,' as our English cousins say. I am retired, living on a modest pension and Uncle Sam's largess."

"Tell 'im why you're retired, professor," James said.

Brian looked at James for a moment, then sighed. "Well, then, as James insists, I was a history professor, tenured, back in Iowa. But I had a small falling out with the dean, so I took an early retirement. At 61 years old, I wasn't ready to teach anywhere else, I came here to live a life of luxury and sin, existing on my pension until social security kicked in two years ago."

The music had started up mid-sentence, and James leaned over to try and hear what was being said. "Did you tell 'im why you was 'retired,' professor?" he shouted.

Brian simply clenched his jaws and looked back at the dancers, who were now doing a line dance. He leaned into Nate to say "And this is why I am here. The lovely ladies of Thailand, may they never grow old and jaded."

Despite their age and background differences, Nate was discovering that he rather liked Brian, even after only a relatively short amount of time and despite his booze-breath. They sat back in silent companionship, enjoying the sight of lithe young bodies moving in rhythmic unison on the stage.

"So which one do you like," asked Brian after a few minutes.

Nate didn't even have to consider it. He had been captivated by one of the girls, a tall, slender girl with long hair and high, good-sized breasts. Her belly was flat and flawless, and her ass, well, he didn't know if he had ever seen such a sweet ass.

"Number 31," he answered, using the number on the small white disk attached to her left boot.

"Oh yes, the lovely Boon. A little reticent, to be sure, sometimes a starfish, but oh so lovely." He paused for a few moments as they watched the lovely Boon do her steps. "Well, would you like to meet her?"

Nate was glad that he could get some assistance in this, because yes, he would like to meet her. And do more with her. "Yea, I think I would."

"No problem."

Brian motioned over the waitress, then spoke into her ear. The waitress walked to the stage and caught Boon's attention, who then knelt down to see what the waitress had to say. They spoke for a few moments, then the waitress pointed back to Brian and Nate. Boon shaded her eyes to see through the bright stage lights. Brian leaned away from Nate and pointed at him. Despite himself, Nate felt his face growing red again. Boon nodded, then continued with her dance.

"Their set's almost over, and she'll join you here. You just bought her a drink, by-the-way."

Boon was pretty hot, no doubt about it. But now that it was set, Nate noticed another dancer, on the other side of the stage who was moving her hips in a way which was probably illegal in some states. His eyes riveted on them, watching her almost naked butt make its siren call. He wondered if he should have picked her instead of Boon. Buyers' remorse, he guessed that feeling was. Well, he had picked Boon, and that was that.

The music stopped and the dancers filed off the stage, most disappearing in a back room. Four girls in rather Mad Max-type outfits came on stage, with wild make-up and wild hair. Each had knee high black boots to compliment the torn-up costumes.

"This is the main event. You're going to like this," Brian said almost conspiratorially.

The four dancers positioned themselves around the stage, stretching for a few moments while waiting for the music. The long strips of fabric hanging from their bikini tops swayed with their movement, revealing tantalizing flashes of bare skin. The dancers who had just left the stage had shown much more skin, but this was more intriguing, more titillating.

The music started with a blare, some heavy rock theme Nate didn't recognize. But the music galvanized the dancers into action. With a lot more energy than the previous dancers, the four girls started gyrating and moving, grabbing the attention of everyone in the bar. One girl jumped into the air to grab two of the poles, one in each hand as she was splayed like a crucifixion. She swung up her legs, wrapped her ankles around the two poles, and then dropped face down, stopping with her nose a few inches from the stage floor. She slowly eased down the rest of the way, bending at the waist, until her back was flat on the floor, before jumping up and into a new set of twists and turns with the beat.

Another girl jumped up to grab two poles as well, holding herself aloft. Spreading her legs, she suddenly came down in a split, her boot heels slamming down with a loud crash. One guy sitting there at the edge of the dance floor jumped up in startlement, much to the amusement of those sitting around him.

None of the girls were dancing in unison, but they danced with awareness of each other, weaving around each other as they strutted the stage, hung from the poles, and did their crashing splits.

Nate was watching so intently that he didn't notice Boon for a few moments as she stood on the floor in front and below him. When she caught his eye, she came up, and as Brian shifted over a bit, sat between the two. There wasn't a whole lot of room between Nate and Brian, so her legs were firmly pressed up against Nate's.

Boon still had her bikini top on, but she had put back on the white shorts and now had a wrap around her hips. She nodded to Nate, then took a sip of the drink the waitress had already delivered. She tried to say something, but the music for this set was so loud that Nate couldn't make it out. So he pointed to his ear with a forefinger and shook his head. They both turned to watch the dancers.

A minute or so later, all four girls jumped in the air at once and slammed down into the splits as the song came to an end. A smattering of applause broke out.

"What is your name?" Boon took the opportunity provided by the lull to ask in a somewhat bored-sounding voice, hand delicately held out.

"I'm Nate," he said, taking her hand in a semi-shake.

"Pleased to meet you." There was a pause, then "Where you from."

"America." He didn't know what else to add there.

"Oh, America number 1," she exclaimed with a little bit of emotion. She gave him a thumbs up.

Just then, the next song started playing, the Stones' "Satisfaction," so Nate dramatically rolled his eyes and shrugged his shoulders. She nodded, and they both turned their attention back to the stage.

To Nate's surprise, a few moments into the song, one-after-the-other, each girl took off her fringe-laden top. Nate had read on the internet that nudity was not allowed in Thai go-go bars, but the four girls were strutting and dancing in only knee-high boots and skimpy thongs.

When the shortest girl, the one with the largest breasts jumped up to do that upside-down thing with the poles, her breasts hung down, towards her face. That was an aspect that Nate had never seen in his short life, and it fascinated him, not just the fact that they were pointing to her face, but that this aspect deformed them in an unusual, but interesting way.

The naked breasts bounced as they danced, and when they did their splits, the breasts positively jumped up and down. Nate had a half-naked, beautiful girl sitting next to him, practically in his lap, but his attention was on the provocative sylphs on the stage.

Nate turned to Brian to ask him about the nudity, but Brian was focused on the stage as well, a hungry-looking expression on his face.

The dancers danced, the watchers watched. Sweat glistened on the bodies of the hard-working girls. As the slimmest of the girls twirled enthusiastically, a drop of sweat flung off her, catching the stage lights as it rose and then fell on the face of a man sitting in a bar-stool alongside the stage. He jerked his head, then with a smile and a deliberate motion, he wiped the drop of sweat off with one finger, then put the finger in his mouth. The guy next to him laughed and clapped him on the shoulder.

As Mick started the final chorus of "I can't get no…," the girls moved to the four corners of the stage. Then at the closing notes, they each went into the crashing splits, boom, boom, boom, boom, one after the other.

The applause was louder this time, Nate joining in, and the girls jumped up, wai'ed and rushed off stage. Topless girls with wild hair wai'ing was both cute and funny, Nate thought,

He looked back at Boon who was holding her drink. When he smiled at her, she gave him a tentative half-smile back.

"Scuse me mate." Dennis was standing up to get out from in back of the table, his ass almost being shoved into Nate's face as he squeezed by. "Gotta go to the loo."

As he lumbered down the steps, James shifted over, bulldozing his own girl as he did until she was shoved up against Nate's free side. "And who's this lov-er-ly?" he asked pointing at Boon.

"Her name's Boon. She's a dancer," he added needlessly.

"No shit, Sherlock! I saw her up there shaking her money-maker." He reached out to her. Boon started to reach toward his hand, but James ignored it and went to her breast, squeezing it. She jumped back as he laughed, "Yes, you gotta QC the merchandise here. She passes!" He laughed louder and looked down at his girl. He grabbed her breast as well. "Yes, she passes, too, but not as good as yours!"

He scootched back to his side of the bench seat, picking up his beer and taking a big swallow. Nate felt a little embarrassed about his actions, but no one else seemed to take notice.

Boon turned to Brian and spoke to him in Thai. Nate looked up at him questioning.

"She wants to know where you're staying."

"At the Holiday Inn, near the Intercontinental."

She obviously didn't need a translation because she spoke right back at Brian again.

"Well, she's direct tonight, I'll give her that. She wants to know if you want to fuck her. If you do, fine, but if not, she needs to find someone else."

This was moving a little too fast for him, but his cock knew the answer to that even if his brain hadn't wrapped around it yet. And being 19 and full of testosterone, his cock took over the vocal chords.

"Yes, absolutely."

Brian spoke again to her in Thai, and she responded. Brian evidently had something to say about that, and they went back and forth for a few exchanges.

"OK, she wanted 2,000 baht for a short-time, but I told her no, 1,500 will do. She agrees. But she wants to leave now."

"I was sort of hoping for a long-time, like all night," he said.

"I don't think that's going to happen. She says she doesn't have the time tonight. So what'll it be? If you really want a long-time, I'm sure you can find someone else."

Nate considered that, then looked down at Boon.

Damn, she's hot, he thought. He wanted her, he wanted to see her body, to touch her, to fuck her, not someone else.

"No, a short-time's OK. That's OK."

Brian relayed that, then touched her upper arm, motioning her up. She stood up and left for the back room.

"So you speak Thai?" he asked the evident.

"Only taxi-Thai, I'm afraid. Enough to get some food, take a taxi, and more importantly, to get some booze and broads." He chose that moment to hiccup.

He picked up his beer and drained it, holding the empty bottle up, pointing it out to the waitress who nodded and went to get another bottle.

"So Nate, what're you doing tomorrow?"

"I don't know, I haven't decided yet."

"Why don't you meet me at the beer garden, say around 1."

"The beer garden?"

Yes, the Soi 7 beer garden. You can't miss it. About 100 yards down the street, just past and across from the little food court. Meet me there around 1, and we'll have lunch. Or breakfast, as the case may be." He laughed at himself, obviously a little tipsy.

Nate considered it. *Well, why not?*

"OK, 1 o'clock it is. See you there."

"Good." As the waitress brought him his beer, he said something in Thai and pointed to Nate. "Well, you'd better pay your bill. I don't think Boon wants to wait after she changes."

A new set of a dozen dancers had made their way to the stage. These were dressed in matching camouflaged shorts and cotton button down shirts, the shirt fronts tied together to reveal bare midriffs. One of the girls had light blonde hair. Nate certainly liked blondes, but with a Thai girl, it just looked odd to him.

The waitress brought back his bill. He took out his wallet before looking at it. Picking it up, he had to look twice to make sure he was reading it right. 1,430 baht?

That can't be right, he thought.

The waitress stood over him waiting. He looked to Brian.

"I think there's been some sort of mistake. 1,430 baht? That's too much."

"Let me take a look at it," Brian told him.

Nate handed it over, and Brian held it up to the light, angling it so he could read the figures. He handed it back.

"No, it's correct. Three lady's drinks, a bar fine for Boon, and six beer." He shrugged.

"Three lady's drinks? Six beers? I didn't order those!" he exclaimed.

"James there said you had these rounds." He cocked his head and raised an eye to James, who was watching them.

"I told you you owed me, so pay up you cheap fuck!" James yelled out over the music.

"Yes, but I thought that was one beer!" To his horror, Nate felt a lump forming in his throat.

Please God, don't let me cry here! he prayed silently.

"One beer, two beer, who gives a shit?" He pointedly looked away, muttering "Bloody septic!"

A feeling of anger crept over him, banishing any chance of tears. He wanted to stand up and refuse, to tell James to go to hell, but he knew he couldn't. He just pulled out two 1,000 baht bills and gave them to the waitress, shame now overpowering his brief spurt of anger.

He sat there in silence, watching the dancers, waiting for Boon. The waitress came back with his change, and in a small fit of pettiness, he took it all, not leaving a tip. She shook her head, but left, and Nate felt a small pang of guilt. It wasn't her fault, after all.

Boon came out of the back room and walked over to him, not sitting down, evidently ready to go. She had on an off-white peasant-girl blouse and a tight pair of designer jeans, and she looked pretty good. That put him in a much better mood. He stood up and followed her out of the bar and to the waiting scrum of taxis and tuk-tuks. Instead of taking any of them right at the entrance, she turned right, walked down 10 or 20 yards, and climbed into a taxi parked there. By the time Nate climbed in, the taxi was taking off.

They both sat in the back, at least a foot between them. Boon sat there staring out the window as the taxi made its way through the traffic and back down Sukhumvit. Despite the heavy traffic, it wasn't too long before they were pulling into the Holiday Inn.

Boon hopped out, and the driver turned to him. "150 baht."

150 baht? It shouldn't be more than 40 baht, he thought.

He looked at the meter, but it wasn't on.

"150 baht," the driver repeated.

Nate looked up at Boon, hoping for some support, but she was staring at nowhere, a bored look on her face. The hotel doorman reached over to Nate's door and held it open. Nate stepped out.

"Can you help me? This man wants 150 baht to take us from Soi Cowboy to here."

The doorman asked Nate to repeat himself, then poked his head into the cab and spoke with the driver. He backed out and said "He say you agreed to the price."

"I never said anything! I never agreed!"

"OK, please wait, sir." He poked his head in again and exchanged some words with the driver. Turning to face Nate, he said, "He say the young lady agree. But I ask him 100 baht OK. He say yes. So maybe you pay 100 baht?"

It was still too much, but instead of dragging it out, Nate took out a 100 baht bill and gave it to the driver. The doorman escorted him up to the door, opening it.

"Welcome back sir," he said cheerfully.

Nate and Boon entered and as Boon went to the receptionist desk, Nate glanced back out the glass front of the hotel. The taxi hadn't left, as he had expected it to do. The driver had merely pulled up a ways, and had parked. He had gotten out and was lighting a cigarette as Nate watched.

He felt a touch on his arm. It was Boon, who then motioned towards the elevators. They got on and went up to the room. As they entered, she pointed to the bathroom.

"You take shower." She simply said.

Nate nodded and went into the bathroom. He left the door open in case Boon was going to join him, then stripped and got into the shower. The hot water felt good, washing away the layer of sweat and street grime. The smell of the soap gave him a little lift.

Well, he could enjoy a shower anytime. Now he had some major fucking to do! He jumped out, half-assed dried himself, then went out to the bedroom.

Boon was sitting at the foot of the bed, and open can of beer in her hands. She had obviously gotten it from the mini-bar. Nate hadn't touched the min-bar himself after looking at the prices. She put the can down and went into the bathroom. Nate could hear the door lock after she closed it.

He picked up the can of beer and felt its heft. It was pretty much full. He shook his head, then lay back. And waited. And waited. Well, it was probably only a few minutes, but it seemed like an awful long time to him.

His rampant cock had softened somewhat by the time she finally came out of the bathroom, towel wrapped securely around her. She sat on the edge of the bed, and when Nate didn't move, she lay down on her back, looking up at the ceiling.

Fully hard again, Nate sat up and moved closer to her. She didn't resist as he took off her towel.

My God, she's beautiful!

Lying on her back, she had essentially no belly at all, actually curving in between her prominent hip bones. Her pubic mound was prominent, with a sparse covering of hair, and her high breasts, with their small, firm nipples seem to defy gravity. Nate may have seen better bodies on the internet, but with the blood pounding, he couldn't remember when right then. He reached out and touched her left breast, marveling at how it could be so soft, yet so firm at the same time.

She caught his eye for the first time since they entered the room. "Condom?"

Nate wanted to enjoy her body for a few more moments, but he leaned back and took out a condom that he had put in the nightstand drawer. He held it out to her, but she shook her head and motioned back to him.

A little disappointed, Nate opened up the package and took the condom out. He had seen condoms before, of course. He had blown them up like balloons before when Steve Prince had brought a box of them one afternoon when he was 13 or 14. He had even taken a vending machine condom one time and had secretively put in on in his bedroom. But last night was the first time he had ever used one in earnest, and An had taken care of putting it on him.

He looked at it carefully, trying to see from the roll which way it went on. He tried to put it on, but it wouldn't unroll. He must have had it reversed. So he switched it around and tried it again. But it still wouldn't unroll. He threw it on the floor and got another one. He tried several times with this one as well, but finally, something aligned right, and it easily rolled on.

He looked down at her. She was lying in the same position, on her back, staring at the ceiling. Nate touched her breast again, and when she didn't respond, tried to maneuver between her legs. She shifted them open wider and he positioned himself.

He lowered himself and tried to enter her. But he didn't make it. Looking down, he could see her small patch of pubic hair, and his cock seemed to be in the right general area. So he pushed forward again, only to slide beneath her down her butt crack. He tried to lean back a little to change the angle, but met with the same lack of success.

He got up on his knees and looked closely between her legs. There, he could see everything, he could see where he was supposed to enter her. Take

Rod A and insert into Slot B. Simple. He lowered himself one more time, and this time, he slipped up over her.

With an exasperated sigh, she suddenly reached to her belly, grasped his cock, pushed it back down, then guided it inside. Nate started stroking, but he accidentally pulled too far out. She didn't give him another chance to find it on his own. She grabbed him again and guided him in. This time, she held onto his ass so he couldn't pull out very far.

She didn't have to hold on long. Within a handful of strokes, Nate came. He groaned and stopped. She looked up at him in surprise.

"Finish?" she asked incredulously.

"Yea," was his sheepish reply.

She slowly pushed him away, out of her. As soon as he cleared her, she scooted to the side, got out of the bed, and into the bathroom. Nate could hear the water running. A few minutes later, she re-appeared, fully dressed.

"I go. You pay."

Nate looked at the clock by the bed. He hadn't looked at it before they started, but he doubted they had spent even five minutes together. She was a stunning girl, but he was rather disappointed on how things turned out.

He got up and got his wallet, taking out 1,500 baht and giving it to her.

"You give me 200 baht for taxi," she demanded.

He looked puzzled. "I just gave you 1,500 baht."

"No, for taxi!" She held out her hand. "Home, far!"

Nate started to argue, but realized he didn't have the heart for it. He just handed her the extra money. She put it in her purse, and left, just like that.

Nate sat on the bed, condom still on him. He waited a few minutes, and sure enough, the phone rang.

"Good evening, Mr. Foster!"

"Yes, everything's all right. She can go."

"Ah, very well, Mr. Foster. You have a good night."

He hung up the phone. The can of beer was still sitting there. He picked it up. It was still almost full, and it certainly hadn't time to warm up very much. With a sigh, he tipped it up for a long swallow.

Chapter 11

Nate found the beer garden without too much problem. He walked in the doorless entry, ignoring the man who stepped up to guide him to a seat. The place had a large central bar area and some smaller bar-type seating arrangements, most with a smattering of older men and some bored girls. Off to the right were some dining booths, and in the second one, he saw Brain waving to him. He walked back and sat down.

"Welcome, my young friend," Brian said, tipping his Chang beer bottle in a semi-salute.

"Thanks." Nate looked around, noticing that there were more girls than he had initially realized, ranging from rather young to fairly old. He looked back at Brian. "Is this a restaurant or a bar? I thought we were going to meet for lunch."

"And so we will. I've already ordered. Here, take this." He handed Nate a menu. "The young pretties here are just an added attraction."

"So they work here, at a restaurant?" Nate was puzzled.

"Well, yes, sort of. These girls are free-lancers. They come in here when they need a few baht to make ends meet, buy a new cell phone, pay the rent. Once a month, or every day, it's up to them. Students, housewives, whatever."

"Really?" Nate didn't know what to make of that. Coming in to work to buy a cell phone?

His stomach was rumbling. He had missed the free breakfast at the hotel, and now he wanted to eat. He finally selected a burger and a coke, giving his order to the waitress.

"Mistake, young man, mistake," warned Brian.

"What do you mean?"

"Well, the hamburger, number one. The Thais, God love them, just can't make a decent burger. I would kill for a Fuddruckers burger now, but I've just learned to do without while I am here. And number 2, a coke?"

In reality, Nate just wasn't in the mood for a beer. But he said "Isn't it a little early for a beer?" instead.

"It's never too early," he replied with a laugh. "It's evening somewhere on the globe, so that's good enough for me."

Another waitress arrived right then with a plate of potatoes and sausage, placing it in front of Brian. "They may be hopeless at a burger, but they do OK on German food." He cut off a piece of the sausage and put it in his mouth. Speaking and chewing at the same time, he asked "So how was last night?"

"It was,…well, OK," he said with a shrug.

"She sure came back to the Longgun quickly." He reached over for a plastic bottle of ketchup, squeezing a generous helping over his potatoes.

"She came back to the bar?" Nate was sure she had said she was going home.

"That she did. She was right back on the stage, and she hooked herself another paying customer."

Nate felt oddly jealous and couldn't explain why. "She wanted 200 baht to go home."

"And you gave it to her?"

"Well, yea," he admitted, now feeling sheepish.

"She got you coming and going. 200 baht will get a girl halfway to Pattaya, much less anywhere here," he chuckled, a piece of potato coming out his mouth to stick in his beard. "Aside for getting taken for 200 baht, was the dirty deed OK?"

"Well, she was beautiful, but she, she didn't seem too into it."

"I warned you, though. I told you she was somewhat of a starfish."

Nate didn't quite remember that, but he still had to ask, "A starfish?"

"Yes, you know." Still holding his fork, he flung out his arms to hold them spread, the motion shooting a small piece of potato across the aisle to land on the back of a girl sitting at the bar. "Starfish. Just laying there while you do all the work."

"Ah, I understand. Yea, she was a starfish." He stared at the potato on the girl's back.

'You'll learn. Just because a girl is pretty, doesn't mean she will give you the GFE. Attitude is better than looks, in the loving department." He grabbed an older girl who was walking past by the arm and pulled her in close. "Right Suri?"

Suri put one hand on his belly, the other around his shoulder. "What you say, Khun Brian?"

Brian looked up at her, put his arm around her waist, and said, "Suri here is one of the best. A real, honest to goodness GFE. No one does it better."

"*Pakwan*, Khun Brian." She pushed away and slapped his shoulder playfully. She leaned over to kiss his forehead, then continued on her way.

"You see, grasshopper, you need to talk to the girls first. Boon is certainly one of the prettier girls around, but she isn't much in the bed department. Don't let your little head drown out your big head. Talk to the girls, and go for attitude over looks every time."

Even with Nate's tiny experience, that made sense. He enjoyed his time with An much more than with Boon, even if Boon was much better looking.

As Brian ate and both of them talked, several girls came up to Brian at different times to say hello or to wai. Several leaned over his belly to kiss his cheek. He responded to each by name, asking questions about kids, family, or school.

"You certainly seem popular here," Nate said, after a tiny girl who couldn't have weighed even 80 pounds came up to squeeze his belly and say something to him in Thai.

"Ah, these are my girls. I love them all." He signaled the waitress for another beer.

"Have you had, you know, sex with them all?" Nate asked breathlessly.

Brian nodded. "Most of them, yes. I try to spread the wealth. Wouldn't be good to grant only one of these ladies my undivided attention. But this," he gestured to take in the room, "this is why I stay here. Where else can someone my age, with my limited funds, enjoy the delectable company of so many choice morsels?'"

Nate looked at him speculatively. "Brian, I'm curious. James asked if you told me why you left your school. I mean this is great, but what happened? You said you had a disagreement with your dean. If this is too personal, I'll just shut up"

"Nah, it's OK." He seemed to gather his thoughts for a moment. "Well, you see, I've always liked the ladies, especially the young and pretty ones. What can I say? And as a professor, the opportunities abound, even if we are not supposed to partake in the delights. I've banged my fair share of co-eds. Gotten lectured for it, too, even if there wasn't any proof."

"Well, unfortunately for me, Leslie McCoy came into my class and my life. She was such a fine piece of blooming womanhood. Every day, with her low-cut tops, leaning over as I walked the aisles. Every day, staying after class to ask questions. Ah, I'm getting excited even now just thinking about her. Well, finally, she comes for office hours one evening, and before too long, I have her out of her clothes and I'm doing her doggie style right over my desk, reports I was grading flying everywhere. Her ass was perfect, and her tits, well, they were pretty perfect, too. Anyway, I finish, and calm as can be, she searches the floor for her report, then gives it to me. She gets dressed, winks, and walks out."

"Did you give her an A," asked Nate.

"You know, I did, but I think I did it because she deserved it. I don't want to think I can be bought off like that. But who knows, maybe I gave it to her because of the sex."

"After that, we meet in my office every Wednesday night and go at it like rabbits. I gave her an A on her next paper, too, as well as a quiz and for a few other assignments. Well, at least I know she deserved the A for the quiz. Pretty cut-and-dried on that." He took another swallow of beer and seemed to be thinking back, remembering.

"On the last Wednesday before finals, she gave me a blow job for the first time. The sight of her red hair covering my lap, well, that was memorable. She finished, wiped her lips with a smile, then reached into her bag and pulled out a binder. 'My term paper,' she told me. She left with one last smile. I was going to lock up and go home, but I picked up her paper and took a look. It was blank, except for a lipstick print on the first page. Nothing written at all."

"So what'd you do?"

"Well, I could've given her an A. I'd already come to the realization that I'd already compromised myself, that I'd already inflated a few of her grades. That would have been the easy way out. But her audacity struck a nerve in me. Then, her smirching during the final exam pushed me into a corner. Her wink was the last straw."

"Lovely Leslie's final exam was gibberish. For one question, she wrote down a recipe for pork chops. I didn't have to think long and hard about it. I gave her an F and flunked her for the course."

"Well, Lovely Leslie was not so lovely when she was pissed, and pissed she was. She came storming into my office a few days later, and the language she had managed to pick up pretty much peeled the paint off the walls, as they say. She told me she was going to go to the dean, and I told her to do her worst. I mean, what could she do? I had the exam and the term paper, and I could deny anything else had transpired. The problem was that Lovely Leslie was also Conniving Leslie. It seems she had snapped a photo of me with her cell phone while I was naked and searching for my underwear, and she gave it to the dean, alleging I had sexually harassed her. The dean had his proof, and I could take an early retirement or face disciplinary action. Although my actions with Leslie might seem to counter it, I am not a complete idiot. I took the retirement."

"Damn! That's some tough shit."

Brian laughed. "Yes, I guess you could put it that way."

"Well, was she worth it?" Nate asked facetiously.

"Yes, I'd do her again in a St. Louis minute! But maybe this time, I'd just give her the A!" Both men laughed uproariously, clinking beer bottle to coke glass in a toast.

Nate's burger and fries arrived. He took off the bun and looked suspiciously at the small patty. Well, it looked OK. He dressed it with ketchup and mayo, then took a bite. It turned out that Brian was right about his assessment on Thai burgers. It tasted more like meatloaf than a burger. But Nate was hungry, so he kept eating.

Brian remained quiet as Nate scarfed down his meal. It didn't take him long.

"You weren't hungry now, were you?" Brian asked sarcastically as Nate ate the last fry. "You know, while it may be hard to believe, given my regal physique now, but I was quite a bit thinner than you one time, many long years ago." He patted his belly. "I was never so muscular as you maybe, but a lot thinner."

At that moment a girl came storming by, eyes blazing in anger. She was pretty, wearing black pants with a ringed metal belt and a sleeveless blue t-shirt. Brian reached out to touch her arm as she passed, saying something in Thai. She swung around in anger, arm raised to hit him. Firmly, but without evident anger on his part, Brian reached out and grabbed her arm, keeping her from lashing out. He spoke quietly, but just as firmly to her in Thai. She hesitated for a moment, then her stance almost collapsed, like a balloon being deflated. Brian shifted over a bit so there was room on the bench seat beside him, and she sat down, arms going around him, tears flowing. In halting Thai, she explained something to Brian as Nate watched, lost as to what was going on. She snuffled and hiccupped, rubbing her nose against Brian's green shirt. She stopped, then sat there for a moment, just holding him.

Brian took his bottle of beer and held it to her, and like an obedient child taking her medicine, she dutifully took a long swallow. Several of the other girls were watching this all take place, and one walked up, put her hand on the girl's shoulder, then walked on.

After she had composed herself, Brian lifted her chin and spoke to her for a few moments. The only word Nate could catch was "OK?" She nodded, wiped her eyes, and stood up. Brian had to shift his body to be able to reach into his pockets, but he brought out something and slipped it to her. It looked to Nate like a 500 baht bill. The girl wai'ed deeply, then started walking to the back where the toilets were located.

Brian looked to Nate and continued as if nothing had happened, "When you get older, and your metabolism changes, you'll probably get as big as me, too."

Nate just stared at him for a second. "You're not going to tell me what that was all about?"

Brian looked up at the ceiling, then let out a big sigh. "These girls, most of them are just trying to get by. And their life is hard. And some of the guys here are fucking assholes. They treat the girls horribly just because they can, just because they think the girls are lower than scum. But you know what? It takes two to tango. If they are buying these girls' services, they are at exactly the same moral level as the girls, the hypocrites." He took a long swig of his beer.

"So what happened there? To that girl?"

"That was Meow. She's 19, did you know that? She can be a little full of herself, but that might be just her defense mechanism. She's a good girl, though. She's got a daughter from her Thai boyfriend who took off when she got pregnant, and not wanting to shame her family, she came to Bangkok, telling them she has a job here. So she lives in a small apartment on Rachadapisek with her daughter, working here most days to pay the bills and to send a little home to her family. I don't think her mother and father even know they are grandparents."

"So why is she so pissed off now?"

"Well, she met a guy here last night, a farang, of course, I'm sorry to say, and he took her to his hotel. She pays a neighbor to watch her kid when she's gone longtime, which she tries not to do too often. Well, he fucks her all night and again in the morning, and he's kind of rough with her, but she puts up with it. Then, when she finally goes to leave a little bit ago, he refuses to pay. He calls hotel security on her, and when she argues, he tells security he doesn't pay for sex. He was just doing her a favor, giving her a good time. Of course, security knows he is full of it, but what can they say? He's paying probably $150 or $200 a night for the room there, and like anywhere, money talks. So they tell Meow she has to leave."

"Wow, that really sucks," Nate said, in a classic understatement.

"Look at this place. Everyone knows that the girls are working here. And Meow even told him her price for a longtime. So he can drop $200 a night for a room, but he has to stiff the girl he grunts and sweats over all night. Fucking asshole!" He drained his beer and motioned for another.

"You know, Nate, the Asians have it right about sex, but western guys like that screw things up. 'Never pays for sex' my ass. I was married to an American girl. Nice woman, gave me two kids. Still love her, in fact, even if she kicked me out. But boy, if I counted out how much I've paid her over the years, and how many times we fucked, well, it would be a lot more expensive than what I pay here."

"Your wife left you?"

"Yes, co-eds, you know." Nate nodded as nothing else needed to be said on that subject.

"Have you ever read *The East, the West, and Sex: A History of Erotic Encounters?*"

Nate looked blank.

Brian sighed. "What was I thinking?" he asked to no one in particular. "It was written by Richard Bernstein, and among other things, it goes into the differences on how the east and the west look at sex. He labels this as the *Culture of the Harem* and the *Culture of Christendom*. In its purest essence, the *Culture of the Harem* considers sex as a normal part of life, divorced from love and family. Mostly men, but people need sex, and to have it outside of the marriage bed is accepted as normal. Women try to please the man, and a woman who is good at it rises in stature. She can catch the eye of the sultan, so-to-speak. An odalisque can even become queen."

"*Odalisque?*"

"A harem girl, a sex slave, if you will. But in the west, we marry, pun intended, sex and love. Marriage is the only way to have 'proper' sex. We look to women as being chaste and pure. We want virgins to marry. Our knights in shining armor fought dragons to save virginal, pure women. Hell, even our god was born of the Virgin Mary."

Although fascinated by his talk, that last comment bothered Nate, and he crossed himself. Brian didn't seem to notice.

"So in the east, sex is a good thing, a normal thing. Paying for sex is fine, and a woman who excels at sex is to be admired. A western girl who excels at sex is a slut."

"Guys like that asshole come in here and push themselves around. They treat the girls like garbage instead of giving them common courtesy and respect. They wouldn't treat a waitress like that, so why treat someone who is giving them a more intimate service?"

"I kinda understand you, but putting all women in a harem? Isn't that sexist?"

"You need to read the book. It's not misogynist. The author does not hate women, and he seems to stick up for women and their rights, especially for the right for women to do as they please."

"I don't know. It seems kinda weird to me, but I guess I can trust you on that."

"OK, enough of the lectures for now. I guess I can't really ever get out of the classroom."

Nate smiled. "Well, I ain't gonna sleep with you for an A, at least."

"Touché, my young friend, touché!"

While they had been talking, Nate's attention kept gravitating to a slender girl with long hair sitting at one of the small bar-like tables. She had been joking with some of the other girls, and her poofy shorts revealed long, attractive legs. Brian caught the focus of his attention on about Nate's fifth or sixth glance.

"Ah, so you find young Tulip to be alluring?" he asked.

"Tulip? That's her name?"

"Well, that is the working name she picked. I don't think I even know her real name. But she's not a bad choice. She's a university student who comes here in the afternoons after her morning classes. Tells her mother she's at the library studying."

That reminded Nate. "Oh, did I tell you? I have a real date with a university girl on Friday. A normal girl."

"All the girls here are "normal" girls, Nate. I take it you mean that you have a date with a non-working girl." He lifted and drained his third bottle, then lifted his arm to signal for another.

"Uh, yea. I met her at MBK, at the food court. She goes to some university near there, Chula–something-or-other."

"You're kidding me! Chulalongkorn?" Brian looked surprised.

"Yes, that might be it. Why?"

Brian raised his hand for a high-five. As he couldn't get too far over the table, Nate had to partially stand up and reach across to return the high-five, which he did without thinking.

"A Chula girl! Nate, my young and obviously magnetic friend, you have just scored on the sexpat's holy grail. A hiso, Chula girl. Stories abound about this very rare species, and some doubt their very existence, but others swear there have been sightings, that they've found footprints or taken grainy videos. Tell me, is she tall, light-skinned, and Chinese?"

Nate was confused. "Well, she's tall, but she's Thai. She speaks Thai. She helped me get my lunch. And I don't know if her skin is light or not. Why?"

"Chinese-Thai, not Chinese-Chinese. No matter. If anyone asks you, yes, she has light skin, and yes, she is Chinese. Of course, not many will believe you having they themselves failed in their own many hunts for this elusive creature."

"I don't know why. She just came up and started talking to me. I didn't have to do anything."

"Oh, the advantages of being young, tall, and good-looking. Enjoy it while you can. Old farts like me, we can only dream of that." He laughed again.

"But that brings us to dear Tulip there. Do you want to meet her?"

Nate looked over at her again. She certainly did look nice. "Yea, I'd like that."

Brian shouted out, catching the group's attention. He pointed at Tulip. Several of the girls pointed at themselves in a question, but after a few hand signals, he singled out Tulip and motioned her over. She smiled, slid off her stool, and came over.

She started to slide next to Brian, but he motioned her over to Nate. With barely a hesitation, she changed course and gracefully sat down next to him.

"Tulip, dear, this is my good friend Nate. He thinks you are *suay mak mak!*"

She laughed and wai'ed, then held out a hand to Nate. "Pleased to meet you." Her voice had a lilting quality which momentarily took Nate's attention from her babydoll face, but her broad smile brought his attention back to it.

Nate was momentarily at a loss for words as he took her hand. But then again, he was usually at a loss for words around attractive young women. After a few moments, he stammered out a greeting, not really too sure what he said, only that she seemed to take it in stride.

Nate had learned that "*suay mak mak*" meant very pretty, and Brian was right on with this comment. Nate did think she was "*suay mak mak.*" Her skin was flawless, her face blemish-free. With her smile, she looked very young, although she had to be at least Nate's age if she was a university student.

"Where are you from, Khun Nate," she asked.

"San Diego." When she looked confused, he added, "California, in the USA."

"Ah, I have a sister who lives in Fresno. Is that close to you?"

"Not really I think it's about eight hours to drive there. "

"Oh so far." With barely a pause, she went on, "Are you here on holiday?"

Brian interrupted, "Tulip, my dear, no need to play bargirl twenty questions. Nate likes you, he wants to take you back to his hotel and enjoy your physical delights."

She looked a little confused.

"He wants to *boom-boom mak mak* you!" That elicited a laugh from her.

Nate hadn't actually told Brian he wanted to take her, but he let it slide because the idea was not without its merits. But thinking back to the hotel, and knowing that Nok was on duty, he didn't really want to take Tulip back there.

"Uh, Brian. I really don't want to go back to the hotel. I read on the internet that there are places you can go for an hour. I'd rather do that."

"You mean a short-time hotel?" When Nate nodded, Brian continued. "Suit yourself, but why pay another 300 baht when you already have a room? Well, if you two young kids insist on making the animal with two backs, let's get your bill so you can scoot off." He signaled the waiter for it.

Tulip leaned in to take his arm in hers. "Oh, you are very strong," she exclaimed, squeezing his biceps. Nate knew she was merely butt-kissing, but still, it felt good.

The waiter brought over the bill and gave it to Nate. Brian did not catch his eye, deciding his beer was more interesting. Nate sighed and pulled out enough for both of their meals and drinks.

Tulip made a short, sharp nod and said, "*Pai*. Let's go."

"You two have fun," Brian called from behind them as they walked out the door and into the street.

With her arm firmly planted in his, she led him to the main road, then down a smaller soi to what looked like a bar/restaurant. In the back was a small reception desk. The bored-looking girl looked up from reading her book and merely said "300 baht."

Nate paid it as Tulip showed the receptionist her ID card and signed a piece of paper. She took the key and led Nate to the small elevator in back of the desk. Up they slowly rode to the third floor and to room 305. It was pretty hot in there as Tulip opened the door and they entered, but after Tulip put the key holder in the slot, the electricity came on and Tulip was able to turn on the air conditioner.

The room was small, barely bigger than the bed in it. Mirrors hung over the bed on the ceiling and over the headboard on the wall. That was rather interesting to him.

"You want to take your shower first?" she asked, handing him a towel.

"Oh, sure." Nate didn't know where to put his clothes so he hung them on the protruding key holder as he took them off and entered the small shower. With a tiny bar of soap, he washed down before stepping out. Tulip had already taken off her clothes and had wrapped herself in a towel. She smiled at Nate and sidled around him to the shower.

Nate lay down on the bed and looked up to the mirror. He thought he looked odd there, towel around his waist. But the perspective was interesting, none-the-less. He listened to her shower, trying not to stare at the flimsy shower curtain. A few moments later, she came out, smiled again, and dropped her towel.

Her body was very, very cute. High, small breasts, a very small waist, and shaved pubic hair. She looked very young, and Nate was rather excited.

She got onto the bed and knelt over him, confidently giving him a full view of all her parts. As she got down beside him and started to stroke him, his attention went up to the mirror. In the image there, he was surprised to see how small she looked lying next to him. Her darker skin made a nice contrast to his rather pale body.

She proceeded to go about her business with skill even if not with great enthusiasm. She gave the impression of being more concerned with her pride of work rather than anything else. And whether it was because of her ministrations, or whether it was because of Nate's attention being captured by the mirror, Nate lasted much longer than he had on the previous two nights. No "slam, bam, thank you ma'am," but rather a hint of the kind of love-making Nate had seen depicted by Hollywood. This is not to say that this was a marathon session of grunting and grinding—it was just Nate's first experience of getting into the rhythm of sex, of feeling two bodies move against and with each other.

When it was finished, Tulip took off his condom and looked at the reservoir tip with what looked like a sense of accomplishment, then threw it out into the small trash can beside the bed.

"*Sabai mai?*" she asked. When Nate shook his head in incomprehension, she added, "Happy?"

"Oh yes, that was great!" he said honestly.

"Good!" She smiled, kissed his forehead, then hurried to the shower. Nate followed her after she got out, and by the time he was getting out of the shower, she was already dressed and sitting on the edge of the bed. He reached into his shorts and took out his wallet, counting out 1,000 baht and giving it to her. She wai'ed deeply before sliding the bills into her purse.

They left the room after he dressed, went down to the reception desk, and gave the receptionist the key. The receptionist counted out some baht to give to Tulip, and together they walked out. Across from the entrance, several masseuses in orange uniforms sat in front of their parlor, waiting for customers. They smiled knowingly at Nate, who felt a flush creeping over his face. He hurried past them and out to the main street.

Tulip stopped him. "OK, I go home now." She pointed up to the BTS station over their heads.

"OK, thank you."

She wheeled away and strode off to the stairs. Nate watched her go, then looked at his watch. It was only 1:45. He'd already gotten laid, and there was the entire evening to go yet. Life was good.

Chapter 12

The next few days ran into each other, one day converging with the next day, time losing its nice, structured organization. Nate slept when he was tired, got up when he wasn't, wandered around the shopping malls and bars, seeking companionship. He met up with Brian each day, and with James and Dennis most evenings. After he asked, Brian steered him one afternoon to a massage parlor with happy endings, and the ending, well, was happy.

But while Nate was full of hormones, while he actively sought out the available companionship for rent, and while he enjoyed the subsequent gymnastics, he began to feel a little jaded. He wasn't sure what else he wanted; he only knew that he wanted it.

He spent another evening with An, trying to recapture the excitement he felt on that first night, but while she was just as enthusiastic, just as skilled, he felt a little disappointed, and he didn't even know why. He tried more encounters, one or two each afternoon at the Beer Garden, and one in the evening. And while he got a little more skilled at the act in the short span of days, he actually enjoyed the experiences a little less. But he could not stop. He was driven to experience as much as he could. And while he enjoyed himself a little bit less each time, it was still pretty good, and he reveled in his new-found pleasures. He just thought it should be a little bit more exciting, a little bit more mind-blowing.

Nate experienced one important change, though. Only a week earlier, Nate could barely hold an intelligent conversation with a women. In an amazingly short period of time, a sense of confidence infused him. He was able to approach girls, to initiate conversations. Nate rather liked Nate 2.0, the new and improved Nate.

He was even able to chat up Nok somewhat. Several times, he stood around to talk with her, moving back when she had to deal with guests, then stepping back up when she was free. He really didn't know what to say to her, so he told her mostly about Oceanside, about school, about his dad. When he ran out of subjects, he felt more awkward, and he made an excuse to move on, telling her each time that he would talk again later. He couldn't tell if Nok was really interested in his company or if she was trapped by her desk and couldn't get away. He hoped it was the former rather than the latter.

On Thursday night, Nate was watching the dancers at the Longgun with James, Dennis, and Brian. He was trading comments with James about one new dancer who seemed to be a little overwhelmed by the scene. She was a tall, light-skinned girl, and the expression on her face left no doubt that she would really rather be doing something else, anything else.

James made a comment about "hiso bitches" when Brian leaned over to announce, "Well, James my cockney friend, ..."

"Liverpool, you bloody twit, I keep telling you I'm from Liverpool," James interrupted, a scowl on his face.

Brian winked at Nate before continuing. "You keep chasing those hiso girls, like that one you said you found at Spasso. Did you know that our young friend Nate here has a date tomorrow with a real Chula girl? The young delectable approached him and asked him out."

James peered at him over his beer for a moment before looking away in disgust. "My bloody arse, you gobshit. This anorak," he tipped his beer to indicate Nate, "couldn't get a hiso Chula girl if he was the last bloody wanker on earth."

Brian took a huge swallow of beer. "Ah, in that you are sadly mistaken. I was with our young Lothario when this vision approached him and basically demanded that he accompany her to dinner tomorrow night. All for her desire to experience his formidable physique."

James shifted his blurry gaze to Nate. "Is that true?" he asked.

Nate chose to ignore Brian's claim to have been there, and focused on his upcoming date. "Yep, I guess it is."

"Bloody bullshit. How do you know she was a Chula girl?"

"Well, you wouldn't know from experience, of course, but it was her charming Chulalongkorn uniform and her quite excellent command of the English language," Brian responded, despite the question being directed at James. Brian seemed to be taking a great deal of pleasure in baiting James "You wouldn't know anything about that kind of girl though. You only make acquaintance with the type of girl you have to pay for her company."

"At least I can do something with the ones I pay for, you fat fucking wanker. And at least I don't start drinking at lunch."

Brian held a mocking hand over his heart. "Alas, you wound me to the quick!"

Nate listened to the banter, feeling his own drink a little much. And with a very uncharacteristic sense of cockiness, he decided to add his own fuel to the fire.

"Well, James, if you weren't such an old loser with no hope left, then maybe you could score on real girls here." He felt exhilarated at being able to dish out some shit, and looked back at his beer in satisfaction. So he didn't notice the sense of outrage which came over James' face. He felt the beer splash on his face, though, and heard him when he started screaming.

"You fucking arsehole. Who the fuck do you think you are?" James stood up, now empty beer glass in hand, dislodging the girl sitting next to him. The girl fell on the floor and started to back away on her butt in panic, not bothering to stand up. "You're the fucking arse-bandit who couldn't even get a whore. I had to get one for you. And you fuck with me now?"

The cockiness Nate had felt vanished like a drop of water on a hot griddle. He stared in horror at James, at the flecks of spit flying from his mouth. Dennis had gotten up and was trying to pull James back, but James easily shrugged him off.

"Are you a big man now?" James leaned over the table, looking down at the still-seated Nate.

Nate felt fear knife through his gut. He thought his bowels would loosen right there. His vision began to tunnel again, as it had so often before in his life. All cockiness was gone, transmogrified into abject fear. He stared at James' hand, wondering when it would hit him.

"Look at this bloody coward!" he crowed to no one in particular, although the entire half of the bar was now watching. "Big as he is, he's a fucking fag. And I'm going to beat his bloody arse."

He raised his fist as if to hit Nate, and Nate didn't wait to see if the threat would materialize or if it was a bluff. He bolted to his feet and ran out the door, heart pounding. Shouldering his way through the people on the soi, he made it to the stoplight before he started to calm down a bit. He looked back, but no one was in pursuit. In humiliation, he slowly walked back to the Holiday Inn, his only consolation a rueful acknowledgment that for the first time, he hadn't had to pick up the tab.

Chapter 13

After awakening the next morning, Nate couldn't seem to get his motor in gear. He knew he should be doing something, so maybe a good workout would help. He got as far as putting on his shorts and shirt when *Meercat Manor* caught his attention, and he got back onto the bed to watch it. That was followed by *Man vs. Wild*, and that provided another excuse to laze away. Even his growing hunger couldn't rouse him. He really didn't want to see Brian after last night's episode, so for the first time during the week, he didn't go to meet him at the Beergarten.

The cleaning lady knocked on his door, but he sent her away and numbly watched a progression of nature shows. It wasn't until he noticed that it was 5:00 PM that he suddenly felt a jolt of anything resembling human life. He had his date with Rattana coming up! He had called her the day before to confirm, and they were going to meet at 7:00 at the Outback in the Silom Discovery Center (with Rattana selecting the location).

After a shower and shave, he put on his jeans and the best shirt he had brought, which wasn't saying much. But it would have to do. He left the room and went down the lobby. Nok waved at him, but he felt unexplainably guilty, so he just smiled and gave a half-wave back before hurrying out.

The late afternoon heat hit him with a physical blow, as usual, and he was sweating rivers by the time the train doors opened and a blessed torrent of cold air hit him. Well, cold by comparison. In the packed car, it was still pretty warm. One stop later, he was at the Siam Center/Paragon/Siam Discovery Complex. Looking at his watch, he saw he was 50 minutes early.

Siam Discovery was a somewhat smallish five story mall with a limited number of shops. Nate wandered the mall, killing time. He reached his five companions-for-the-night threshold after about five minutes, so he was pretty bored by 6:45 when he stationed himself in front of Outback and waited.

And waited.

And waited.

He kept going over his conversation with Rattana in his mind. Yes, the date was for 7:00, he was sure. And this was the only Outback at Siam Discovery. He wandered in twice to see if she had somehow snuck in without him noticing it. Each time, the waitress tried to seat him, and each time, he smiled and ignored her before leaving to take up his post again.

Thoughts of his senior prom, where Alicia Jenkins had invited him as a joke, only to stand him up, started to creep into his head despite his efforts to banish them. He made himself a promise that he would wait until 8:00, and if she didn't show, he would leave. The closer he got to 8:00, the more those thoughts made themselves felt. 8:00, and still no Rattana. He decided to give her another 5 minutes. When those five minutes were up, he gave her five more. But when those were up, he had to admit that he had been stood up. He slowly left his position and started to walk off to go to MBK to eat. As he was going down the escalator, he heard his name called out, and there was Rattana going up the other escalator. She had come after all!

He got to the bottom and hurried around to the other side to go back up, but as he was going up, there was Rattana again coming back down. She laughed and told him to stay on the upper floor. A minute or so later, she was coming up, and they met at the top. She wai'ed him.

"Sorry to be late, Khun Nate. Traffic was very bad."

Nate wondered at that. From what he knew, her university was only about half a mile away, so traffic couldn't have made her over an hour late. But he wasn't going to belabor the point. His stomach chose that moment to growl loud enough for her to hear.

"Well, I guess we should eat, OK?"

She nodded, and they went back into the Outback, finally letting the waitress give him a table. Sitting down, Nate used the menu as a shield, not knowing what to say. The menu items looked somewhat like what he would see at an Outback back in the US even if the prices were higher. He was very hungry by now, but the steak prices seemed high, so he ordered a burger instead. Rattana ordered pork ribs.

With the ordering out of the way, Nate was forced to look at her. She was dressed quite nicely, with a blue silk top which did nothing to hide the curves of her breasts. Nate was excited knowing that soon enough, he would be touching them. She smiled at him and began the chitchat, asking him about his day and what he had been doing over the last few days. Nate left out the bar-related events, and that left what he could talk about a little on the light side. But Rattana didn't seem to notice. She listened intently, asking about why he used certain phrases or words. That made it a little disconcerting to Nate, but he suffered each interruption well.

The waitress was very gracious, coming over regularly to see if things were OK. Nate would have been much happier had she come with his order, hungry as he was, but he appreciated the effort.

Nate was going into greater detail about his jewelry store junket, which seemed to surprise Rattana to no end, when the food came at last. It looked like a pretty good burger, at least. He poured on the Heinz ketchup, which was the only one he used at home, and took a bite. Well, looks weren't always a good indication on taste. It had the "Thainess" he had experienced before, something which made it a rather poor burger. At least it was calories and bulk, so he wolfed it down anyway.

Both of them focused on their food for a few moments, conversation fading away. Rattana delicately used her knife and fork to slice small pieces of the rib meat off the bones. Nate would have just used his hands to pick the ribs up and gnaw on them, so he found Rattana's methods rather endearing. Not that this observation slowed him down on his own attack on his plate.

Nate had long finished when Rattana finally put down her knife and fork. Nate looked longingly at the bits of meat still left on the bones, but he thought better of asking her if he could take a chew on them. She precisely folded her napkin, then looked back up at him.

"When you told me you were 'fed-up' with the people at the jewelry store, do you mean you were 'bored?'" she asked almost as if they hadn't paused in their conversation.

Nate sighed. He wasn't up for this English class, and her questions about prepositions and participles had him confused. He had forgotten most of that. But to spend a night with her, he would willingly discuss the past perfect tense, whatever that was.

"No, 'bored' means that you are tired of it, but not upset. 'Fed-up' means more of angry, sort of. You don't like it, I guess."

"I thought 'bored' had a meaning of being upset." She wrinkled her brow as she thought about it.

"No, not really. Not really upset or angry. Just, bored."

They went on with her prodding him to talk to her, to tell her about his adventures, not just in Thailand, but back in the US. He started talking about boot camp, and the military phrases had her stymied. She had never heard of most of them, and she kept stopping him to ask for their meanings. The waitress came by for the umpteenth time to refill their water glasses, but Rattana didn't seem to notice nor acknowledge her. He paid the bill, and still she couldn't take the hint, still she wanted to talk.

Eventually, she seemed to run out of steam. She picked up her purse and asked, "Should we go now?"

At last, he thought. Now they could get to what he really wanted, and what he really wanted was covered in a blue silk blouse. He almost knocked over the table as he jumped up.

They left the restaurant flanked by the staff wai'ing and thanking them for coming. As they walked, Nate was wondering if he should take her hand. After riding down the escalator, he had just about gotten up the nerve to take her hand when she turned to him, hand outstretched to shake his.

"Thank you, Khun Nate. I learned much from our conversation. I hope we can meet again."

Nate took her hand by reflex, but he was floored. She was leaving?

"Uh, I was hoping, I mean, I'd like to...uh, I want to stay with you more," he stammered out.

"Oh, my parents do not allow me out late. I have to get home. But we can meet again. Maybe for lunch. You can call me. Now I have to go home." She glanced at her watch. "Well, OK, bye." She smiled at him and turned to walk away.

Nate watched in stunned silence as she walked away. This was not how he had envisioned his evening! What was he going to do now?

He briefly considered heading off to Soi Cowboy or Nana, but he didn't want to run into James. Brian, neither as he would then have to explain why he wasn't with his Chula girl. He thought about it, then figured that he could take a night off. Maybe he'd just head back to the hotel and call it a night.

At least it was early enough that the BTS was still running. He got onboard and rode back to the hotel. Walking down the steps at the station, he looked east, towards Nana and the rest, considering once more if he should make the trek. But a quiet night really did sound good, so he shook his head and walked over and into the hotel.

As he started off towards the elevators, he looked, as was his usual, to the reception desk to see if Nok was there. She was, and he caught her eye. She waved with a big smile.

Nate faltered, then stopped. He looked back at the still smiling Nok. He was attracted to her, that was for sure. He would love to spend some time with her. That was equally for sure.

Nate was not the sort of guy who could easily chat up women. But his week in Thailand had germinated a seed of change. The girls here liked him. They told him he was handsome and strong. They went to bed with him. That seed of self-confidence has sprouted into a small sapling. It was no mighty oak yet, but it was at least something.

He looked up at the ceiling, took a deep breath, and screwed up his courage. Turning, he walked over to Nok. She looked up again and smiled.

"Khun Nate! I hope you are having a good night."

"Yes, yes I am. I was just going to go relax now, watch some television."

He stood there looking at her while she looked at him expectantly.

Not like this! This is the old Nathan. Be aggressive, be a man! he thought to himself.

Steeling up his nerve, he looked her directly in the eyes. "You know, you are beautiful."

She pushed back a few inches, eyes widening in surprise.

He paused, trying to get his thoughts together. "I mean, I've seen some hot girls here, but you are the hottest." Saying the words like that seem to release something in him, making him feel empowered.

"Khun Nate, I don't think …"

"Really. You're hot, and I think we should hook up," he interrupted.

Nok's eyes narrowed and she moved back a few more inches, smile gone.

"Whaduyah say, Nok? Can we hook up?" He reached out over the counter to take her small hand in his.

Fire suddenly blazed in her eyes. She jerked her hand back, then leaned forward. "Mr. Nate! I am a good woman! I graduated from the university. I am not a bar girl!" She paused, anger making her breath come in gulps. "You *farang*, you think all women want you, that all women sex you. You come here to my country, you throw money, you get girl, you get boy, for selfish. You think you better than Thai!" In her anger her normal, well-spoken English evaporated.

Nate was taken aback. Despite her anger, despite his growing horror, though, he couldn't take his eyes off her heaving chest.

"You want me because you want to sex me!" She was furious, despite keeping the volume down on her voice. The tone carried though, and two other receptionists looked up, wondering what was going on.

"Go back to bargirl for that. I know you take joiner every night. I see. I am good Thai girl, not for you!" she said with finality.

Nate looked at her now in horror. "No," he protested, "I don't think that, I mean, I don't want that!"

Of course, she was exactly right. He did want to fuck her. That is why he came over. And now to have it thrown in his face like that, well, his little sapling of self-confidence was cut off at the roots.

He stared down at her, mouth agape. "I… you…"

Fight or flight took over, and as usual, for Nate, his *modus operandi* was flight. He wheeled about and ran, around the corner, sticking his hand in a closing elevator door to keep it open, then jumped inside to the surprise of the elderly Japanese couple already there.

He rode it up to his room, and with shaking hands, he had to swipe his key card five times before the green light indicated success and he could enter. Without turning on the light, he made his way in the dark to the bed and flopped down on it. He felt the familiar pounding of his heart, the cold sweat on his brow.

How could he have done that? In an intellectual way, he knew the bargirls he had been meeting were in it for the money, and they would have been with him as long as the baht held out. And Nok certainly was not a bargirl. But somehow, even after only a week, he had begun to lump women together, as objects for his own use. He knew this wasn't right. His mother taught him better than that. Yet he did it, anyway. He wasn't fit to be with a woman, he knew. Shame filled him with remorse.

He didn't know how long he lay there, wallowing in his self-pity. It wasn't fair. He was a good guy. But no one understood him. Not his dad, not the Marine Corps, not girls in general. An hour passed. Two. He didn't know nor care.

His sulk was interrupted by a soft knocking on the door. It didn't really register with him until it happened again.

"I don't need anything," he called out, thinking it was the turn-down service.

The knocking started again. With a groan, he rolled off the bed and went to the door to tell the maid to go away. He opened it and stood in surprise as Nok stood there, bowing her head when she saw him.

"Khun Nate, may I come in?" She looked up and down the hall.

Nate merely stood aside as she entered stopping in the entranceway. She moved to close the door, before noticing the darkness. Nate quickly turned on the light.

She looked nervous, wringing her hands together.

"Khun Nate," she began, "I must apologize for my actions. You are our guest, and I was wrong. I cannot talk to our guests that way."

Nate just nodded.

"I don't know what you were thinking, what you wanted, but I should not treat you like that."

"It's OK." The guilt meter was getting pegged now. Nate had been wrong, Nok had been right. Yet here Nok was apologizing to him.

"I am not supposed to be here in the guest rooms. But I needed to apologize. I hope you can accept that."

Nate nodded again.

"Some guests, well, they do come here to have sex with girls or boys, and they do treat them bad. And they do think that all Thais are like that, to sell themselves for money." Nate's feeling of guilt grew even stronger, if that was possible. "But Thailand is not all like that. Thailand is a wonderful place of peace, tradition, and happiness."

She looked up at him and seemed to gather herself. "Khun Nate, tomorrow, I will take my holiday and go home for a week. I think you should see the real Thailand. I invite you to come with me and see my home, my family, my village. This is the real Thailand. Not Patpong." She looked at him to see his reaction.

Nate stepped back. Go to a village? But he rather liked Bangkok. He liked Nana and Soi Cowboy. But he felt guilty about what had happened, and he didn't want to admit that he wanted to stay where he could get laid. Looking down at her, she looked so lovely, even concerned as she was. She was simply gorgeous. And maybe at her home, well, maybe a little romance could blossom. That was what made up his mind.

"I would be honored to visit your home," he said, bowing his head.

Her smile made an immediate comeback. "I am happy about this. I think you will learn about my country. I have to go now. I shouldn't be here. But I will come back tomorrow at 11:30. I will meet you at Emporium, at the information desk. Is that OK? So you check out of your room and meet me there."

"Why not here?" he asked.

"I cannot! Not with hotel guest. Please, Emporium?"

"Oh, OK."

"Thank you Khun Nate. I will see you tomorrow." She slipped him a note with her phone number and stepped back to make a formal wai, which Nate tried to emulate. She turned, opened the door a crack, and looked out, checking for anyone watching, then quickly left.

Well, he hadn't planned it, but Nate was on his way to the countryside!

Chapter 14

At 11:20 the next morning, Nate was standing at the information desk at Emporium, backpack beside him. He had checked out of the hotel, paying for the one night not covered by his dad's award program, then boarded the BTS for the short trip to the upscale shopping center.

By 11:45, he was getting fidgety. The two girls behind the desk had by now taken him as part of the landscape, so he stood to the side and waited for Nok. Had he checked out in vain? Should he go back and check back in?

Finally, shortly after noon, he felt a swell of relief as Nok walked up, a pink roller bag in tow and a very large plastic shopping bag in her arms. He almost didn't recognize her at first. Her hair was hanging down, and her jeans did a much better job of showing off her assets than the green Holiday Inn uniform. But her smile was unmistakable, and Nate broke into his own smile as she walked up to him.

She gave a short bow of her head. "Khun Nate! I am happy you are here!" She looked a little sheepish. "I thought maybe you decide not to come."

"Oh no, I said I would, and I am a man of my word."

"Well, OK! I am happy." She indicated with her free hand the main doors of the shopping center. "Shall we go now?"

Nate nodded, took the bag out of her arms, and followed her out, taking note of the way her jeans framed her small butt. He rather hoped that he would be able to sample some of that in the very near future.

They left the cool inside for the fierce sun radiating off the pavement. Nok held her hand over her forehead in an ineffective sunshade as they moved down to the waiting taxis. The next taxi saw them and popped the trunk. Nate grabbed Nok's roller bag and put it in the trunk, intending to put his backpack there, too, but most of the trunk was filled with a large cylinder, probably the natural gas to power the taxi. So he put the bag, which seemed to consist of two good sized boxes, in the front seat, then pushed his backpack into the back seat and climbed in, only then realizing that the backpack was separating him from Nok. He should have gotten in first then brought in his pack. Then he would have had an excuse to sit close to her.

The taxi was blessedly cool as Nok gave the driver their destination, and off they pulled into the traffic. Nate was very aware of Nok sitting next to him, her jeans-clad legs just a few inches away. But she just watched out the window as they rode along, so he did the same. Traffic was heavy, but eventually they crossed a large river over an impressive-looking bridge, then moved onto an elevated highway. They were able to drive quicker then, and shortly, they were back off the elevated road and were pulling into a large bus station.

Nate paid the driver and followed Nok inside the station where a bewildering array of ticket booths greeted them. Nate couldn't make heads nor tails of them, but Nok made a beeline for one of them and got in line. When they made it to the window, she told the person on the other side of the window their destination, then turned back to Nate and told him 450 baht. Nate handed her a thousand, and she smiled and thanked him, paying the agent and getting back 100 baht.

"Thank you, Kuhn Nate," she said with a smile, handing him back the hundred.

Nate hadn't really planned on paying for her ticket, but it was only 450 baht, and it made him look generous, so he just smiled in return.

Tickets in hand, Nok led him to a seat, one of about 20 plastic, armless chairs all connected to each other. "Are you hungry? Thirsty?"

Nate was nineteen years old, so he was always hungry. "Sure."

"OK, you wait here."

He sat there watching the flow of people. An old couple, the woman barely moving with short, halting steps was escorted by a patient man, her arm in his. Nate watched them, wondering what it would be like to be old, to be limited in motion. He wondered what they had experienced in life, what they would have looked like when he was a young man courting her. Did they have kids? Did they have a full life?

Two young girls in school uniforms pushed past them, not giving the old couple even a glance as they talked and laughed. The couple just continued their slow progress.

A few seats down, a middle-aged man was low in his chair, head back over the edge of it. He snored intermittently, but no one seemed to take notice. He was dressed in what Nate would consider workman's clothes: khaki cotton pants and a polo shirt with what looked to be a company logo on the breast. His heavy work shoes were caked with a light-colored dust.

Nok came back with a plastic cup filled with a pink liquid and a Styrofoam container. He thanked her and took a sip of the drink. It was sickeningly sweet, like liquid candy. Nate quickly put it on the floor next to his seat. He opened the food container. It looked like a jumble of vegetables and some sort of processed meat. He took a hesitant bite. It tasted pretty much like it looked. This wasn't like anything he had eaten in Thailand so far, and he wasn't too enthralled by it. But food was food. He smiled at Nok as she looked at him questionably, which elicited a smile back from her as she dug into her own food.

After finishing, Nok got on her cell phone for some extended conversations. Nate just sat there staring until Nok got up at last, motioning him to stand up as well. He followed her as she made her way to the correct bus. They placed their bags under it and got on, making their way back to their assigned seats. Nok had the window and Nate the aisle. He would have liked to be able to look out the window as well, but given the limited room and their respective sizes, perhaps it was better this way.

The bus was finally loaded and backed out of the station. The air conditioner tried dutifully to cool the bus interior with limited success, but at least it was not sweltering. Up in the front of the bus, a small television screen came to life, and one of the US-made Jackie Chan cop fish-out-of-water movies came on. Nate settled back to watch, but the sound was so low that he couldn't make anything out. He caught a few words, but they seemed to be dubbed in Thai. Even without sound, though, Nate's attention was on the screen as they pulled out onto a major highway. He settled back into his narrow seat for the trip, very aware of Nok's arm pressed up against his. She looked up and gave him her high-wattage smile.

The bus was crowded, but not unduly uncomfortable. With Jackie kicking his way through dozens of LA bad guys on the television and Nok at his side, the trip was not nearly as bad as he had expected. Jackie gave way to a Thai martial arts movie, and without the sound, it made just as much sense as the previous video. And before that video was finished, the bus was pulling into a station. Nate tried to see a sign which would tell him where they were, but he couldn't spy one. As the bus stopped, he got up, joints creaking, and made his way off the bus, stopping to grab their bags. The station was nothing much: an open courtyard-looking terminal with half-a-dozen buses of various degrees of maintenance filling about half of the parking slots. Nate followed Nok as she navigated through the terminal's interior and through the front doors.

They walked across the street to where a line of pick-up trucks with seats in the beds were parked. Nate followed in a daze as she moved unerringly towards one, asked the driver a question, then motioned for Nate to hop in the back. The hard wooden bench was pretty uncomfortable, and he hoped the ride would not be too long.

"We'll take this to your home?"

"Oh no, but this will take us to the outside of my village. Then we will walk in. Not far."

After about 20 minutes, the pick-up was completely full and it took off, weaving through the traffic. While nowhere near as crowded as Bangkok, there were a surprisingly large number of cars and motorcycles creating a localized traffic jam. The difference was that unlike in Bangkok, after about 10 minutes of horn-honking progress, the traffic opened up and the pick-up began to gather speed. Nate tried to look over his shoulder at the city, but that posture was uncomfortable, so he gave up and just looked ahead.

An old lady sitting across from him gave him a toothless smile. He smiled back, but not knowing what else to do, he tried to avoid eye contact with her. That was difficult though, and each time her gaze captured his, the smile-exchanging was back in force.

"This is a famous wat," Nok told him, pointing to a large temple complex. Nate turned to see it. "King Rama IV walked to here when he was a young man and meditated. You know meditate?" Nate nodded. "He was a monk here, and he gave money to make the temple bigger. It is very famous."

Nate had seen a few wats in Bangkok, but surrounded by large buildings, they looked smaller, more circumspect. This one, on the edge of the city, looked much grander. He would have liked to take a look around.

The pick-up, or *songthaew*, as Nok called it, moved into country. Nate got a few glimpses of fields and forests. But mostly, he watched the people on the bench facing him, trying to avoid granny's eyes. They passed a few small settlements with half a dozen or a dozen homes, but most of the route was country. The driver seemed to think nothing of driving down long stretches in the oncoming lane, slowly passing other cars. Nate couldn't see in front of them, but he was quite uncomfortable imagining oncoming cars hurtling at them for a fiery collision. No one else seemed concerned though, so he tried to suppress his anxiety.

The pick-up finally slowed down and entered what looked to be a small town. The pickup pulled up to a small market area, and two thirds of the passengers got out.

"Is this your home?"

"No, this is the city. My village is more far."

Nate bent down to look around. "City" seemed a generous label for the place. The market was about a full city block, but none of the buildings surrounding it were more than two stories tall. The road next to the market was jammed with cars, trucks, motorcycles, and pedestrians. Nok pulled out her cell phone and made a call, but offered nothing else to Nate, so he just stretched his legs out and waited.

The pick-up waited at the market for about 15 minutes until oncoming passengers, laden with packages, filled up the empty seats. Most seemed surprised to see Nate sitting there. The driver threw his cigarette out the window and started the engine before pulling out and slowly worked his way through the congestion and out on the main road leading out of the "city." In minutes, the pick-up was lumbering along a decent road surrounded by fields. Nate settled down for a long drive, but shortly after leaving the city, Nok reached over and pushed a button on one of the supports , eliciting a buzzing sound. The driver pulled the truck to the side of the road, and Nok motioned for Nate to get out. Trying not to step on toes, he carried the packages and stepped off the truck and stretched. Looking back, he could see the city off in the distance over the rice paddies. Nok had said it was "far," but it couldn't have been more than a mile-and-a-half or so away.

"Khun Nate," Nok called out. He turned to look. "This is my family."

Standing at the side of the road were several people. Oldest were an elderly man with a big grin on his face and an equally elderly woman. But where the man was rail thin, the woman was on the hefty side. A middle-aged woman dressed in a pair of loose cotton pants and a white blouse stood with one hand on the shoulder of the old man. Another version of Nok was there, and hiding in back of her and clutching her skirt was a small girl of maybe 4 or 5 years old.

"This is my grandmother and grandfather, and this is my mother. This one is my sister, and in back of her is my niece." She moved over to give her niece a hug. She started speaking in Thai, all Nate was able to make out was "Khun Nate."

Except for the little one, they all wai'ed him, and he awkwardly tried to wai back.

Nok's sister looked down at the little girl and said something to her. The girl buried her face in her skirt, and Nok gently took her hands and brought them forward. The little girl relented and brought them together in a quick wai which Nate returned. The adults laughed.

"Now we walk." They picked up the bag and suitcase and started trudging down the side road, down past some rice paddies and into some trees. Nate could see some coconut palms, but many of the trees were uniform in size and planted in neat rows, deep trenches dug out between the rows. He wondered what they were.

In amongst the trees were several homes. People watched the small procession. One man yelled out something, and everyone laughed. Nok glanced up at Nate quickly, so he figured the comment had been about him.

Dogs came up to sniff at them. Nate was not too comfortable around dogs as a rule, but these were wagging their tails, so they did not seem to have ankle biting on their canine minds.

More homes came into view as they walked. Some were small, square, concrete homes. Others seemed to be wooden and built on platforms. Beneath these homes were sleeping dogs, chickens, broken-down and half-disassembled motorcycles, hammocks (some occupied), and various other signs of the human condition.

As they walked further into the village, Nate could see the top of a tall, ornate building ahead. It had to be the local wat, but before they reached it, the procession turned off the road and into a small concrete house.

"Welcome to my home, Nate."

He looked around, blinking his eyes to adjust them to the dim light inside. He was taken a bit aback. The concrete exterior extended to the interior as well. The floor was a smooth concrete. The walls were concrete, resplendent with cracks. A few desultory pieces of furniture reminding him of garage sale rejects were placed in front of an old television, wires running higgelty-piggelty along the ceiling and down to the set. A low concrete wall separated the "living room" from the kitchen area, which looked to be nothing more than a table with a small propane burner on it. A pot was bubbling along on top of the burner, steam rising into the air. A huge clay pot was next to the table, and a small beat-up refrigerator was up against the back wall. To the side, a small closed-off room was evidently the toilet. Turning around, he saw two rooms, obviously the bedrooms.

He smiled at Nok and said, "Very nice," thinking how lame that must sound.

She watched him closely. "I know this is not the Holiday Inn. Is it OK for you?"

"Sure." He smiled awkwardly back at her, knowing that his smile looked forced.

"This is a typical Thai house, so now you already know more about Thailand," she laughed. "I will change clothes now, so maybe you want to change too?"

She ushered him into one of the small rooms. There was a lone mattress on the floor, a light with a wire going up the wall and over the top to the other room, and a small dresser. Nate took off his pack and decided what to wear. It was brutally hot, so shorts it was going to be. Grandpa had on shorts, so he thought it should be OK. He put on a t-shirt and waked back out.

Granny came up and started non-stop Thai while Nate looked on hopelessly. He figured she was trying to get him to sit, so he sat on the deck-chair-type seat in front of the television and just looked up at her. Nok came out of the room and to his rescue. She also had on a pair of shorts and a white t-shirt with check boxes for the words "Small," "Medium," and "Fat." The "Fat" box had a large red check. No truth in advertising there, he thought. Nok was not fat in the slightest.

"She wants to know if you want a drink," she told him.

"Uh, sure, I guess."

Nok said something to Granny who smiled and waddled over to the fridge and took out a Coke. She opened the can and put in a straw before handing it to Nate. He hadn't drunk a soda in a can through a straw before, and as he took a sip, it seemed to taste different. But Coke was Coke, so he figured it had to be his imagination.

Gramps came over and stood in front of Nate, smiling but saying nothing. In the afternoon light streaming in the window, Nate could see a serious scar running down the side of his head. Nate felt uncomfortable as he stood there staring at him, but after a few moments, he just walked off.

Squeals of delight, which were the same in any language, came from the little girl as she opened the packages he and Nok had brought. Nate hadn't really looked at them, but he could see now the largest was a computer. The little girl had opened the box top and was trying to pull out the CPU. Nate jumped up to grab it. He didn't want to think what would happen if it fell on the concrete floor.

Nate eased the CPU out of the box. The little girl held her hands clasped in front of her, eagerness evident on her round face. He looked around to see where he should put it, and Nok hurriedly cleared a space on the table. With nothing better to do, Nate decided to hook up the computer.

As far as computers went, it wasn't much. A simple CPU, a small monitor, a mouse and a keyboard. When he asked Nok where he should plug it in, there ensued some heady discussions in Thai. Finally, the wire to the television was unhooked, then re-routed to the table. Nate shuddered to think of the quality of the power, but at least Nok had brought a surge protector, so maybe it would be OK.

Nate held his breath and turned on the power. The computer booted up, and everyone crowded around. The little one sat on a wooden crate so as to reach the keyboard, and Nok spent the next few minutes showing her how to use it. Despite Nate not understanding Thai, it was very evident that her niece kept on insisting that she knew how to use it. She took the mouse from Nok and brought up a game. Soon, the entire household was crowded around, laughing and clapping as she made her way through a colorful maze.

Nok stepped back and stood next to Nate. "She has learned computer in school. We have no internet, but my mother has ordered it from ToT. Next week it comes." She paused. "Do you think this will make Nidnoi a better student?"

Nate sort of took computers for granted. He shrugged, but said "Sure, of course it will."

"That is good. Nidnoi, she is smart, and she must get into a good university."

"But she is what, five years old?"

"She is seven. But we need to prepare her now."

Nate thought it might be too early to worry about that, but it wasn't any of his business. The women watched Nidnoi for a bit, then drifted around the table and started getting to work cooking. Nate thought there was an awful lot of food for dinner.

"All of that food is for dinner tonight?" he asked Nok.

"No, it is for the wedding."

"Wedding?"

"Yes. The wedding. I told you this, I am sure. My friend will get married tomorrow, so we must prepare the food tonight."

Nate thought back. He was sure that no wedding had been mentioned. But it might be interesting to see how the Thais celebrated it. He wandered over to see what was being cooked. None of it looked familiar. An opening in the wall, not really a bona fide door, let Nate see outside to where Granny was tending a fire with another bubbling pot on it. Nate ducked to step through the opening. Granny grinned and started jabbering about something, putting her nose over the pot and miming smelling. Nate leaned over and took a sniff. It wasn't bad, but it didn't smell appetizing, either. Nate smiled though, and rubbed his stomach. Granny cackled and kept speaking to him, even after he broke away and wandered around to the back of the house.

A white chicken with three dusky chicks scurried out of his way in panic as he rounded the corner. One chick bounced up against a low wire fence surrounding a rectangular pit filled with black, black water. Nate stepped over the fence and was immediately assaulted with a vile, sewer smell.

The pit was too well-tended not to have a purpose, and when Nate saw a small hand net, against his better judgment, he figured there had to be fish in there. The water was viscous, almost mud. A small polypropylene bag lay up against the house, the image of a fish on it, so he stepped back over the low fence, looked inside, and took a small handful of the pellets he saw. Moving back to the little pond, he threw them in.

At first, there was nothing. He was about to leave when a few swirls disturbed the surface of the water. So there was fish in there! How they could breath in that muck, how they could survive in that cesspit was beyond Nate.

He continued his circuit of the house. Beyond the fish pond was a small raised platform, two walls and a roof protecting it. He looked inside and saw a dirty foam mat and a blanket.

"Nate! Do you want to go to the market?" Nok came around the corner.

"Sure, why not?' he looked back at the dirty mat. "What is this place?"

"Ah," she said with a laugh. "That is for my grandfather. When he is drunk, my grandmother will not let him into the house. He has to sleep here. It is good for him, yes? And very good for my grandmother, yes times two!"

She leaned beside him to look in. "Very nice. Maybe you will sleep here tonight, too?"

Nate looked up in alarm before seeing the smile and twinkle in her eyes. "Ah yes," he agreed. "Better than the Holiday Inn!"

Nok laughed and took his arm, leading him back to the front of the house. It felt good to have her arm around his like that.

Both put on their shoes which were at the door, then she pointed a small motorcycle, motioning for him to get on. It seemed she expected him to drive. Nate had been on a bike a couple of times, but not enough to feel comfortable. But he couldn't admit to that.

He straddled the bike and looked down. OK, the key was there, just like he remembered. He turned it, then pulled in on the clutch. Giving a short prayer, he flipped out the kick starter and kicked down as hard as he could. The little bike roared, well, maybe not roared, but mewed to life. Nok settled on the bike behind him. She put her hands on his butt and pushed.

"Khun Nate, you are so big! Make room for me!" she told him with another laugh.

He scooted forward a bit, very, very conscious of Nok's body pressed up against his. He needed to get going. He eased off the clutch and turned the throttle. All that happened was the mewing became a little louder. Then he remembered that he had to kick it into gear. He tried to remember the gearing on a bike. Was it up or down for first?

He pulled up with his foot, then released the clutch again. The bike lurched forward and died, Nok smacking her head into his back. He turned to look at her and she raised a hand to her mouth.

"*Mai pen rai*," he heard.

Pulling in on the clutch, he started it once again. This time, he slowly let it back out again, and with a few fits and starts, he was smoothly into first gear. And first gear was just fine with him as he slowly made his way down the tiny road to the main village road. Despite his rising panic, he was able to move the bike into second, then third gear, even keeping it upright.

When they reached the main highway, he thought they would be going to the town, and the thought of doing that on the small bike frankly terrified him. But Nok pointed him to the left, and he drove in that direction for only a hundred yards or so to where a line of rickety stalls lined the edge of the road. This was the "market."

Nok jumped off the back of the bike as Nate turned the key, relieved in having made it this far in one piece. With no helmet and just his running shoes, he felt woefully under-protected. He started to follow Nok as she went down first to a vegetable stand where she grabbed what looked to be a bunch of weeds, and then to a meat stand where raw meat sat on a table out in the now fading sun. He wondered how long the meat had sat there, and how many flies had paraded across the meat's surface. She bought some ground meat, probably pork, and together they went back to the bike. Nate felt a little more confident this time, despite Nok motioning him to stay on the same side of the road on which they went to the market, facing oncoming traffic. But once they turned off the main road and were back in the village, he was able to enjoy the feeling of Nok in back of him. He started to enjoy himself. But too soon, they were pulling into her mother's house, and Nok was off and back cooking. Nate was left on his own.

Chapter 15

Nate stared at the wall, the faint glimmerings of dawn finally beginning to make themselves seen. He had been awaken by low voices and sounds of people moving about outside his door a couple of hours earlier and hadn't been able to fall back asleep.

The night before had been a little boring, to be honest. Nok had tried to pay attention to him, but with the bustle of preparing food, he spent quite a bit of time sitting on the main chair alone, with grandpa sometimes coming over to stare at him, a goofy smile on his face. Nidnoi's father came over, evidently after work, and everyone shared a cup of soup; then he, his wife, and Nidnoi left for the adjacent concrete house. Nok unplugged the computer and ran the wire back to the television, then turned it on for Nate to watch, but the snowy picture was incomprehensible to Nate. It looked like a soap opera of some sort.

When granny took off her shirt to splash water on her arms and chest to wash, Nate took that as a cue to go into his room. He told Nok he was going to bed while trying not to stare and granny's pendulous breasts. He assured Nok that he was OK, just tired. And he was tired. Early as it was, he quickly fell asleep on the thin mat.

Having been awake now for what might have been a couple of hours, Nate decided it was time to get up. He slipped on his shirt, then peeked outside. No one seemed to be up yet. He tiptoed to the toilet but hesitated before going inside. Looking around and seeing no one, he quietly walked out the side door, and on the other side of the fish pond, relieved himself up against a small tree. He knew he would have to manage the Thai toilet sometime, but the tree seemed a better option at the moment.

No sooner had he finished, though, that he heard approaching voices.

Spinning around guiltily, he moved away from the tree as Nok, her mother, and her grandparents came from around the corner of the house with what looked like miner's helmets on and some tools in their hands.

"Khun Nate!" Nok exclaimed. "Did you sleep well?"

"Uh, yes, I did." He looked at them in curiosity. "Where did you go?"

Nok stopped as the others trooped into the house. "We had to tap the rubber trees. Even with a wedding, we need to tap them in the season."

Nate didn't quite understand, but he let it go.

"Khun Nate, do you want to help for cooking?"

"I can't cook," he admitted.

"No, not cook, I mean. But helping." She pointed to the long-handled net lying up against the concrete wall of the home. "You can catch some fish for us. We need ten, I think so."

She moved over to pick up the net and a plastic basket, then motioned to the pond.

Nate looked at the pond with distaste. It was really nasty. "I can do that."

Nok beamed him her smile again and went into the house.

Nate walked over and picked up the long-handled net leaning up against the side of the house. The net itself was connected to the spindly wooden handle with numerous windings of wire. It did not feel very firm. He stepped over the low netting, then stepped up to the edge of the pond. Peering into the dark water, he wondered how he was supposed to catch anything.

Tentatively, he lowered the net into the pond, making a half-hearted sweep before bringing it up empty. By swirling the water, the rank miasma rose up to assault his nose. He wondered how anything could live in that poison.

Taking care not to get too close, he lowered the net into the water again. He pushed it deeper and deeper. Originally, he thought the pond might be a foot or so deep, but it was clearly deeper than that. He had the net in almost three feet, and it was not touching the bottom. Something in the dark water bumped against the net, the shock waves travelling up the handle and into Nate's arms. He twisted the handle, bringing the net to what he hoped was horizontal, then quickly brought it up. As it cleared the surface, he could see a dark wriggling shape. A good-sized fish, perhaps 3 or 4 pounds struggled feebly in the net. It was somewhat long and cigar shaped. Looking around, he spotted a large basket, so he moved the fish over and dumped it in, careful not to get splashed.

It took awhile, but eventually, Nate had caught the 10 fish. He didn't know if there were 100 or 2 fish left in the pond, but he had his quota. He put down the net and picked up the basket. Trying to hold it away from his body so the fish could not flick water at him as they struggled, he took it inside and set it on the counter.

Nok beamed her megawatt smile at him again. "Thank you Khun Nate!" She reached in to examine the fish. "They are beautiful. These are lucky fish for us."

"Lucky? Not too lucky if they are going to be part of the wedding meal," he replied with a smile.

She looked up at him for a moment before breaking into a laugh. "Not lucky for them, lucky for us! These are our Queen's fish." She reached back to brush a wisp of hair away from her face, her now fishy hands leaving a small spot of fish slime on her cheek.

"You mean they belong to your Queen?"

"No, our Queen loves us, and she told us to grow fish. She taught us how. It is good business for us. So now, these lucky fish will be good for the marriage. Very lucky for them. Maybe they will have many babies together."

Nok's mother reached over and took the basket, arms not even straining at what had to be 35 or 40 pounds. Lucky fish or not, she dispatched each one rather quickly with an experienced slash of her knife. She gutted each one, then took a wooden skewer and ran it up the body of each fish. After rolling them in what looked to be salt, she put them aside on a plate.

Nok looked up at him, a pensive look on her face. "Khun Nate, can you please change your shirt?"

He looked down at his black t-shirt, wondering if the AC/DC logo was somehow frowned upon.

"In Thailand, to wear black at a wedding is bad luck for the new couple."

"Oh, OK. No problem." He went into his room and changed into his one button-down shirt. He hadn't actually planned on wearing a t-shirt, thinking that was too casual. In fact, he worried that he would be underdressed. He hadn't planned on needing any nice clothes on the trip.

He came back out to Nok's smile. She motioned to a large tin-looking pot in which some sort of stew or soup bubbled away. "Khun Nate, can you please help me?"

Nate picked up the pot, which was lighter than it looked. Nok grabbed up a smaller pot, then Nate followed her out the door. The sun was all the way up by then as they made their way to the small road in front of the house. Nate moved up so he was walking side-by-side her.

An old man was lounging in front of the house across the street, shirtless and in a pair of faded shorts. He called out something to Nok, and she brought the pot up a bit and nodded her head as if she was wai'ing him.

They reached the main village road, and directly across from the intersection, a large canopy was placed in an open lot. Under the canopy and surrounding it were a large number of card tables and folding chairs. To one side were some long tables, and it was to here that Nok led him. She motioned to a round metal ring with hot charcoal inside, and Nate carefully placed the pot on it. An old lady behind the table gave him a toothless grin and spoke to him in Thai. He just nodded, smiled, and stepped back. In the distance, he could hear some atonal music and drum beating.

"Now we will see the parade!" Nok exclaimed happily. She took Nate by the hand and led him away and onto the road. She dropped his hand and skipped several steps like a child, clapping her hands and laughing.

"Hurry, hurry!"

A procession of sorts came into sight, and Nok hurriedly joined it. A number of people surrounded a young man, nicely dressed in a white shirt and pants. As they clapped several men played metal flutes of a sort, clanged small cymbals, or beat on drums. The man walked seriously, which was at odds to the people surrounding him, who were swaying with their shoulders as they clapped and walked along.

Nate joined in the clapping, then stole a glance at Nok. She was radiant, simply beautiful. Nate couldn't help but wonder if someday, a ceremony like this would be held for the two of them. The music brought him back to reality. The best that could be said of it, in his opinion, was that the people seemed to like it. The droning nature of it and lack of a discernable melody was not quite to his liking.

With the groom as its focal point, the rest of the procession milled about, shifting concentrations like some slow moving school of fish. Other people came out of their homes and joined in. By the time they reached the canopy, there had to have been over a hundred people in the throng.

To Nate's surprise, they did not stop at the canopy but moved to the front yard of the house next to it. Blocking the way was a barricade made of two short posts and some ribbon. Guarding this barricade was a 5-year-old moppet, resplendent in a Thai costume, arms crossed. The groom knelt next to her and pleaded. She gave her head an exaggerated theater shake. He asked something else, and she gave the same shake, this time reaching out to shove him away. Some of the crowd yelled out to him as the others laughed. Finally, he reached in his pocket and took out a new 100 baht note. He gave it to the little girl, who quickly wai'ed, then pulled the ribbon off one of the posts, allowing the groom to advance.

A few steps further was another set of posts and a ribbon. A teenager dressed in blue jeans and a white cotton top stood guarding it. With more comments and laughter from the peanut gallery, the groom took out another 100 baht note and handed it to her. She pointedly did nothing. He reached into his pocket again and took out more cash, but this time, it was a 500 baht note. She wai'ed and took down the ribbon.

In front of the door was yet one more barricade and a slightly older gate guard. This one was wearing a nice business-type suit. Inside the open door, Nate could see a large number of people waiting and watching, with who had to be the bride right in the front.

The groom unhesitantly took out a 1,000 baht note and handed it to the toll-keeper. She held up the bill so everyone could see, then took off the ribbon, allowing the groom to enter the house. The crowd broke out into applause.

The bride stepped forward and went into a deep, graceful wai. She had on a stunning red silk dress which hugged her figure, cinched at the waist with a large ornate gold belt. The dress was off the shoulders, but one shoulder was covered by an intricate shawl which fell all the way to the ground.

Nok pulled Nate down so she could say into his ear, "That is my classmate, Gung. She is lovely today, I think so."

Nate had to agree. "Yes, she sure is." He looked down at Nok's slim figure and wondered how she would look in such a gown.

Nok kept his arm and turned him towards the tables as the wedding party disappeared inside the house. The rest of the crowd milled about, finding seats. She sat him down, then went to the tables where her mother and grandmother were among others getting the food ready for serving. Someone hooked up a sound system and Thai popular music soon filled the area.

Nate started to lean back, but he felt the plastic chair start to give, so he hurriedly leaned forward, glancing around to see if anyone noticed. He caught the eye of a young man sitting two tables over. The guy was glaring daggers at him. Nate looked around to see if there was someone else in the man's line-of-sight, but no, he was the subject of the guy's evident ire. Feeling very uncomfortable, he looked away and studiously avoided glancing back over. He was relieved when Nok came back with two plates full of food.

Nate thanked her and ravenous, eagerly checked out the offerings. On top of all the food was a fish-on-a-stick. Despite the charring, he recognized it as either one of the fish he had scooped up or its very close cousin. Thinking of the foul water, he pushed the fish aside, determined not to eat it. The rest of the food was quite bland and not very flavorful. The best that could be said of it was that it was nourishment (he hoped.) But when Nok asked him if it was good, he smiled and nodded his head.

Other people kept coming by to talk with Nok. Nate felt rather superfluous, only wai'ing at each introduction before sitting back and being ignored. But Nok seemed to be enjoying herself.

Nok had brought him a plastic glass of beer, which he slowly sipped.

Other men were gathering over at a table in the corner where something stronger was obviously being served. Nok's grandfather was prominently entrenched there, quickly downing one glass after the other. He started a slow dance to the music, although dance was probably a pretty generous term. He lifted each foot up in turn and used the hand not holding his drink to make vaguely Thai-like movements. As he moved out into the sunlight, the huge scar on the side of his head became very evident. Nate had wondered about it before, but now it seemed even more prominent.

He touched Nok's arm. "What happened to your grandfather?" He made a motion along his own head.

Nok only hesitated a moment. "My *Pu*, he was very *mao*, very drunk one night. And he was arguing with that man there, his friend." She pointed to another older man pouring himself a drink. "So they argue on who is still young, who is still strong. My *Pu* said he is so strong, no one can hurt him. So Pi Tom took a big knife and boxed my *Pu's* head with it. We had to take him to the hospital with the knife still in."

Nate looked at her in amazement. "He had a knife in his head? Was he badly hurt?"

"The doctor told us he would die. But maybe *Pu* was right. He is very strong, and he lived. But now, he is a little *tingtong*."

Nate looked at the happily dancing man. "What about his friend? Did he get arrested?"

"Oh no, they are friends. And they were drunk. So *Pu* did not complain to the police."

Another person came over to greet Nok, so Nate didn't have a chance to respond to that. He watched as Pi Tom came over to Nok's *Pu* and pour him some more Thai whiskey.

Time passed slowly. He caught the angry guy glaring at him a few times, but he tried to avoid his gaze. A few of the people who came up to talk to Nok made comments to him, seemingly oblivious to the fact that he didn't have a clue as to what they were saying.

The music stopped and someone shouted out to the people. Everyone got up and moved closer to the house.

"It is 9:09, the lucky time to get married." She pointed to the house, but Nate could not see anything.

Everyone simply stood around, chatting in small groups. After a short wait, the bride and groom came out the door, followed by a monk in saffron robes. The newlyweds gave a deep formal wai together as the crowd clapped. They almost had to make the wai together as they were tied together with a string of flowers. They moved to an open area under the canopy and sat on cushions while the rest of the wedding party started to mingle with the guests.

Several people took turns speaking into a mic, evidently wishing the couple good luck and a happy life. Nate sat back down at his seat and poked around his plate to see if there was anything good left to eat which had escaped his notice earlier.

After the speeches, people started going up in turn to congratulate the newlyweds. Nok took Nate by the hand and stood him up, then joined the end of the line. She handed him two small pieces of string. When they got to the front of the line, he saw what they were for. Each well-wisher tied a piece of string around the wrist of both the bride and groom.

Feeling very awkward, he stepped up and tied the first piece of string around the groom's wrist. The groom looked up and thanked him in English. He moved over to the bride, but his fingers didn't want to cooperate, and he fumbled around, doing only a half-assed job of getting the string tied. The bride also thanked him in English.

Sure that all eyes were upon him, Nate slunk back to his chair and sat down. Nok did not seem to notice his discomfort. Another foreign man came up to join the party, a pretty young girl in a fairly revealing dress on his arm. The girl waved at Nok happily and came over to say hello. The man was probably in his 30's. His head was shaved, and he had on a tight t-shirt which prominently showed off his impressive musculature. His biceps threatened to rip his sleeves apart. He had on some old-fashioned running suit pants and what looked to be brand new Nikes. He gave Nate a rather condescending glance before looking away. Without a doubt, the man looked dangerous. Nate didn't want to have anything to do with him.

After a few minutes, the man pulled on his companion's arm, pointing to the drinks. She stopped talking to Nok, and the couple moved off to the table where the girl poured him a glass of whiskey. He quickly drained it and motioned for another. Nate looked over to see a small frown mar Nok's face.

"Who's that?" he asked her.

"She is another classmate. Her name is Nong. She works in Pattaya, and that is her boyfriend. He is Russian man."

"You don't like him, do you?"

"*Mai pen rai.*" She shook her head, then refused to say anything else.

Nate spent the next hour pretty much doing nothing. Nok would intermittently stop talking with her friends to turn to him to ask if he was OK, which he assured her he was, then go back to chatting with various guests. He wondered what was happening back in Bangkok.

The Thai guy who seemed to take a dislike to him kept looking over. That was making him feel a little nervous. He finally had to know more.

"Who is that guy over there?" he asked Nok.

She looked over, trying to see who he was indicating.

"That guy, in the green shirt."

"That is Wit," she replied simply.

"Well, why does he keep staring at me? With that angry look on his face?"

"*Mai pen rai*. It is nothing."

"Really, I want to know."

She hesitated, then gave a shrug. "Do not worry. He is uneducated. He never went to the university, he is ignorant. And his girlfriend, she got a new boyfriend, a farang. So now he doesn't like farang."

"But I didn't have anything to do with that!"

"I told you he is ignorant. He thinks because you have white skin, you are here to steal Thai girls. Forget him."

The bride and groom started making the rounds of all the folding tables. They looked rather sweet together. Nate really didn't have marriage high on his immediate list of things to do, but he stole another glance at Nok, wondering if she might be his match.

The happy couple eventually made it to their table. Using decent English, both thanked Nate for coming.

"I am very happy to be here. You have my congratulations," he assured them.

As they moved to the next table, Nate stood up to stretch. He was happy to be with Nok, but he wondered how long they would be staying. He moved over towards the food, but Nok's grandfather snagged his arm and pulled him over the booze table, pouring some whiskey into a plastic cup and giving it to him, his fetid breath washing over Nate in a cloud of alcohol. Nate raised the cup and took a tiny sip, then nodded appreciatively despite his real desire to just throw it out. Several of the older guys clapped him on his shoulder. The Russian guy was at the table as well, getting another drink, but he gave Nate a snort of, well, not disdain as that would indicate he thought something of Nate, but more like dismissal.

Nate stayed with the older men, not understanding a word they said, but nodding as if he did, laughing when they laughed. He wondered what they were saying, what was funny. Surrounded by people, he was somehow feeling alone.

Wit came walking towards the table. Nate felt the beginnings of panic, but he merely stepped to the side, controlling himself. Wit just probably wanted a drink. And as Wit went up to the table, Nate felt a sense of relief. Wit took two plastic cups of whiskey, then turned back.

Nate wasn't sure what happened next. The Russian guy might have stepped forward from where he was standing, or maybe he hadn't moved. Nate wasn't sure. But when Wit turned around, he bumped into the Russian's arms, the whiskey in the Russian's cups splashing over his light green shirt.

Wit stared down at the wet stain on his shirt. The Russian guy dropped the plastic cups, then sort of flicked his finger over the wetness before breaking out into a derisive laugh. Nate thought it was the laughter that did it.

Wit purposely splashed one glass of whiskey, getting a small bit on the Russian, his face livid with anger. The Russian stopped laughing, looked down at the tiny wet mark, then back up at the angry Wit. Without warning, his fist lashed out, connecting with Wit's chin. Wit dropped as if poleaxed. He fell bonelessly, head bouncing off the hard-packed dirt, legs bent underneath him. The others around the drink table didn't seem to realize what had happened for a moment. They looked down at Wit as if surprised to see him laying there.

The Russian looked at Wit for a second, then casually reached down and grabbed the back of his shirt collar, lifting his head up. Very calmly, he swung his hand, slapping the unconscious Wit's face with a backhand, then a forehand. Wit's head snapped back with each blow. The Russian dropped Wit, then casually reached over him to take a plastic cup of whiskey and turn to walk away.

What scared Nate most of all was the entire casual nature of the Russian's actions. He didn't look angry. He didn't look upset. His attack might as well have been the swatting of a mosquito. The entire incident sent a shiver down Nate's spine.

As the Russian made his way calmly back to his table, others started to react. Some rushed to Wit and laid him flat, gently slapping his face. One or two guys started taking a step towards the Russian, and Nate thought they were going to jump him, but others held them back. The rest of the people pointed and jabbered away in Thai.

The Russian reached his table where his girlfriend was engrossed in conversation, not realizing what had happened. He jerked her upright by the arm. Her feet got tangled up with her chair as a look of alarm crossed her face. Holding her half off the ground, he slowly finished off his cup of whiskey, then looked around the gathering. The place got quiet. With a slight smile, he nodded to the bride and groom, then strode off, dragging his girlfriend with him. He reached his car, unlocked the door, and almost threw his girlfriend in through the driver's side before getting in himself. As he backed away, the gathering broke back into talk.

Nate hadn't realized he was holding his breath. He took a deep one, then looked back over at Wit. He didn't like the young man, but what had happened to him was brutal. Nate couldn't help but to imagine that huge fist coming to connect with his face, what that would feel like. He broke out into a sweat.

The wedding party disintegrated pretty quickly after that. Nate just stood there until Nok came over to sweep him up and take him back to her house.

Chapter 16

Nok's *Pu* was seemingly the only one in a good mood back at the house. He was still three sheets to the wind, and he kept mimicking the blow to Wit, then acting out Wit's fall. He seemed to think it was pretty funny, but his wife kept scolding him. Nate just stood around watching and listening as everyone seemed to discuss the incident.

Finally, Nok, looking a little disgusted, grabbed Nate by the arm and dragged him outside.

"We need to go to the market." She pointed at the motorcycle. "You drive."

Nate wanted to ask her about what happened, but he sensed he should just be quiet for now. He sat on the bike while Nok got on behind him, arms around his waist. The bike started on the first kick, and he slowly made his way to the main village road. The awning was still up, and a few people were gathered in small groups, but most of the people had left. He turned left and drove to the main road. Expecting to turn left again, he was surprised when Nok raised her arm around him and pointed off to the right. Nate hesitantly crossed the traffic lanes and hugged the far left side of the road, driving slowly to the town visible in the distance.

Nok's body felt wonderful up against his back, and he quickly forgot the unpleasantness of the incident at the reception. He started to let his mind wander a bit and he imagined just what pressure points on his back corresponded to what parts of Nok's body, and as a result, he drifted over a bit too far and started kicking up the dirt on the shoulder of the road. He quickly brought the bike back and started to concentrate on driving.

Before too long, they were entering the outskirts of town. Riding in a small village was one thing. In town the extra cars just raised his anxiety levels. To make matters worse, there seemed to be no regard for traffic laws. Cars, motorcycles, vans, and pushcarts were making their way willy nilly. He even had to stop once as a pickup pushed slowly down Nate's lane against the traffic. Nate was a cautious driver back in Oceanside, but here, he was almost frozen.

With one arm around his waist, Nok used her other arm to point this way and that as they made their way to the market in the center of town. It was with a huge sense of relief to him when he reached it and Nok pointed to an area where he could park.

Nate had seen the market from the back of the passenger pickup the day before, but as he followed Nok up to the market proper, his senses were bombarded with a cacophony of sounds and a myriad of images. On the ground in front of the open-sided market structure, flower vendors competed with toy vendors who competed with old ladies with plastic tubs filled with live fish. As he approached, one catfish-looking fellow made a valiant effort to escape, jumping the bucket and squirm-crawling across the concrete pathway. Market-goers merely stepped over the escapee as they entered and exited the market confines. Nate stopped to watch for a moment, wondering if the fish could somehow make it to some sort of safety, some waterway, but the heavyset older woman gutting fish hit the shoulder of a young teen who jumped up and chased it down, dumping it back into the plastic tub.

In a moment of panic, he suddenly realized that he had lost Nok. He quickly stepped up, scanning over the heads of the people until he spotted her slender figure up ahead. He pushed his way through the milling throng of shoppers until he caught up with her. She was closely checking what looked like weeds to him. At least they were not anything he immediately recognized as food. She eventually made her choice, but by what parameters she made them, he didn't have a clue.

She absentmindedly handed him the weed-filled plastic bag and took his arm to lead him further into the depths of the market. The market was stifling hot, not only from the sun beating down on the tin roof, but the huge number of jostling, milling people. Nate started to sweat heavily.

When Nok stopped at a meat stand, one of several down the row they were walking, Nate had to wonder about the sanitation of the meat. Chunks of pork were laid out on a metal table. Some desultory flies, too bothered by the heat to be very active, walked over the various cuts. Both Nok and the vendor, a shirtless middle-aged man, didn't seem to notice the flies. Nok pointed at what looked like what would be pork chops if the chunk of meat was sliced, and the vendor popped that into another plastic bag. Nok gave that to Nate as well.

The market looked to have about 5 or 6 long aisles, maybe 100 or 150 stalls all told. Nate followed Nok past more meat and fish stalls, vegetable stalls, fruit stalls, stalls for spices and bottled sauces, for toys, for household goods, for baby clothes, for tools, for adult clothes, for eggs, for Thai music cd's, for lottery tickets—for just about everything needed by a typical Thai household, he figured. And business seemed to be booming.

Nate was beginning to feel claustrophobic. There were just too many people there, too much jostling, too much pressing. With the smells and the heat, it was getting to be too much for him. He needed some air.

He tapped Nok on the shoulder, interrupting her examination of some shirts. "I need to get out of here for a bit, get something to drink, OK?"

She looked up at him with concern on her face. "OK," she agreed. "Over there is a Seven. I will be there soon." She pointed out of the market.

With relief, Nate made his way out, then saw the 7-11. He entered it, the air conditioning a welcome respite. Walking towards the back, he opened the coolers and picked out a Pepsi. He held the cold can against the side of his face for a moment, relishing the feel.

"Kinda hot out there, huh?"

Nate turned to see a 60-ish man, a white foreigner, standing next to him. He was a slender guy with a shock of white hair. His hand was sticking out. Nate took it without thinking.

"Mike Whiting," he simply said as he shook Nate's hand.

"Nate Foster."

"So what brings you to our little neck of the woods? Not too many farang get out here."

"I just, I mean, I came out here from Bangkok. I went to a wedding." Mike's simple question had Nate somehow flustered.

"Here in town?"

"Uh, no, out aways, in a village. I came with a girl, and…."

"Ah, you've been hooked!" Mike gave him a knowing smile.

"No really," Nate insisted. "I know her from my hotel, and she invited me, so I came. She's not my girlfriend or anything."

"But you want her to be, right?" Mike kept digging.

Nate didn't say anything.

"Knew it!" Mike said with a laugh. "Don't fret it. We've all been bit by the Thai lady bug." He clapped Nate on the shoulder.

Nate paid the cashier for his drink. "What're you doing here, Mike? On vacation?"

"No, I live here. Married, got a kid, a house."

That took Nate a little by surprise. He looked back at him. "Really? You live here?"

"Yepper! Just a little different from OC. Oklahoma City," he added, after seeing the puzzled look on Nate's face.

"I'd guess so! So what do you do? For work, I mean."

"Work? That's a four-letter word here!" Mike said with another laugh. He pulled Nate back from in front of the cashier so another patron could make her purchase. "No, I'm retired. Thirty years with the OC police force. Came out 9 years ago and just stayed."

"You came here?" Nate couldn't imagine anyone coming out to this out-of-the-way place.

"Here? Heck no. No, I did the same as everyone. Went to Pattaya. Boozed and barhopped my way for a year before I found my wife. This is her home town, so we came here to get married, then stayed."

There was an awkward silence for a few moments. Nate took another swallow of his Pepsi and looked out the sliding glass door of the 7-11.

"So how long you gonna be here?" asked Mike.

"Not sure. I'm sort of taking things as they come."

"You staying here? At our wonderful lone hotel?" The sarcasm was heavy in his voice as he said "wonderful."

"Oh, no. I'm staying out at the place with the wedding. Maybe only a mile away, though."

"Out on the highway? That little place? I don't even know the name of it. How is it there?"

"Actually, it's a little rough. And the food! Blech! I thought I liked Thai food, but not this."

"That's because you like Farang-Thai food. Restaurant food. Local food ain't nearly so good. Tell you what. What're you doing now? You free? Why don't you come to my place for lunch?"

Nate was not the kind of guy to just go somewhere with a person he just met. But being two Americans in the middle of a sea of Thais, he felt an automatic kinship to a degree. But then there was Nok. What about her? He wanted to be with her, but then again, it was a little tense back at her house.

"That sounds tempting, but I'm with someone. We rode together," he said reluctantly.

Mike probably heard that tone of reluctance. "She probably won't mind. Where are you going to meet her? We can ask."

"Right here, I think. And I guess so. Why not?" He felt a bit of anticipation creeping over him.

They chatted a bit while they waited. Nate told him about Oceanside, but left out boot camp. Mike told him about being a cop and a National Guardsman. Within ten minutes, Nok emerged from the market and started across the street to meet him.

"Here she comes," Nate informed Mike.

"Whoa! I can see why you followed her out here to Suphan Bumfuck. She's stunning," Mike told him, evident awe in his voice.

Nok looked up at Nate with a smile before taking in Mike. The smile stayed, but with a hint of curiosity tingeing it.

"Uh, Nok, this is Mike. He's from America, and he's invited me to his house for awhile. Is that OK?"

Nok looked over at Mike, then said, "Of course Khun Nate. You can do whatever you want. I am not your mother to tell you no, right?" She laughed.

"But I don't want to offend your family. Is it OK?"

"Of course. I will wait for you here and shop."

"It is OK, Nok. I will take him back. No need for you to wait," Mike told her.

She hesitated bit, looking unsure. "You can find my home?" she asked Nate.

"Sure I can. I can see your village from the road outside of town. No problem."

"Well, OK. I will see you there. We will have dinner with my family."

"Thanks!" Nate exclaimed, feeling for a moment like he was 8 and his mom had just given him permission to go to the beach with his friends. He handed Nok the key to the bike and the packages, then followed Mike to his pickup, a huge thing for the small roads of the town.

He clambered in as Mike pulled out and slowly made his way through the crowded street and over to a crossroad. He turned right and drove perhaps 200 yards before turning right again down a small street with about 5 or 6 small but western-style houses.

"Welcome to Soi Farang," Mike told him.

Nate looked back. He could still see the edge of the market. He could have walked the distance in a couple of minutes. Considering parking, walking would probably have taken less time than taking the truck.

"Soi Farang" was about 50 yards long. One side of the street opened up to a large lot, full of trash and overgrown weeds. On the other side were five white houses with small fenced front yards. Each house seemed identical to the one next to it. It was a little slice of suburbia injected into the Thai cityscape.

"Why do you call it 'Soi Farang?'"

"Five homes, five farangs. So that is what the locals call it. I guess it is better than 'Farangtown.'"

He pulled in front of a gate at the second house and honked his horn. He waited a moment, then honked again. The front door opened and a

30's-something woman came out and opened the gate. She was on her cell phone the whole time. Mike parked and both of them got out. The woman was already back in the house as they went to the front door and entered.

While the house looked like it could be American from the outside, inside, it had an undefined "un-western" feel. Maybe it was the flat white tile floor. Maybe the complete lack of wood trim. Maybe it was the sparse furniture. Nate couldn't place his finger on it, but the house had a foreign feel. Or if this was a typical Thai interior, then maybe the correct term was a domestic feel. Regardless, it would not fit in back in Oceanside.

Nate had a Hmong friend back in Oceanside, and while his house was a carbon copy of Nate's on the outside, it had a vaguely foreign feel inside as well. And while that home had heavy wood accents and this one was stark and plain, the somewhat disjointed feel was similar in both places.

Mike motioned for him to sit on an Ikea-like sofa. "Do you want a beer?" he asked.

"Sure," he replied. He looked around as Mike walked past the woman who had opened the gate, now sitting on a stool in the adjoining room, still on the phone. Mike turned the corner and disappeared from view, then reappeared a few moments later with two bottles of Heine. He handed Nate one, then sat down on a chair which matched the sofa.

"So, welcome to my castle," he said, sweeping one arm around. "And over there, on the phone, that's my wife, Bo. Like in Bo Derrick. But not a '10,' I'm afraid."

Nate didn't understand the reference, and the comment about Bo whomever sounded rote, as if he had made the same comment a thousand times before. He nodded to Mike's wife, but she was oblivious to them, more intent on her conversation.

Nate sat sipping his beer, not knowing quite what to say. But he felt uncomfortable in the silence. He felt he had to break it.

"So how long have you been married?"

"What, 7 years, I guess. We met 8 years ago, then lived together in Pattaya for a year before tying the knot and coming out here. Second time around for me."

"Second time. You were married before?"

"Yea. Back in OC. Married for 26 years. I've got three kids, too. All grown now, and two of them have kids of their own. You are looking at a genuine grandpa here," he said with a smile.

"Do you see them, I mean your grandkids?"

"I go back once a year at Christmas-time and spend a week or two there. It's hard with the bitch living there, though." He paused for a second. "I guess

I should say 'ex,', but after getting our house and half of my retirement pay, I'm still a little bitter."

Nate didn't know what to say about that, so he just kept silent.

"And they don't like Bo. I took her home once a few years back, to meet my kids, but Angie, that's my ex-wife, she wouldn't even come to the kids' houses when me and Bo were there. And my kids, especially Mike Jr., well, they wouldn't accept her. So now I just go home alone. Leave Bo here."

They both took a long swallow each and avoided each other's eyes for a moment.

"But hey, enough about my sob story. You hungry? Want to eat?"

"You bet! The food at Nok's house is kinda crappy, if I gotta be honest."

Mike laughed. "Yea, not like back in a Thai restaurant back at home." He turned around and yelled out "Bo! Bo! Lunch!"

Bo didn't seem to acknowledge Mike, but she got off her stool and disappeared behind the wall to what Nate assumed was the kitchen.

"So how do you like living here?"

"It's good. Oh, you miss things from home, and you get frustrated by the Thai way of things, but it's good. With only half my retirement, I can live good here. And Bo is a good wife. She takes good care of me. I go to Bangkok every second Saturday of the month for a VFW meeting, then stay over night and have a little fun with some other guys from the post. A little Soi Cowboy action, if you know what I mean."

He looked over to see Nate blush. "Oh, I see you DO know what I mean." He laughed. "I mean, I've got a pretty wife, I'm living the good life. Where else can an old fart like me live like this?"

Nate tried to picture his dad living like Mike, out in the Thai countryside. His mind couldn't capture the picture. And his uncle? No way. Even with his kids already out of the home and into the Marines, he simply could not imagine Uncle Bedford being that far away from his family.

Mike's wife came in with two plates and set them on the table before going back into the adjoining room, cell phone still plastered to her ear. As she walked off, Nate could see part of a tattoo showing on her shoulder.

They both got up and moved to the table. Mike's wife had made two sandwiches.

"Isn't she going to eat with us?" asked Nate.

"Who, Bo? No, she doesn't eat farang food, and I don't eat Thai. She'll eat soon with one of her friends."

Nate pulled up one side of the bread to see ham with sliced cucumbers. He hadn't eaten a sandwich with cucumbers before, but he took a bite. It wasn't bad. He downed it rather quickly. He looked longingly at the half of a sandwich Mike hadn't eaten yet, but he didn't say anything.

"So you don't eat together?"

"No, not usually. We don't like the same food, and she doesn't speak English, so we don't have much to say."

"She doesn't speak English? How do you talk? Do you speak Thai?"

"Nah, not really. I have a few words. I mean I can buy beer and get the truck filled, but I never learnt Thai. And she never learnt English. But she knows what I want. We get along."

Nate thought back to when his mom was alive, at how she and his dad would have long conversations about any number of subjects. Having only been exposed to that, he sort of assumed that was the norm. To live with a wife and not talk with her was a new concept to his world view.

The front door suddenly opened and another woman walked in. She wai'ed to Mike and walked back to his wife who finally put down the phone.

"Ah, the sister-in-law. Not a friend today. Guess I was wrong."

"She just walked in without knocking?"

"Welcome to Thailand. I bought this house, but I can't own it, and it's in Bo's name. I guess that makes it a family property."

"You can't own it?"

"As I said, welcome to Thailand. Farangs can't own a house here."

"That doesn't seem fair."

"Bingo! Give the man a star."

Another woman walked in the door, a small girl in tow. They both wai'ed as they passed and went back to his wife.

"Well, I was right after all. Nan is coming for lunch, and with her kid, too. Nan got pregnant by a farang, an Aussie she thinks, so the kid's got light skin, and all the women gush over her. They all think she's gonna be a movie star when she gets older, making ma and the grandparents rich."

Laughter broke out from the kitchen area.

"This is getting to be a hen party. Let's get out of here and meet some of the neighbors. Take your beer."

As they walked out, yet one more woman, an older one, came through the gate. Mike gave a half-wai as he passed.

"The mother-in-law," he whispered to Nate.

They walked to the next house and entered the yard.

"Hey Till, you in there?"

"Come on in," shouted a voice from inside.

They entered the front room, the exact same layout as Mike's with similar furniture. A tall, heavy-set man sat on a couch, a small boy sitting beside him with an open book between them.

"English," directed the man.

The boy jumped up and deliberately and precisely said "Good afternoon, gentlemen."

"German!"

"*Guten tag.*"

"Thai!"

"*Sawadi krup,*" the boy said, following that with a deep wai.

"Good job Klaus. Come give me a hug."

The boy jumped back on the sofa and gave the man a death hug around the throat.

"Ah, you're too strong! Go get your mother before you kill me."

The boy laughed and ran upstairs. The man stood up and offered his hand to Mike, then to Nate.

"Welcome, welcome," he said with a slight accent. He looked to Nate. "and you are…?"

"Nate. Nate Foster. I'm an American."

"Well, welcome Nate Foster, American, to my home."

"Too many women at my house, so we came over to bother you."

"I can see you have your drinks, even if you call that Dutch swill beer," he said with a laugh. "Come, come, sit. So Nate," he asked after they had sat down, "what brings you to our small city?"

"What do you think?" Mike interrupted before Nate could answer. "I saw his young lady. Quite a babe!"

Nate started to blush as Till laughed.

"Yes, it is always the lovely Thai women who bring us all to our doom, right?"

"He's even staying out there in one of the villages."

"Oh, you are dedicated. Or in love. Or maybe just lust?"

"It's not like that…" Nate started to argue.

"Of course not, young Nate. You are just interested in Thai culture," Till broke in with a twinkle in this eye. "You have no interest in anything more from your ladyfriend."

Nate had to smile. "Well, maybe a little more interest than that," he admitted.

"Nothing wrong with that."

A very attractive woman came down the stairs, being pulled by the boy. A girl, slightly older-looking than the boy, followed. The woman was stunning in a very simplistic way. She had on a white cotton blouse and tan shorts, but her most arresting feature was her smile.

"Nate, please let me introduce you to my wife, Nok. Behind her is my daughter, Giselle, my princess, and you have already met Klaus."

That was three Noks Nate had met. He wondered how common the name must be. Nok smiled and gave a deep wai.

"Good afternoon," she said haltingly. Giselle repeated the phrase, but much smoother.

Till spoke to his wife in Thai for a moment, and after listening, she looked up at Nate with interest. Both kids jumped onto the sofa next to their dad, the girl at his side and the boy next to her. Giselle took his arm and held it protectively as she watched Nate. Nok came to the edge of the sofa and leaned over a bit, leaning into the sitting Till, arm on his shoulder. Nate had to admit that the four of them made a pretty picture.

"And this is why I live in Thailand," he said, nodding his head to encompass them all.

Giselle pulled her father's head down and whispered into his ear. He listened, then asked her "Why don't you ask him yourself?"

She shook her head and shrunk back to use his arm as a shield.

"Come on, *liebchen*! You can ask."

She murmured something which Nate could not hear.

"He could not hear you. A little louder, please."

"Do you have horses, sir?" Nate could barely make out.

"I have ridden horses, but I don't have my own," Nate told her.

She smiled and squeezed her father's arm tighter.

"She is going through a horse phase now, and when she heard me tell my wife you are an American, well she thinks all Americans live on ranches and ride horses."

Nate caught her eyes. "Well, if you ever come to America, I can take you out to ride horses."

She squealed with delight. Till turned to evidently translate what Nate had said to his wife, and she smiled at him in appreciation for making a little girl's day.

"OK, you two. How about you two go out to play, and let us visit here?"

They both stood up on the sofa and kissed his cheek before running outside.

"I am always amazed at how you train those kids. My kids were never so well behaved," Mike said as they left.

Nok slid gracefully to sit beside Till.

"Oh, they can be hellions, to be sure. You caught them at a good time."

"Yea but it always seems to be a good time."

"Well, if they are angels, then it is from Nok. If they are devils, it is from me."

Nok merely sat through the exchange, one of Till's hands clasped between the two of hers, her body angled into his. She had a smile on her face, but Nate could see that she wasn't catching much of the conversation.

As the conversation drifted from generalities to generalities, Nok kept drawing Nate's attention. She and Till seemed quite obviously happy with each other, and when the kids ran in to show them some sort of lizard they had caught, the domestic picture was really quite sweet. His thoughts turned to his Nok, wondering what it would be like to have her sitting next to him in the same way, wondering about children. It seemed like an attractive idea to him.

As Nok got up at Till's urging to get them a "real beer," he couldn't help noticing her nicely shaped butt, and he looked away in embarrassment. She came out with four bottles of a German beer, handed three of them out, then took the fourth before settling cat-like next to Till.

"How's that?" Till asked, holding up his bottle. "Much better than that Dutch crap, huh?"

Nate couldn't really tell the difference, but he agreed anyway. As he felt comfortable with them, he decided to ask their opinions on what happened at the wedding. He told them the story.

"You said a Russian guy?" asked Mike.

"Yea, that's what Nok told me."

"A Russian guy, from Pattaya. Probably Russian mafia. Sounds like it."

"But why wouldn't anyone do anything?"

Mike looked at Till before answering. "This is Thailand. And the Russian mafia is pretty strong here. All those Russians like to get away from the cold, and they launder their money here. And they pay off the police, of course. So probably, no one wants to piss off the mob. You could report it, but nothing will get done, and maybe something else happens."

"That doesn't seem fair. I mean, he just clocked the guy."

"Life isn't fair," Mike responded as Till nodded his head in agreement.

"I love Thailand, don't get me wrong. But as a farang, you just have to accept certain things. And challenging the mafia, Russian or Thai, is just one thing you don't do."

"But why the Russian mafia? I mean, this is Thailand, right?"

"Oh, the Thai mafia has the power, that's right. But the Russian mafia, or I guess mafias, plural, pay off the Thai mafia to work here. Honor among thieves, you know. So they get to do here almost all that they do back home in the Motherland. "

Nok interrupted to say something to Till, who looked at his watch. "Ah, football is on. Bundesliga of course, Mainz against Dortmund."

He got up and went to the front door, calling out for his kids. They came rushing in and ran to the adjoining room, clamoring onto a sofa there.

"You can watch soccer here?" asked Nate.

"Well, mostly Premier League. The Thais love Man U. But we can get other matches, too. This is an early match back in Germany, so it is later here."

"Not much real football," Mike added. "ASN shows a few games, but you got to get up at 1 in the morning to watch."

"You two want to join us?" Till asked as he and Nok started to move into the other room. "We only have the one couch there, but we can pull in some more chairs."

"I think we'll let you Euro-trash watch. We Americans like real sports," Mike said with a laugh.

"Yes, I have watched with you. Your American football, you need armor to play." He stepped back over, hand out to shake. "Well, good to meet you Nate. You are of course welcome here anytime."

"Thanks. And you have a lovely family."

"Ah, yes, that is the secret to a happy life." He winked at Nate. "Just don't tell everyone else about our paradise here. We don't want to be overrun by the rabble."

Mike gave Till a salute. "Well, we're off on our neighborhood watch."

The two of them left and walked out into the still hot sun, seemingly hotter after the cool of Till's air conditioned house. They turned further down the soi, passed the next home where an older white man and an older Thai woman were doing some gardening. Nate expected to be introduced, but Mike took him past and on to the next house where he walked up and tried the front door. It was locked, and they walked around in back and tried the back door.

"This is Rob's house, but he's back in Farangland now, so we try to come over and check on the house every day."

"Oh, that's what you meant by the neighborhood watch."

"Yea, and all looks well. Till had his house broken into a couple of years ago. Got his television, stereo, and such."

They moved to the next house and did the same routine. "And this is Jorge's home. His wife and Rob's wife are sisters. And while Rob is back home, Jorge had to take the two sisters to Hua Hin for the weekend."

He looked over to the last house in the line. "I don't see his car. Hey Marco, you there?" he shouted out. "Marco?" He looked to Nate and shrugged. "Looks like Marco's out. Too bad. He's a good guy."

They got back on the soi and started walking back to Mike's house. "Sorry you only got to meet two of us."

They passed the older man and woman again. This time, the man looked up to glare at them as they walked.

"What about him?"

"Who, Mark? That's Mark Masterson, or Mark Bastardson, as we call him. We don't have anything to do with him. He's another American, but a real asshole."

"You don't even talk to him?"

"Believe me, if you knew him, you would understand. Hell, I've tried to hold my dog over his fence so he can shit in his yard, but the damn dog can't shit while in the air," he said with a chuckle. "I'd stick my own ass over the fence and do it, but the bastard would probably shoot me. And his wife's just as bad."

Nate glanced back at the old man, who continued to glare at them.

"Well, what do you want to do now?" Mike asked.

Nate looked at his watch. "Maybe I'd better get going back. I mean, they're making dinner for me. Not that I haven't appreciated this, though."

"OK, bud. No problem. Let me get my keys."

They went into the house, and Mike wrote his phone number on a piece of paper.

"You give me a call if you need anything. OK?"

"Sure, and like I said, I really appreciate all of this."

They clamored into the pickup and backed out of the drive. Mike's wife came out to close the gate, and as they drove off, Nate looked back to the still glaring Mark Bastardson.

Chapter 17

Mike had left him off near Nok's house, but after being told that dinner would still be some time yet, Nate wandered out to the road. There was still trash from the wedding around, and a few kids playing, but most people had drifted away by then.

Ahead, he could see the tall, ornate tower of the wat. His feet seemed to guide him there. The gate was open, but he didn't know if he was allowed in, not being Buddhist. No one was around, so he hesitantly stepped in.

Aside from some extremely mangy dogs, the place was deserted. The center of the wat was a wide open space of hard-packed dirt. To the left was a large temple building. It wasn't as big or as elaborate as the buildings at the Grand Palace in Bangkok, but it wasn't a slouch, either. Nate wasn't an expert, but he thought he recognized some of the same sort of carvings and decorations as he had seen at the Grand Palace.

On the other side of the temple building was a line of small stone structures, some raised on short columns. Each one was maybe 4 feet cubed. He walked closer and saw small photos of people on some of them, and flowers and burnt incense on the ground. He realized these must be tombs or monuments to the dead. Feeling like he was intruding, he hurried back towards the temple.

A brown dog, most of the fur gone from his body came up to him. Nate felt a flash of fear as the dog approached, but it merely sat in front of him before starting to scratch his head with his hind leg. Nate hesitantly reached down to pet the dog, which began to wag its tail. The fur on his head was filthy, and Nate wanted to rush somewhere to wash his hand. He walked past the dog, which turned and followed him.

In the back of the compound was a lower building, open in the front.

Nate peered in to see a large room covered with what had to be religious art. To the right of the room looked like what had to be a souvenir shop. Nate wanted to step up into the room, but he lacked the courage to do so. Instead he wandered further to the right until a large drum caught his eye.

The drum was suspended from the upper crossbeams of a small pavilion. Four wooden legs reached up to support a carved roof which protected the drum from the elements. Nate tentatively walked up to the drum. He hesitantly reached out and tapped on the drum with his hand.

A voice broke out behind him. Nate whirled around in panic to see an old monk standing there, his wrinkled skin barely covered by his bright orange robe. He was hunched over, and he couldn't have weighed more than 120 pounds.

He spoke again in Thai, but Nate merely shook his head and held out his hands from his side, palm up. The monk spoke again, and once again, Nate couldn't answer.

Understanding seemed to dawn on the monks face. "*Engrish?*" he asked.

"Yes, yes, English. American."

The monk reached out and grabbed his arm, going off again in Thai. He kept waving one arm in a semi-circle, trying to convey something. Eventually, he seem to realize that he wasn't getting through. He grabbed Nate's arm again and started leading him off. Nate wondered if he was in trouble. He contemplated making a break for it. The old monk certainly could not hold him. But he meekly followed instead.

He led Nate to a small wooden shack where there was a desk and chair. He picked up something off the desk and showed it to him. It took a moment, but Nate recognized it as a calendar, even if he couldn't read the month. The monk kept pointing to it.

"Yes, calendar. I know."

The monk was more insistent. Then Nate realized that he was pointing at one day on the calendar. It took him a moment to figure it out, but the monk was pointing at the next day.

"OK, OK. Monday."

The monk smiled and pulled out a watch from under his robe. He pointed at the 10 on the watch, then at Nate, then at the ground. He repeated this several times. At last, Nate began to get the point. The old monk wanted him to return tomorrow at 10:00.

Anxious to get out of there, Nate began to wai.

"Yes, OK, I will come. I will be here 10 AM."

The monk looked closely at him before breaking out into a smile. He let go his deathgrip on Nate's arm, and Nate continued to wai as he backed out of the room. He walked to the gate of the wat, looking back to see the monk watching him, a smile on his face.

It seemed like Nate had a date for the next day.

Chapter 18

"Khun Nate, are you awake?" Nok's voice filtered quietly into his dream state.

"Uh, yea, wait a minute." He sat up and rubbed his eyes. What he really wanted to do was to lie back down and sleep. Why he had agreed to go out and tap rubber was beyond him. Last night, after dinner, it had sounded fun when Nok had asked him. Now, at zero-dark-thirty, things felt different.

He struggled putting on his clothes, then walked outside to where the others were eating some rice and cold vegetables. Nok's mother handed him a bowl, which he quickly downed despite the somewhat insipid taste.

Nok handed him what looked to be a miner's helmet, complete with light. He put it on, but it sat on top of his head instead of fitting over it. Nok laughed, too happy a sound in the early morning darkness, and adjusted the band inside. He put it back on, and this time it fit normally. She handed him an empty bucket.

Nok, her mother, her sister, and her grandmother and grandfather trooped out with Nate in tow. He would have started singing "Hi ho, hi ho" if he had had more energy.

As he stepped out into the darkness, he turned on the light at his forehead, then followed the bobbing lights in front of him down the road. As the way narrowed, branches brushed against him. They walked quietly down what was now no more than a path for about fifteen minutes before they pulled off and stopped.

Nok turned to Nate. "This is our farm. First, we have to, what you say in English, 'score' the trees, to make them bleed. You can come with me."

The family split up. In the darkness, it was hard to see, but it looked like the rubber trees were in neat rows, deep ditches separating each row. Nok went to the first tree in their row, then took a curved knife. In the light of her headlamp, she pulled the knife down along the bark in a spiral, paralleling marks of previous cuts. At the bottom of the cut, she drove in a small metal tube, then hung what looked to be half of a coconut shell on the tube at the base of the cut. She looked back at Nate, the light on her helmet momentarily blinding him, then moved off to the next tree. She scored that tree in a similar manner.

After watching her do this to six or seven trees, Nate wanted to try.

"Can I give it a shot?"

"You can do it?"

"I think so. It doesn't look hard."

Nok handed him the knife. "Start here," she said, pointing to a spot on the tree.

Nate applied pressure to the knife, trying to draw it down. The knife dug in deep, and Nok reached out to take his hand.

"Not hard. Only kiss the tree."

He eased the pressure, then brought the knife down. Instead of a nice spiral, he made a deep gouge going helter skelter down the bole of the tree. Nok quickly grabbed the knife from his hand.

"I think I should do this. And we let this tree rest, OK?"

Nate was embarrassed, but he didn't say anything. He did pick up the coconut cup at the base of the tree, though, and put it on the tap after Nok set it.

In the surrounding areas, he could see glimmers of other lights moving between distant trees. The whole village must be out on their own plots.

They worked down the row, then moved up several rows once they finished and started over again. It probably took two hours for the family to tap each of the trees and then gather to share some hot, well, lukewarm tea from a plastic Coke bottle. It was still dark.

"Why do you get up so early to do this?"

"In the night, when the tree sleeps, the pressure is high. So we get more rubber now. If we do in daytime, we get smaller rubber."

Nate wasn't sure he understood, but he let it go. They stood around talking softly for another fifteen minutes or so as the eastern horizon began to show signs of the coming day.

"OK, Khun Nate, now we get rubber." She handed him a medium-sized bucket. "Come with me."

He followed her back to their rows. She took off the coconut cup and pulled Nate's bucket close, turning the cup over so that a white, milky sap slowly oozed out and into the bucket. It took a bit of time, but the cup eventually emptied. They moved to the next tree and repeated the process. About three quarters of the way down the row, Nate's bucket was full.

"Now go empty this in the large bucket," Nok told him, pointing back to where they had initially gathered.

Nate trudged back, found the larger bucket he had brought, and poured his load into it. He walked back to Nok, turning off his light as dawn had made itself fully felt. They emptied their first row and went to their second, Nate making two trips to empty the smaller bucket. Nok's grandfather and grandmother were moving slowly, so after finishing off their rows, the Nok and Nate helped those two finish their trees.

It was full morning by the time they met back at their staging area. There were two full buckets with sap. Nate picked up one while Nok's sister picked up the other. They started back, Nok's sister giving way to Nok, then her mother as they took turns carrying the load.

As they reached the main road, they converged with two other groups carrying their own rubber. Good natured shouts were exchanged, then they all trooped together to a concrete-floored shed. Nok showed Nate where to place his bucket. One lady reached over to grab Nate's bicep, saying something which had everyone break into laughter. She mimed a biceps flex to Nate, which brought even more laughter.

Each bucket was weighed and the weight entered into a log book. Then they were dumped into what looked like large cake molds, the kind his mom used to use to bake. One lady poured a bit of clear liquid from a plastic container on top of the white sap. When the last of the rubber was poured, everyone seemed to relax, and several bags of snack food were brought out. Nate was offered some, which he took. He had no idea of what it was, only that it was salty and crispy.

Gossip seemed to be the order of the day. Nate couldn't understand a word, but it had the rhythm and feel of gossip. Ladies would poke the rubber, gauging the consistency while not missing a word said. Finally, the sap must have been ready. Each cake was taken out and put on the floor where people would walk on them, flattening them. Nate had seen wine being made by feet in some old movies, and there was that famous old Lucy show where they did it, but this was different. He took off his shoes to try it, feeling the clammy rubber give under his weight.

Once the rubber was flattened, it was fed into a machine which looked like a huge pasta maker. This one lurched back and forth as the cylinders turned, but out came flat rolls of white rubber, each with a cross-hatch pattern. They looked like car mats. Each one was laid on a drying rack. Other mats were already there, obviously from previous days' gathering, and the nice white had turned to a dirty goldish brownish.

Nate looked at his watch as the last one was put up to dry. It was 8:30. Back in Bangkok, he would still be in bed.

"We are done, Khun Nate. Do you want breakfast now?"

His stomach growled its assent as Nate followed Nok back to her house.

Chapter 19

Nate looked up from the computer to his watch which he had placed on the table. At Nok's request, he had been slowly going over some basic computer skills with her niece. Truth-be-told, she already seemed to know what to do, but Nate wanted to please Nok, so a teacher he was.

It was almost 10. He was supposed to go to the wat, if he had understood the old monk correctly.

"Nok, I think I am supposed to go to the wat now. The monk there told me to be there."

Nok looked over at him in surprise. "You talk with the monk?" she asked.

"Yea, I didn't tell you. But yesterday, before dinner, I went there, and the monk there told me to come."

"The old monk or the young one?"

"I didn't see a young one. It was an old guy."

"Then you must go. He is an important monk." She got up from where she had been chatting with her mother and walked over to him expectantly.

Nate had planned on going alone, but he welcomed her company. They walked out of the house and moved off to the main village road.

"I did not know you were interested in Buddha," she remarked. She looked over at him to gauge his response.

Nate didn't really know how to answer. He was a die-hard Roman Catholic, but he knew he shouldn't be dismissive. "Of course I am interested. I want to know more about Thailand, and more about you."

He took a chance with the last comment, but it didn't seem to register with her. Instead, she took his hand, swinging it back and forth as they walked like young schoolkids. Within five minutes, they were walking into the compound. There were more people there this morning, but the dogs were the same. Most lay in the shade of one of several trees, but one curious black-and-white mutt came up to investigate them.

Nok led him to the building in the rear in search mode. She finally spotted her target and quickly led Nate to the old monk who was talking to a middle-aged man. He looked up at their approach and broke out into a smile. Nok broke into a deep wai which Nate tried to copy. Nok spoke to him in Thai, and as they conversed, Nate just stood there. The man who had been talking to the monk put in his two cents' worth, then the three of them, Nate in tow, walked over to one of the smaller buildings on the far right of the compound. The monk called out as they approached one of them, and in a moment, a younger monk came out. He wai'ed the older monk, and it was only when he straightened back up that Nate realized in surprise that he was a white guy. They spoke a few words in Thai, then the young monk held out his hand, western-style, to Nate.

"I'm Ken," he said in a perfect American accent. "*Luang Pa*, what we call the senior monk here, tells me you want to learn about Buddhism."

Nate stared at him. It seemed so unreal listening to perfect English coming from a shaved-headed, orange-robed man. "I just, I mean, I was here yesterday, and that monk, he told me to come here today."

Ken the Monk simply smiled and nodded his head. "Some of these senior monks, well, they know what you want even before you know it yourself. Why don't we take a walk together?"

Nate felt uncomfortable, being this close to a Buddhist monk. He was Roman Catholic, after all. Not Buddhist. And he was happy with his church. But he fell in beside Ken as they moved away from the others. Nok started to join them, but the older monk put his hand in front of her, not touching her, but clearly stopping her from following them.

"So, where're you from?" Ken asked him.

"Oceanside, California."

"No kidding? Really? I'm from Poway!"

Nate momentarily forgot about Ken's orange robes. "Poway? We hated Poway! All the Emerald Brigade crap!" He paused for a moment. "Oh, sorry, I guess I shouldn't say that."

"You mean that you hated us, or 'Crap?'"

"Well, both."

"Don't worry about it, *mai pen rai*. I used to love kicking Oceanside's ass, so we're even."

"You can say that? I mean, 'kicking ass?'"

Ken laughed. "Oh, we are supposed to keep calm and all of that, but then again, we're all human, and I am sure the Lord Buddha himself would not have gotten too upset with a little strong language."

They moved closer to the temple building. "So, did you play ball for the Pirates? You are certainly big enough."

"Yea, I did." Nate didn't tell him he was mostly a bench-warmer. He hurried to deflect any further questions about his less-than-stellar football career. "What about you? You play for the Titans?"

"Cornerback for football, but my passion was wrestling."

"Yes, you guys were pretty good at wrestling."

"Pretty good?" he asked in mock-outrage. "Just the best program in the state! I was CIF champion and third in the state!" he added with pride.

Nate wondered how a high-school wrestler ended up in Thailand as a monk. "So how, I mean, ..."

"So how did I become a Buddhist?"

"Well, yea."

"After Poway, I got a scholarship to Cal Poly. Full ride. I was going to be a star, you know? But away from home, well, I sort of fell to drinking, a little drugs, you know how it is."

Actually Nate didn't know how it was, but he didn't say anything.

"And the girls, oh my God, the girls. I fucked my way through whole harems of them. I even got one girl pregnant, then pretty much forced her to get an abortion." He paused for a moment, seemingly lost in thought. "Anyway, I wasn't doing well in classes. Skipped most of them. And then I popped positive on a drug test and was kicked off the team. Lost my scholarship. Dropped out. Typical sad story. I went back to Poway and moved back in with my folks. I got a job at the WalMart there, but got fired after punching out one of my co-workers. It was probably for the best, 'cause I was using my salary for drinking and even tried meth."

"So how did you get here to Thailand?'

"Well, I may have been a drunk, but I was still an athlete, at least in my mind. And I needed to burn off stress, so I took up biking. I rode my bike, sometimes 100 miles in a day. So once, I was up north of Escondido, up in the mountains, and on some small road, I saw what turned out to be a wat, right in SoCal. I rode in curious, and took a break. I started talking to one of the monks there, an American, and we seemed to hit it off. I think he saw my inner turmoil. To make a long story short, I started riding up there once a week, then twice, then three times. I finally asked to stay awhile, and bada bing, one day I realized that Buddhism fit me. I converted, and it saved my life. I stayed there for 6 months, then they brought me out here to Thailand so I could further my journey."

"But what about your parents? I mean, what did they think of you becoming a monk?"

"Well, we weren't a very religious family. My father is Jewish, and my mother a Lutheran, but really only in name. They thought my choice was a little strange, but I think they saw I needed it; otherwise I would be in jail or dead. They don't like me living so far away, and my mom wants grandkids, but they support me."

They now stood in front of the temple. "Do you know, this temple is almost 150 years old? And see that tall tower in front?" he asked pointing. "That has a fragment of the Lord Buddha's bones in it. This is really an important wat."

They stood there looking at the tower. Nate had seen bone fragments of saints in a few cathedrals, so the concept was not foreign to him. But with Buddha's bones there, he guessed that was more like having bones of Jesus himself. And those would certainly be kept at the Vatican in a huge crypt or something, not in a stone tower in some small village church.

"So, how do you like it? I mean, living like this."

Ken thought for a moment before answering. "The biggest thing is that I am at peace with myself. No more demons. Yea, I miss the food, and I miss the girls. I miss television, especially during the NFL season. But I don't miss the stress, I don't miss what I had become."

Nate allowed himself to smile. "I think missing the girls would be the hardest."

"Oh, maybe it once was. But now, I think it's the food. We go out in the morning with our bowls, and the people come out to fill them with food. But, you know, some of these people just can't cook! What I would give for a hunk of prime rib, or even a burger sometimes."

Nate looked at him in surprise. "You mean you miss the food more than the girls? I know food's important, but girls?"

Ken started walking again, and Nate had to follow.

"There was a really famous monk here, Ajahn Chah. And the senior monks serve as 'masters' to the junior, and sometimes not so junior monks. Well, the Venerable Ajahn Chah was a master to an English monk named Ajahn Brahm, a pretty VIP in the monk hierarchy himself. He goes all over the world teaching about Buddhism, getting awards and such."

He stopped for a moment. "Sorry, I'm rambling here. Anyway, when I was new to Thailand, I was in a car with Ajahn Chah and Ajahn Brahm. We were just tooling along, going to a meeting, and Ajahn Chah suddenly turned and looked back at me, telling me I was thinking about a girl."

"Well, he was right. I had been thinking about Lorrie right then. Lorrie was, well, let's say a mighty fine example of the female form. She and I had some great times together. But here I was, with one of the most accomplished monks in the world, and he caught me thinking about a girl, about sex. How he knew, I wasn't sure. I was really embarrassed. But I didn't want to lie, so I admitted it."

"He looks at me and says, 'It is OK to think about women.' I was shocked. I couldn't believe he said that. "

"Then he goes, 'If you want, you can write her and ask for something of her, to remind you of her.' I remember my heart fluttering when he said that. I was thinking, a lock of hair, maybe. Like in the old days."

"'Did you love her?' he asked me. I didn't know what I should say, so I just told him yes. 'All of her? Did you ever tell her you loved everything about her?' I told him sure I had said that. All guys say that. So then he goes, 'I want you to send her a plastic carton, then ask her to shit in it and send it to you.'"

Nate stopped to stare at Ken.

"Yea, exactly my reaction. I looked at the Venerable Ajahn Chah Bodhinyana Mahathera in utter shock. Send me her shit? Then he goes, 'If you love everything about her, well her shit is part of her, right?' He looked at me so seriously before he broke out into laughter. Then I laughed, and Ajahn Brahm laughed."

"So now, when I get feeling the urge, I get thinking of that, of getting a Tupperware full of shit, and you know? The urges ain't so bad anymore."

Nate still stood there looking at him. A smile slowly came over his face and he broke out into laughter, Ken joining in.

"I never really thought of it that way. I just can't imagine some bishop telling a new priest that back at home," Nate said between chuckles.

"Ajahn Chan had a way about him. He constantly surprised people, but you know, there is truth in what he said. I just wish I could've been around him more."

"Do you see him anymore?"

"No. Unfortunately, he died shortly after that. But as one of the most important teachers of the Forest Tradition, we study his words all the time."

"Forest Tradition?"

"The type of Buddhism we practice. Are you ready for a lesson in Buddhism?"

Nate stepped back, arm out, palm facing Ken. "I'm Catholic!"

Ken laughed. "And? You think we are going to feed you to the tigers to convert you?" He reached out and slowly lowered Nate's arm. "Even Roman Catholics can learn about Buddhism. And they can take from it as well, as they deem fit."

"Well, OK," he responded, sounding none-too-sure of himself.

Ken laughed again. "I'm not going to bore you with the whole history of the Lord Buddha himself or everything about Buddhism. But you know there are two main types of Buddhists?"

Nate shook his head no.

"So we don't even have a foundation here. OK, the two main branches of Buddhism are the Theravada, or 'School of Elders,' and the Mahayana, or 'The Great Vehicle.'"

"But I thought you said you were the Forest Buddhists."

"Forest Tradition, but that is part of the Theravada branch. Most of south-eastern Asia follows Theravada, while China, Korea, and Japan follow Mahayana. But whatever branch, we all believe there are three ways, what we call the 'Three Jewels:' the Buddha, the *Dharma*, which is the teachings, and the *Sangha*, which is the community, to break the cycle of suffering."

"'Cycle of suffering?'"

"Sorry, I keep forgetting that Americans are not really taught much about Buddhism in school. Buddhists think that life is an endless cycle of suffering. We call that the '*dukkha*.' If you can break this, you can enter '*nirvana*.'"

"I've heard of that. But I thought '*nirvana*' was great sex or something."

Ken looked surprised for a moment, then broke out laughing again. "Sex? No, not hardly. Nirvana is sort of the Buddhist version of heaven, I guess you can say."

They had reached the hanging bell, and Ken motioned for Nate to sit on the wooden platform.

"Isn't karma part of Buddhism?" asked Nate hesitantly.

"Ah, so you do know a bit about Buddhism, whether you realize it or not."

"Yea, what goes around, comes around, right?"

"I guess that is one way to put it. If you do good things, you will be rewarded. Do enough good things to outweigh the bad, and you might achieve nirvana. With karma, we hold a different view than the Mahayana Buddhists. They think you can chant away bad karma, like a confession in your church. We don't. We believe karma is sort of a part of nature. Think of it this way. If you eat lots of cake, you get fat. If you exercise and eat less, you lose weight. Same with Karma. Do good, and it is the intent which is important, not the actual action, and you will benefit, do bad, and it will come back to hurt you."

"So what about your Forest Buddhism?"

"Well, we are more traditional. We live a much more austere life, doing away with most of the trappings of modern life. We eat only once, and that has to be before noon."

"You eat only one meal?"

"Yea, I told you it was hard," he admitted with a wry smile. "Look, I don't want to get into a deep religious lesson, but I have to get some things out so you can understand where I'm coming from. Let's see, where to start? OK, Lord Buddha was the first person to reach enlightenment."

Nate wasn't 100% sure what enlightenment was, but he thought he had a basic idea, so he didn't interrupt.

"He gave us four truths, what we call the 'Nobel Truths.' The first is that life is suffering. That is the *dukkha* I told you about. The second is that this suffering is caused by cravings. The third is that suffering ends when craving ends. And the fourth is that you can become liberated from the suffering by following the path given to us by the Buddha."

"I don't get it. Cravings lead to suffering?"

"Let me give you an example. You're young, full of hormones, ready to fuck just about anyone, right?"

Nate still felt uncomfortable with Ken's use of language. He wasn't Buddhist, but Ken was religious man, and he felt religious guys shouldn't be so earthy, so crass. But he nodded in agreement.

"And when you can't get laid, you suffer, right?"

Nate nodded ruefully.

"Well, if you weren't horny, would you spend those same miserable nights awake, thinking about girls and getting laid?"

"I guess not," he admitted.

"Well, that is a very simplistic example of suffering caused by craving. It is the wishing for something that isn't there. And the Lord Buddha gave us the way to rid our cravings, to end our suffering. We call it the 'Nobel Eightfold Path.'" He looked at Nate to see if there was any recognition. When he saw none, he went on. "This is what pulled me towards Buddhism, and the Forest Tradition in particular."

"The first two paths have to do with purifying the mind. A person should try to see reality as it really is, not what it appears to be. And the second is to have an intention to freedom and harmlessness."

He saw the confusion in Nate's eyes. "Don't worry about that one now."

"The second group has to do with ethics and morality. A person, should be truthful, but in a non-hurtful way. He should act in a non-harmful way, and he should have a job which is not harmful."

"And the last group has to do with mental discipline. Everyone should make an effort to improve himself. Everyone should create an awareness to be able to see reality, without cravings or aversion, and people should meditate to be able to achieve all of this."

"Seems kinda hard to me. All I have to do to get to heaven is accept Jesus Christ and let him wash away my sins."

"Yea, but even a mafia killer can do that. And that doesn't make sense to me. Buddhism forced me to examine myself, to try and become a better person. And it allowed me to make myself a better person. Oh, it's hard. I still have cravings. Many of them. But with the Forest Tradition, we focus on meditation, we live without too many material things. We don't tempt ourselves with things which will result in cravings. We try to live an ascetic life."

"But what about pleasure? What about craving a burger, then biting into it. What about that?"

"Well, some masters have said that it is OK to enjoy food. Even the Lord Buddha said that we need to eat enough to be healthy. But we don't need to be hedonists. That's what causes cravings."

"You can boil all this down to knowing yourself, trying to be a better person, and doing no harm."

"So you are a vegetarian? And you don't kill mosquitoes and things?"

"I think you are thinking of some Hindus. No, you can kill a chicken to eat, for example. But many Buddhists are in fact vegetarian."

Nate leaned back a bit and thought for a moment. "What about people? I was going to be a Marine. My dad's a Marine. He killed people. What about him? Does he have bad karma?"

"Remember when I said it was the intent that mattered, not the action? If your dad killed in order to bring about a greater peace, or if say, a policeman shoots a kidnapper to keep him from killing his hostage, well, the intent is right. But yes, we do teach that killing people is wrong, so you have to look at the intent."

"How come not everyone does the same as you monks?"

"Well, we have a list of things you should try to do or not do. Everyone shouldn't kill, steal, lie, have sexual misconduct, or get drunk or high. That's for everyone all the time. And that's basically good enough. But monks got to take it to the next level. For us, the sexual misconduct means no sex at all. And we can't eat after noon, we can't wear jewelry or make-up, and we have to sleep on a bed and sit on a chair which isn't luxurious."

"What?" he asked in amazement.

Ken laughed. "Yes, that last one is sort of strange, even to me after all these years. But I gotta accept all of them to get the benefit of the ones which have changed my life. I'm gonna be this way forever, but all Thai men do this at some point, maybe for a couple of weeks, maybe a couple of months."

Nate didn't think he could cope with that. He couldn't even complete boot camp, after all. He let his gaze wander, and he caught site of Nok sitting patiently on a bench, watching the two of them.

"I don't want to pry, but *Luang Pa* seemed to think you were troubled. Are you?"

Nate was about to instinctively tell him to mind his own business, but then he thought why not. He wasn't ever going to see this monk again. He had to formulate his thoughts first, though.

"I'm, well, I told you I was going to be a Marine. But I got dropped, and now my dad, well, he's a lifer, and I know I disappointed him."

"Why did you fail boot camp?"

He felt the familiar sense of shame creep over him. "I'm a coward," he admitted quietly.

"Tell me what happened."

Nate went over the pugil stick incident, finding it easier to talk as he went along. Ken was a good listener.

"Maybe you just aren't violent," Ken said as he finished. "Maybe you just didn't want to hit that other guy."

"No, I didn't have a problem with that. I just didn't want to get hit myself."

"Or maybe you didn't want to fail."

Nate had to admit that there could be some truth to that. Failing might be worse than the pain of a beating. Pain would fade, but shame lasted much longer.

"I'm just not too good at that sort of thing."

"Have you looked at yourself?" asked Ken.

"What do you mean?"

"I mean, you are huge. You've got muscles on top of muscles."

"Oh no, not really," he replied, taking a moment to stretch out one arm to look at it.

"I'm not some sort of psychologist, but it seems to me that you simply lack self-confidence. You clearly don't have a grasp of reality, that's for sure."

"Maybe," Nate acknowledged with a frown.

Nate knew intellectually that he was a big guy, bigger than most. But he didn't feel big. He certainly didn't feel tough.

"I'm not trying to convert you, but you could take a lesson from Lord Buddha. You need to be able to get a grasp of reality. And the only way you are going to do that is to get to know yourself, understand who you are. You can pay a real psychologist a zillion dollars to help you, or you can meditate. Whatever, but I think your view of yourself is skewed. And if you don't know who you are, what you want in life, well, your subconscious will know, and then the cravings will become stronger and stronger. And that will cause more and more suffering."

"The Dalai Lama... you know the Dalai Lama, right?" he asked, then continued when Nate nodded his head. "The Dalai Lama said 'Self-confidence is knowing that we have the capacity to do something good and firmly decide not to give up.'"

When Nate didn't seem to acknowledge that, he added "OK, how about this one. Eleanor Roosevelt said 'No one can make you feel inferior without your permission.'"

That one hit closer to home. Nate did give others permission to make him feel inferior.

Despite the relief he had felt on admitting to someone that he was a coward, the talk about knowing himself and self confidence was beginning to wear on him. He needed time to digest some of what Ken had been telling him. Oh, not the history lesson on Buddhism. But how it might pertain to him.

He stood up. "Um, I gotta go. I mean, thanks for your time, but I need to get back now."

Ken smoothly stood up and wai'ed as Nate held out his hand. He quickly switched to shake at the same time as Nate switched to his own wai. Ken reached out to grab his shoulder.

"Handshake," he said with a laugh. They both shook.

"Take care, Nate. And you can reach me anytime through *Luang Pa* if you want to talk."

Nate turned and walked away, feeling unsettled. Even Nok's smiling face as she rose to meet him wasn't enough to change his mood

Chapter 20

Nate was still contemplating his meeting with Ken when he woke up the next morning to trudge after the rest to tap more rubber. He had decided that there was a lot of truth in what Ken had said, and he wanted to talk more about it, but as much as he liked Nok, he wanted to keep that separate from her. Nok seemed to understand that he was in a contemplative mood, and they worked mostly in silence.

After they were done with the rubber and back at the house, Nok came up to him.

"Today, we will go to see Thai nature. You will like it, I am sure. OK?"

"Sure. What kind of nature?"

"You will see."

She put together some food, putting each dish in plastic bags, then putting them into a small backpack. When she was done, she motioned for Nate to follow her. She checked the gas level on the motorcycle, then got on, waiting for Nate. It was a little awkward with her sitting there on the back of the seat, but he managed to get his leg over and sat down. He started the bike and moved slowly down the lane. He was getting better, more sure at this. As he pulled onto the main village road, Wit looked up at them, his face a massive bruise. He slowly lifted one hand and extended his middle finger. Well, either the Thais used the same gesture or Wit was "bi-gestural."

As they got to the highway, Nok pointed to the left. He picked up speed, very conscious of Nok's arms tightening around him. They felt good, as did her body pressing up against his back.

He drove along the edge of the road, only moving out when an oncoming bike came at him against traffic. He was nervous as the big trucks zoomed by, the air of their passage making a vortex which seemed to want to pull them into the traffic. Some cars blasted past them doing what had to be a hundred miles an hour. A few times, dogs ran out from roadside shacks, barking and feinting at their legs. Nok didn't say anything, but when the dogs came, her arms tightened around him even more. That made Nate feel a little protective. He even tried to kick at one dog, to show her he was capable, but that almost caused a crash, so he quit. The dogs never actually bit at them. At some invisible line discernable only to them, the dogs would pull up and trot back to their territories.

They rode for almost an hour when Nok pointed to a road off to the right. He made the turn, and slowly they left the valley and started to gain in elevation. Within 15 minutes, Nok guided him to a drive and into a parking area. She hopped off, and Nate, back aching a bit, followed.

The parking area was mostly grass and some naked dirt. Surrounding it was a dense forest. Butterflies flitted in the sunshine. A wide path led into the trees, and Nate followed Nok to a wooden booth where a middle-aged lady sat reading a book.

"We have to pay here," Nok told him.

Nok asked the lady something, then looked back at Nate.

"It is 220 baht."

Nate gave her the money, and she received two receipts. Nok handed them to him, and he glanced at them before putting them into his pocket. One had a "20" on it, the other a "200."

He held them out to Nok. "Why the difference?"

"Oh, I am Thai, so I pay 20 baht. You are farang, so you pay 200 baht," she answered nonchalantly.

"We pay different prices? For the same thing?"

"Yes, you are farang."

"That's not fair!" He wanted to say more, but held his tongue.

He was in a sour mood as he followed Nok. Even the sight of her rounded butt in front of him was not going to make a difference.

They moved into an open clearing where people sat on benches, drank from plastic bottles, and chatted with each other. Small children ran in circles, screeching whatever kids screech. A dull roar could be heard, but Nate wasn't quite sure what it was.

Nok led Nate to a raised platform. He looked out to see a huge lake down below him some distance away. He couldn't see the ends of the lake due to the hills and trees, but the far shore had to be a mile or two across the water. Small boats plied back and forth. There looked to be some submerged trees in the water, so this had to be a reservoir. A big one, though.

Nok took Nate by the hand and led him back towards the trees on the side of the clearing. Two old ladies sat on a bench in the sun, and they smiled as the two of them walked by.

A wooden bridge was ahead of them, and as they entered the coolness of the shade, the roar became more pronounced. Coming closer to the bridge, Nate could see that the roar was a waterfall. The stream fell over a cliff to fall maybe 100 feet into the gorge below. Mist rose up in the air, a rainbow forming where the sun could peek through the canopy. It wasn't the largest falls he had ever seen, but still, it was impressive.

"It is beautiful, am I right?" Nok asked him.

"Yes, beautiful."

He looked over at her. *Not as beautiful as you*, he thought.

And she was beautiful, looking down at the roaring water, a little girl's delight on her face. He pulled out his camera and took a photo of her, the falling just beyond her face. For all his attempts at artistic photos at the Grand Palace, he knew this simple photo would be much, much better.

"I love this so much," she remarked.

They stood on the bridge for some time, not saying anything, just taking in the glory. Finally, she took his hand and led him across the rest of the bridge and onto a path going up stream. The dirt was hardpacked, but wet with moisture. They moved higher into the mountain, the stream rushing by them.

He wasn't sure how far they had climbed, but through the trees ahead, he could see another set of falls. This one wasn't as high, maybe 5 or 6 feet, but it was wide. Set in a horseshoe, it had to be 20 feet across. While it didn't have the power of the taller one below, it had a degree of serenity about it.

There was a wooden bench facing the falls, so they sat down on it while Nok slid off her back pack. She took out one of the plastic bags, two plates, and two spoons. Taking the rubber band off the bag, she tipped the contents evenly onto the plates, then handed one to Nate.

The light mist made it cool under the trees, and that made the ground pork dish seem a little clammy to Nate, but he wolfed it down anyway. Nok took tiny bites, chewing each mouthful deliberately. Nate glanced sideways to watch the muscles in her jaw work.

He ached to talk to her, but he didn't know what to say. Ken had told him he should be more self-confident, but he wasn't sure where to start. She must have felt his gaze as she suddenly looked up at him and smiled.

"So, Khun Nate. You have seen my family. You have seen a marriage. You have seen this waterfall. You have talked to a monk. I wanted to show you real Thailand, not Nana Thailand. What do you think?"

Nate actually missed Soi Cowboy, especially when he was lying on his mat in the room all alone at night. But while socially inept, he was not that stupid.

"I love this, Nok. I am so happy to be with you now, here." He wondered if she would notice the "with you" part of his sentence.

"My country, my Thailand, is wonderful. And Nana, my country is not Nana."

"I know. And I really like your country. Maybe I can live here." He wanted Nok to make an offer, to at least agree with him.

"I know America has many things. I can see it in movies. But when you go back to your home, I want you to tell your friends about the real Thailand."

That didn't seem like an invitation to him. He wanted to bring the conversation back to the more personal.

"What about you," he burst out before contemplating his words. "What do you want with your life."

"Me? You want to know? I just want to be happy."

"What about a family?"

"Oh of course, I want to marry to have children. I want to have a happy family to take care of me when I am old."

"Who will you marry?"

She laughed. "Some nice man. Good heart, not butterfly." An iridescent blue butterfly chose that moment to flit by them.

"Like that?"

She laughed an punched him lightly in the arm.

"So what else?"

"Good job, handsome. Tall."

Well, at least he was tall, he thought. He looked at her wry smile as she looked up at him. Was that some sort of hint, that he was the one for her?

She jumped up and put their trash back in her pack.

"Come," she ordered him.

They continued to walk upstream. At intervals, there were more waterfalls, each with its own character. Most of the next few falls were cascades covering more distance horizontally. But where the path ended, the stream split above it into two branches to fall over the rocks. Nok carefully stepped down off the path and jumped to a rock on the far side of the nearest split. Nate felt his heart rise to his throat, but he had to follow. His legs were long enough that he didn't really have to jump, but still, he nervously found his footing.

They were now on what was essentially a small island, the creek emerging from the dense forest above them to split and fall, then flow around the island before both branches joined again, back into one stream to continue its descent. A lone tree was on their little island, and Nok went over to where it hung over the water. A large rock poked out of the water a foot or two off the island and a couple of yards from the base of the falls. Nok dropped her back pack and took a careful step to stand on it. She stood there, looking at the water, making a pretty sight. The falling torrent caused eddies of air which flung her hair around in circles. She turned back, her face beaming, and motioned for Nate to join her. The rock looked a little small for both of them, so he just went to the edge and stood there. She nodded, then squatted down to try and reach the water, her butt a perfect upside-down heart. Nate could hardly keep his eyes off of her.

She stretched one leg out to the side to try and reach lower, but she still couldn't quite reach the flowing water. She turned around and smiled, brushing her now damp hair off her face. She held out her hand, and Nate took it as she prepared to step back off the rock. As she took the first step, though, her back leg slipped and she fell into the water. Nate had her hand, but the quickness of her fall kept him from holding her up. She fell butt first to sit in the water, which was only about two feet deep. The flow on the near side of the rock was not that great, so she really was in no danger, but panic struck Nate as he hauled her up by the arm, lifting her in the air to deposit her on solid ground.

Nok looked down at her soaked frame, then up at Nate with a huge smile. She broke out into a laugh, then hugged him.

"I think you save my life!"

"Are you OK," he asked in a worried voice, pulling back out of her embrace a bit to be able to look down to her face.

"I am OK. *Mai pen rai.* Just took a shower, I think. Now I am so clean." She laughed again, a trill of excited delight. Laughing caused her body to shake a bit, something Nate was extremely aware of with her in his arms.

Nate wasn't totally convinced that she was OK. But she did feel good, and she didn't seem to be upset.

"Maybe we should start back now," he told her.

"OK, if you want."

She picked up her backpack, but Nate took it from her. He tried to put it on, but the straps were adjusted way too tight. He couldn't lower his arms, and the pack stuck on the back of his head. Nok burst into laughter again.

"Bend over for me."

He complied, and Nok slid the pack back off his head. She squatted again, loosening the straps.

"Here, try it again."

Now the backpack slid on, and Nate only had to slightly adjust the straps to make it comfortable. They moved to the base of the little island, and Nok unhesitantly jumped back over to the bank before Nate could move to help her. Nate took a deep breath and made the jump as well.

Nok stood there waiting for him to clamor back up to the trail. Her wet shirt was clinging tightly to her body, making her breasts stand out prominently. She was shivering slightly, and that made it even harder for Nate to ignore them as they slightly jiggled. He was both relieved and disappointed when she turned to walk, facing away from him.

They had a leisurely walk back down the trail. They met up with one young Thai couple, obviously infatuated with each other, as they walked up the trail, hand-in- hand. The girl was slightly pudgy, and not really attractive to Nate, but the tall young boy was obviously happy. They barely acknowledged Nok and him as the two couples passed each other.

Nate turned to look at them as they passed, walking together so closely that their hips kept bumping. He looked back at Nok walking in front of him. He felt a yearning in his soul. Was this love? Did he love her? By the time they had reached the bridge at the first falls, he had decided. Yes, he loved Nok. Now he just had to gather the courage to tell her.

In typical Nate fashion, though, he said nothing as they walked back to the motorcycle and got on for the ride back. As Nok put her arms around him, he thought he could feel her still wet body more distinctly. He wanted that body, he wanted her. And he thought, hoped, the feeling was mutual.

Chapter 21

The ride back was pleasant. It was nice to have Nok holding him, and the colors of the countryside seemed more vibrant somehow.

They had seen several sections of roadside stands along different stretches of the highway. At one group of stands, the attendants, mostly girls, waved signs as if in beat to music, or even danced to get the attention of the passing motorists. Nate slowed down a bit to look, and Nok tapped his shoulder to stop where one young girl of maybe 15 was gracefully dancing while twirling a small sign mounted on a long stick. These stands were all for mangos, and Nate bought a few, two of which they ate right there at the side of the road, sweet juices dripping off their chins. Nate acted like he was put upon when Nok took out a tissue and wiped his face, but secretly, he enjoyed the attention. He wondered why all the stands on that stretch of the road were mango stands. It seemed to him that it would make more sense to have a variety of offerings. But each grouping of stands, which popped up every few miles, seemed to all sell the same thing.

The sun was just about ready to set by the time they pulled into Nok's village. Before they reached the small soi which led to Nok's home, they saw that a good portion of the village had gathered at the same lot where the wedding reception had been held. Nok tapped his shoulder again and motioned for him to stop.

Nate pulled over and after Nok spritely hopped off, he gratefully swung his leg off the bike and stood up, butt protesting. He wasn't used to such long rides in anything other than a car, and Nok's little bike vibrated quite a bit more than Nate's family car back in Oceanside.

Several young boys were playing soccer with a bright pink plastic ball, some plastic coke bottle serving as goal posts. They ran back and forth, calling out to each other as some of the older people watched while chatting with each other. Nok's grandfather squatted off to the side with two other older men, engrossed in conversation and smoking cigarettes. He was fairly animated in what he was saying, and the other two men frequently broke into laughter. He didn't notice the two of them arriving.

Three of the younger women called out and motioned for Nok to join them. Nate followed in trace. Wit was among the people gathered, but after one sneering glance, he looked away.

A child of possibly 4 years came up to Nate and solemnly looked up at him. He might have come to just over Nate's knee, but not by much. Nate smiled at him, but that garnered no response. The child, bare-chested and bare-foot, just stood there, hands clasped together, staring at him. Nate didn't know how to react, but the child finally turned and walked off.

Nate didn't understand a word of what was being said, but it was pleasant there all the same. There was a community spirit which seemed to emanate the informal gathering, a spirit not often found back in southern California suburbia.

A silver SUV pulled up, and Nong and her Russian boyfriend got out. Nong hurried over to join Nok and the other three girls while her boyfriend took a long swig of a beer he was carrying, then stood alone watching the soccer players. He nodded as one youngster kicked the ball between the goalposts from halfway down the makeshift field.

Nong seemed happy to be with the others, smiling broadly. The same could not be said about the Russian. He seemed quite bored. He had on a different color set of running pants on, but his tight tank-top seemed the same as what he had worn at the reception. A few of the Thais nodded at him, but he kept focused on the kids. Wit stood up and left the area, not looking back as he walked down the road. Nate caught the Russian giving the retreating Wit a look, a satisfied smile momentarily taking over his face.

Nok's grandfather had evidently completed his story and noticed Nate. He motioned Nate to join them, so Nate wandered over. Nok didn't seem to notice him leaving.

One of the other men offered Nate a cigarette, which he turned down. He then took a small bottle of whiskey out of his pocket and offered that to Nate. He accepted that and took a swallow, controlling by force of will the shudder which threatened to overtake him. The men nodded and got back into the conversation.

Nate stood there, smiling, but once again, not understanding a word. At least he was not understanding with a group of men, not a group of women, and that made him feel a little less conspicuous, a little less of an outsider.

Nok's grandfather started to sing a song, his feet moving in an odd sort of shuffling dance. He looked up to Nate and motioned for him to join in, not seeming to notice when Nate remained quiet. The other two men joined though, and they started their own version of the shuffling dance. They moved around each other in a sort of weaving pattern, one hand holding their cigarettes, the other doing a crude version of the hand motions of traditional Thai dancing. The soccer ball bounced over from an errant kick, hitting one of the men on the foot, but they didn't seem to notice it. One of the boys ran over to retrieve the ball, picking it up and starting to leave before he stopped, faced the oldsters, and mimicked them with exaggerated motions before running back to the game. Nate laughed out loud. Kids were kids no matter where in the world they lived.

He watched the boy run back. The Russian was still standing there as he drained his beer. He threw the bottle over his shoulder, then walked back to his SUV. He looked in the back for a moment, probably for another beer, and not finding one, he called out to Nong. Her back was to him, and she didn't respond. He called out again, and Nong, obviously trying to make some point to Nok and the others, didn't seem to notice. The Russian slammed shut the car door, his face twisted in anger.

He marched across the lot to where Nong was still talking. He yelled out something again, and Nong turned her head to see him, then said something back to him before turning back to her friends. The Russian then grabbed her by the arm and swung her around before backhanding her across the face. The sound of his hand across her face cut through the general din. She fell to the ground and fearfully looked up to him, hand against the side of her face where he had struck her.

Everything seemed to stop. The soccer game, the old guys dancing. Nok and the other two girls stepped back. The Russian reached down to grab Nong's arm and pull her up. She resisted, cowering, but she could do nothing against his strength as he started to drag her back to the car.

Nate wasn't sure how he got there, but suddenly, he was standing in front of them, blocking the Russian's way. As the Russian looked up at him, the familiar fear took over Nate, begging him to turn and run. He couldn't believe he was there, and as tunnel vision took over, he was afraid he might faint.

The Russian dropped Nong's arm as a sneering smile came over his face.

"What you do? You think to protect this whore? You Gallahad?" the Russian asked him in heavily accented English as he squared up in front of Nate.

Nate just stood there. His mouth opened and shut a few times, but despite his best effort, he couldn't force any words out. He started trembling and breaking out into a cold sweat.

"I thought not. Big Amerikanski, but big gay. *Podkabluchnik!*" He dismissed Nate, turning back to grab Nong's arm again.

That dismissal touched a nerve in Nate. The guy didn't even think enough of him to consider him as any sort of threat. In a rush of emotions, Nate's past surfaced like a tsunami. All the times the other kids at school picked on him. Alicia's cruel prom practical joke. Recruit Anderson trying to kill him in the pugil stick ring. Getting dropped from recruit training. James getting on him. Wit's sneering. Now this. It all came boiling to a head in a conflagration of intense anger, remorse, and conviction. He didn't deserve all this hassle in his life.

In a flash he thought of Ken's advice of only the day before, how he had to be true to himself. How he had to find his own place in life. How all men are faced with certain crossroads in life where they have to decide just who they are and where they are going.

A strange sense of calm, controlled determination came over Nate. His trembling stopped. His tunnel vision vanished, and at the same time, everything slowed down. As if a switch was flipped, he saw things in an intense clarity. A clarity not only of the physical world, but also of his inner self.

The Russian started to turn back to him in slow motion, pulling Nong around. From the core of his body, starting in his toes and gaining power like a gathering storm, Nate pulled back his arm, cocking the strength he never realized he possessed. He paused only a moment as the Russian took in the change in Nate, of his looming fist.

His eyes widened in surprise as he dropped Nong's arm and started to bring up his own fists. He was a natural born fighter, a person used to physical conflict, and his reflexes were superb. But once Nate released his fist, once he let fly, there was no force on earth which was going to stop that swing.

Nate's fist ploughed forward, hitting the top of the Russian's hand raised to block him, then connecting with his jaw. The look of growing anger on the Russian's face disappeared in a flash as he dropped to the ground in a limp heap, knees buckled forward, body laying back. Nate's fist continued on its journey, the momentum pulling him forward a step, on top of the crumbled heap of Russian mobster.

Nate took his foot off the unconscious Russian and looked at him in Wonder, taking in his suddenly misshapened face. Nong scrambled up, looking at Nate in abject fear. She got to her feet and ran, the only person moving for a few seconds. All eyes went from Nate to the Russian and back.

Like turning on a faucet, everyone spoke at once. No one came directly up to Nate, who slowly looked at his reddening knuckles. He shrugged and calmly started walking back to Nok's house. He was all the way back and going through the door before Nok caught up to him.

Chapter 22

He walked through the doorway and sat down on the beat-up chair. He was frankly amazed at how calm he felt. He looked again at the knuckles of his right hand. They were beginning to ache., but he was reveling in the feel of that. He was pleased with himself if somewhat astounded.

"Khun Nate, this is not good," Nok said in a worried voice. She came up and knelt on the floor in front of him.

"He had it coming. I had to do something," he simply said.

"But here in Thailand, it is not our business. And now, our village will have problem."

She moved his hand so she could look at it, then scowled. She got up and went to a drawer in the kitchen, grabbing some bandages. She took some out and tried to place them on each knuckle. They didn't fit easily. Nate reached over with this left hand and stopped her.

"It's OK. They don't hurt."

She looked worried.

"Why do you say there will be problems?"

"Khun Nate, you don't understand. He is a big man in Pattaya. He is mafia. He will tell his mafia friends to come hurt us, to hurt our village."

Her anxiety was actually begging to register with him. "They will come here?"

"Yes, I think so. They will want to hurt you, to hurt us. They need to be powerful. Maybe they pay police to take you, too."

Nate was feeling a little full of himself, a little powerful. But even in his calm euphoria, he realized that he could not stand up to a group of mobsters or the police.

"So what now, what do we do?"

"You need to go now. Go back to America. Maybe they can't touch you there."

His heart fell. He had been considering staying in Thailand, staying with Nok.

"I have to leave?"

"Yes, I think so. Not forever, but now."

He considered it. He started feeling the familiar panic begin to bubble into his consciousness, and it took an effort of will to suppress it. But panic was evolution's way to letting a person know that danger lurked. He shouldn't be paralyzed by panic, but he should listen to it. But he didn't want to leave Nok.

"Will you come with me?"

"Yes, I will take you to the airport."

Nate meant more than just that. He wanted her back in Oceanside with him. But right then, Nok's mother came in and shot some rapid-fire Thai towards her. She looked scared.

"Get your pack, Khun Nate. We need to leave."

He got up and went into his room. It only took a few moments for him to stuff his things into his backpack. He came out to find Nok already at the front door, peering out along the soi back in the direction of the gathering. She saw Nate and took his hand, urging him to hurry. She got on the bike and waited for Nate to get on as well.

"Your farang friend, from the market. You can find him?" she asked.

"You mean Mike? I think so. Yea, sure I can."

She started the bike, then turned left, back towards the rubber trees. After a short bit, she turned off on another tiny soi and crossed the main village road 100 yards further down from where they had been, closer to the wat. Nate could see the people still gathered around and what looked to be the Russian now laying prone.

They went down another small soi similar to the one on which she lived, passing a few small houses in the trees. A man came out to stand at the edge of the soi. In the dimming light, Nate couldn't tell who it was for a moment. Then he saw it was Wit. He gathered himself for anything that Wit might try, but Wit just smiled at him with a nod and lifted his hand again, although this time, it was his thumb which was raised.

Nok reached the main highway and turned right towards town. As they entered, he directed Nok to Soi Farang, and they stopped at Mike's house. They walked up to knock on his door. When Mike answered, Nate was still in his mixture of calm acceptance of what happened and his anxiety of what might happen, and he was content to let Nok speak. Nok tried to explain what had happened, but her English was suffering

Mike stopped her and told the two of them to follow him. They went to Till's house, going in when Till came to the door. Nok went on in Thai, excitedly telling him what had transpired.

Till kept looking at Nate, but he let Nok finish. Finally, she stopped, chest heaving.

"You took out that man with one hit?" he asked.

"One hit? Who?" interjected Mike.

"Seems our young friend here took out a Russian mafia don, almost killed him with one punch."

"Holy shit!"

"That would be an accurate assessment, my friend."

"Why did you do that?"

"He deserved it." Nate simply said.

"He deserved it? He deserved it?" he asked, his voice getting louder the second time he said it. "How the hell did he deserve it?"

"He was beating up a girl."

Mike looked at him in wonderment. "Well, I've got to say, you're the man. But now you're fucked. Those guys play for keeps, and if you hurt one of them, they've got to hurt you back, harder."

"Nok says they might come out to her village."

"Not 'might,' will," Till put in. "These are serious people, and they can't afford to look weak. The local gangs would move in, challenge them, maybe the Chinese gangs, too. They've got the money to buy the police, but so do the rest. They have to be strong."

"So now what? Nok thinks I need to get back to the US."

Mike and Till looked at each other, while considering, then both nodded in agreement.

"Yea, that's probably best," answered Mike. "We can take you to Swampy, but catching a plane at the last second is gonna cost you."

"I've got an open ticket on United. I can go anytime."

"An open ticket?" he repeated. "That's good. If they've got a seat, you get it. And the flight is at 6:50 AM, so we can get you there in time."

"You mean now? Tonight? I was hoping to stay a little bit longer, maybe in Bangkok."

Till shook his head. "Not a good idea. They've got the police in their pocket. So your name and description is going out. Tomorrow morning is probably OK, but you don't want to get picked up at immigration on assault charges. Even the honest police are going to arrest you if you are charged, and you will be, I can guarantee you. No, you've got to leave now."

"But they don't know me, they don't know my name," he protested.

"They know your first name, right? Or someone in the village does. And they can find out where your girlfriend here works. You said you stayed at her hotel, right? Not hard to find out your name."

"And they don't need to find you in Bangkok," added Till. "You've got to fly out, so they will have a watch list with you there."

Nate sighed, accepting defeat. "OK, I guess I got go back." He looked over at Nok, who had gone quiet listening to the three of them speak.

He had a sudden thought, more of a hope.

"What about Nok, though. Should she come with me? They can get her, too."

"Khun Nate, I can't ...."

"Nah, she's safe as long as you're gone," Mike spoke over her. "She, well, everyone in her village, they can just say you're gone, that they kicked you out. The Russians ain't gonna declare war on a village for something you did, not if the people there publically say they already dumped you."

"They could," put in Till.

"Not for this, you think?" asked Mike.

"Probably not. It would cost them with the police, and if Nate was gone, there would be no point. Just a waste of bribe money."

Nate looked at all three who in turn were staring at him.

"OK, I get it. Let's go then."

"You coming, Till? I can give him a ride to Swampy."

"It's getting late. I don't want to be away from the kids all night. I think you can take him." He turned to Nate. "Good luck!"

Nate took his hand and shook it. He looked back at Mike.

"OK, let's do it."

Chapter 23

Nok flipped her cell phone shut.

"He is in the hospital now. He will get well, but in many months. Now he must eat his dinner through a straw."

Nate merely grunted.

"And Nong is back with him. She is crying."

"Crying? He hit her! Why is she back with him?" he asked.

"She loves him."

"What about the police?" asked Mike, driving his big SUV down the expressway.

"They have Nate's name, and they want him, but I think no one tells he is gone now."

"Well, we'll be at Swampy in ten minutes. Nate can check in, then hang around for his flight. He's gonna be OK. Aren't you, Nate?"

"Yea, I'll be fine."

He looked out the window at the lights of Bangkok. The ride had been uneventful. There were cars on the road, but traffic was moving. He looked back at Nok, in the back passenger seat. He would have rather been sitting there with her, but that would have left Mike alone up front, like a chauffeur.

As they passed the streetlamps, the light moved to reveal her face before she fell back into the darkness between each one. Other than her phone call back to her village, they hadn't said much on the trip.

He wanted to talk, he wanted to make sure she knew how he felt, but his new-found courage didn't extend to revealing his personal feelings. And with Mike there as well, he was even more reticent. He hoped he would have time with her alone at the airport.

The expressway widened as signs pointed the way to Suvarnabhumi. They exited along the left in a broad expressway in and of itself, going around a huge curve which was framed by two of the largest billboards Nate had ever seen. The Samsung one was particularly large.. A few minutes later, they came up on the terminal. Airlines were assigned to each debarkation point, so they drove slowly until they saw the sign for United.

Nate and Nok got out and came around to the driver's window. Mike held out his hand.

"You take care, now, you hear? And later, when all this blows over, you come back and see me, OK?

Nate shook his hand.

"Sure will, and thanks for this. I really appreciate it."

"No problem, we farangs need to stick together, you know?" He looked to Nok. "You go in with him, honey, make sure everything's OK. I'll park on the bottom floor. We've got each other's numbers, so give me a call when you're coming out, and I'll let you know where I'm at."

She nodded, and they turned to walk in. Looking at the big board, Nate found his flight and was directed to the "L" aisle. When they tried to walk in, the attendant told Nok that the area was only for passengers.

"Khun Nate, I will wait over there," she said, pointing to the other side of the check-in area.

Nate walked over to the counters. It was still well before the flight, and only a few counters were manned. No one was waiting in line. A woman waved him over.

"Good morning sir," she said cheerfully. "May I have your e-ticket and passport please?"

"Um, I don't have one. I mean, I am not on the flight yet. I have an open ticket."

He handed his paperwork to her, which she looked at in confusion.

"Just a moment, please, sir." She called over to another agent who, after a few exchanges, motioned Nate to come over to her.

"You have an open ticket, sir?"

He handed her his paperwork. She looked it over.

"Mr. Foster, thank you for being a Premier Executive. What day would you like to leave?"

"Today, if I could."

She looked at her computer screen. That should be no problem to Narita. We are not full on this flight. And let me check." She hit a few keys, intent on her keyboard. "You are going to San Diego, right?"

"Yes, ma'am."

"Going through San Francisco, that is open, too. I am happy to be able to help you with this."

She printed out his tickets, took his bag and checked it in, putting an orange priority flag on the luggage tag. She handed him his three boarding passes and gave him his seat assignments.

"You will have to claim your luggage in San Francisco and go through immigration, then check your luggage back in for your continuing flight to San Diego. Thai immigration and security checks are that way," she said, pointing to her left. "And as a Premier Executive, you are welcome to use our lounge. It opens at 4:00 AM, so you have a little time before then. Have a pleasant flight."

Nate thanked her and walked over to the left where Nok waited for him.

"You are OK? You have your flight?" she asked.

"Yea."

They walked together to the immigration area. A woman was checking boarding passes at the entrance.

"Here I must leave you, Khun Nate."

Nate had wanted to spend the rest of the wait with her. He hadn't realized she could not go into the terminal. But he didn't want to say goodbye.

"Oh, but I don't have to go in yet. Maybe we can wait out here together?"

"Khun Nate, Khun Mike is waiting for me, and we need to drive back."

He felt crushed. Standing there in the terminal was not quite how he imagined saying goodbye. Well, it was only goodbye for now, he thought.

"OK, I understand. I, uh, I'm happy we met."

She looked up at him. "I am happy, too. I hope I showed you the real Thailand. I hope you will tell your friends that Thailand is not Nana Plaza."

"Yea, of course. I know. I just want to say, you know, I want you to know, I like you," he managed to get out.

"You are a good man, Khun Nate. I like you, too." She didn't go beyond that simple statement.

"And I want, maybe if we can, I want to see you again."

She hesitated. "If you come back to my hotel, I will see you. You are always welcome to Thailand."

He screwed up his courage. "And maybe you can come visit me in America."

She laughed. "Oh, it is very difficult for Thai woman to get visa to USA. And I have my work here."

Nate felt crushed that she had laughed at his suggestion. He tried to recover, but didn't know what to say.

"Khun Nate, you should go," she told him, pointing at immigration.

He had been planning a long passionate kiss goodbye, a kiss full of promise for the future, but her response put him off stride. He dug within to gather his nerve, and before he could falter, he grabbed her shoulders and leaned forward for a kiss.

Nok turned her face, and Nate ended up kissing her cheek. She pulled back out of his grasp and made a deep wai. "*Sawadi kha*, Khun Nate."

Feeling his face turn red, Nate did the only thing he could. He wai'ed and responded "*Sawadi krup*."

Nok looked back up at him, gave a little wave, then turned and walked away. Nate watched her, but she never turned back to look at him. She went to an escalator and disappeared from view.

Nate sighed and turned to go through immigration and security. Once through, he had some time to kill before the lounge opened. He walked the length of the huge terminal, and was happy to see a Burger King at one end. He got a Whopper Meal, the first enjoyable food he had had for several days.

Wandering back, he found an internet café. With some hesitation, he logged in and opened his hotmail. There were a number of messages for him, but the ones which caught his eye were from his dad. He didn't want to open them, but he knew he was only postponing the inevitable. He opened the most recent one first. He was ready for storm, so he was surprised to read it.

> *Nathan,*
>
> *I see where you are now. I got my credit card statement online, and I see the ticket to Thailand. I don't know why you went there but its OK. Take your time. Get yourself rite. If you want, let me know your OK. Let me know when your coming home. Im not pressuring you but when you get home I talked to Gunny Simpson. He retired and is a manager at the Home Depot in Carlsbad. He can give you a job. Or you can go to school or do what you want. Everything is OK. You are my son and I am always proud of you.*
>
> *I am fine. Don't worry.*
>
> *Love,*
>
> *Dad.*

Nate felt his throat constrict. He was so worried about how his dad would feel about him getting kicked out of boot camp, out of the Marines. That short e-mail took a huge load off his mind. His relief was palpable.

Eventually, the lounge opened, and Nate went inside to snack on dim sum, some sort of rice and chicken soup, and small tuna sandwiches until boarding. He made his way to the gate and took advantage of the priority boarding to get his seat.

He watched the rest of the passengers board, the families, the backpackers, the single men. He wondered if he had seen any of those men at Nana or Soi Cowboy. A 30's-something man in a coat and tie took the aisle seat, leaving an empty seat between them. He nodded to Nate, stowed his coat in the overhead bin, then sat down. Nate wasn't up to a long conversation, so he was happy when the man leaned back and went almost immediately to sleep.

The crew went through their briefs, and the big 747 pulled back and moved down taxiway to the runway. Pulling into position, the pilot ran the engines up, the plane shuddering slightly. With a release, the plane lurched forward, gathering speed until it lifted off the ground. The plane banked right, and Nate could see the dawn breaking over Bangkok, the city lights still on. He watched out the window as they left Bangkok behind. When he couldn't see the lights any longer, he turned forward. He was leaving Thailand.

Chapter 24

"Exit on Oceanside Boulevard?" the Cloud Nine driver asked him.

"Yea, just go straight for awhile."

Twenty-four hours after leaving Bangkok, he was almost home. Being in Oceanside, the furthest away, the shuttle driver had taken the other passengers to their homes and hotels first. Now it was just the driver and him in the white van.

The flight back to San Diego had been long, but Nate hadn't minded. It had given him time to think about himself, about where he was in his life.

Nate had always been afraid of pretty much everything, especially after his mother died. He was afraid of danger, to be sure. He was afraid of the physicality of confrontation. But he was also afraid of trying new things, of taking on new tasks. He wasn't sure if that was a fear of failure so much as a fear of the unknown. And he had to admit to himself that he was always going to be fearful. But what was new to him was the realization that he didn't have to be a slave to his fear. He could confront it and conquer it.

He looked down at his right hand, now slightly swollen and sore. He flexed his red knuckles, feeling the pain in them. But instead of fleeing the pain, he somehow reveled in it. This was a physical proof that he could defeat fear. His hand was his trophy.

What had amazed him most was that he had been quaking in his shoes, but once he had made the decision to hit the Russian, a sense of calm had come over him. He wondered if his fear was based on the prospect of confrontation, rather than the actual confrontation itself.

Ken had been right when he said that each individual had to find himself, to get a grip on is own reality. For a guy who had left his life in the US, who had nothing that most people thought important, he seemed to be doing OK.

196

Nate was not about to abandon the church, but he thought he might study up some on Buddhism, maybe find that wat near Escondido. If a couple of hours with a monk could affect such a positive change in him, who knows what else he could learn?

"Turn right at the light," he told the driver.

In just over a week, Nate had gone to another country on his own, gotten laid, fell in love, and hit a man. He was not the same Nathan who had been kicked out of bootcamp.

He thought of An, his first woman. He immediately had an erection as he remembered her touch. Yes, he decided he rather liked sex. He was going to have to do more of it. He was happy to be home, but he also wished he was at Nana right then. It would be the best of both worlds if Nana or Soi Cowboy could somehow be transported over to Oceanside. He smiled at the thought. He would have liked to spend another couple of days there before coming home, getting in a few more fucks, but things got beyond his control.

But as good as An was that first night, Boon, Tulip, and the others, well, they weren't quite what he had hoped. It was like jacking off. Oh it was great masturbation. The girls were much better than jacking off to internet porn. But there wasn't the connection he had imagined.

But he had gained confidence, he admitted to himself. He had held conversations, he had been a little aggressive even, and he had talked openly about subjects he would never have imagined he could. He wanted to try out his new-found confidence with girls back here in Oceanside.

And that made him feel guilty, like he was cheating on Nok. Nok, Nok, the lovely, alluring Nok. His heart still ached a bit for her, but on the long flight back, he realized that he had created a relationship in his mind, a relationship which was not as he thought. Oh, he thought Nok liked him in her own way, but she had never given any real indication that she felt romantic towards him. Her arms tight around his waist were so she wouldn't fall off the motorcycle. Holding his hand as they walked was what she did, to him, to her niece, to her friends in the village. She was older than him, and Nate got the feeling that in Thailand, young women did not have relationships with younger guys. He had come to the conclusion that Nok had invited him to her village, partly in response to her blowing up at him that evening in the hotel, partly just as she told him, to show him a different Thailand.

Nate realized that what he had on Nok was a crush. The old Nathan would have been horrified at this, embarrassed. But the new Nate just smiled.

It took three people to make him a man, maybe four if you counted the Russian. But the Russian was merely a foil, merely a tool in his journey.

An made him a man in the common, puerile sense of the phrase. And while Nate planned on trumpeting up An with his acquaintances, he realized that this was the least significant part of his change. Sex was fun, great even. But being a man did not depend on whether he had slept with anyone or not. Sex was nothing special, nothing unique. With over six billion people in the world, each one of them a result of two people fucking, well, there was a lot of it going on. Nate fully intended to add to that mass of bodies coming together, but that would not define him as a man.

Nok had made him a man in the emotional sense. Before Nok, he had never thought much about women and relationships except for his constant sexual fantasies. He classified women in two categories: fuckable and not fuckable. But the feelings that Nok had awakened in him went beyond that, and made him realize in his heart, not just as an intellectual abstract, that women are more than just a receptacle for his sperm. They were much more. And while Nate was not ready to rush to the altar, he now looked forward to getting married someday, to have kids. He wanted an emotional relationship.

And Ken had made him a man who knew himself, who understood who he was. Ken gave him the tools to examine himself and make decisions, to change instead of just going with the flow and accepting everything coming his way.

It probably wasn't accurate to say that Ken and Nok "made him" anything. It was probably better to say that Nok gave him the experiences, and Ken gave him the advice which allowed Nate to "make himself" a more mature person, better able to interact with the world.

Thailand had been good to him as things turned out. But it could have been most anywhere. And now that Nate had started on a new phase of his life, had matured into a more capable person, it was up to him to keep that process going, to continue to learn and better himself.

As he told the driver to take the next left, they drove past Stephanie Card's house, and Stephanie was out in the driveway in lime green shorts and a white shirt washing her father's car. Stephanie was somewhat of a nerd, a thin girl who was more wallflower than social queen. But Nate and Stephanie had been friends when they were young, playing around the neighborhood. Her butt looked kind of cute as she bent over the hood of the car. Nate did not really think that Stephanie was his fated love, but you had to start somewhere. Maybe he should walk over this evening to say hello to his old friend.

Despite his commitment to be the new Nate, not to retreat to the old Nathan, he wasn't sure what he was going to do next. His departure from Thailand had been abrupt, and he had no concrete plans. He had dismissed the offer from his dad about the Home Dept job when he had read it, but maybe that would be a good idea. He could take it, giving him the time to make up his mind. And he knew he needed to pay his dad back for the charges he had made, so the salary would help.

On the flight back, he briefly considered school, but he didn't think that was a good choice for him. He even considered enlisting in the Army, or maybe the National Guard. He thought Nate could make it through boot camp where Nathan had failed. But he realized that he probably was not suited for the military, despite his pedigree. So the more he thought about it, the better Home Dept sounded, at least for the time being.

The driver turned onto his street. Looking ahead, Nate could see his dad's old GrandAm in the driveway. He was home, then. Nate had hoped to be able to get home first to prepare himself for meeting him.

He felt the familiar rush of panic begin to form, threatening to rise up and take over. He wasn't going to let it happen. He took a deep breath and pushed back, forcing the panic back, pressing it into a small ball that he could ignore. The panic was still there. He could sense it. But it couldn't explode to take over him. He could control it.

The van pulled into the driveway. Nate got out, paid the driver, and shouldered his backpack. He walked up the steps and pushed open the door.

"Dad, I'm home!"